Praise for
Kristina Riggle and
Real Life & Liars

"With ease and grace, Riggle walks the fine line between sentimentality and comedy, and she has a sure hand in creating fun, quirky characters."
—*Publishers Weekly*

"*Real Life & Liars,* Kristina Riggle's sumptuous and rich debut novel, examines the complications that arise in family and marriage, love and heartbreak. With lush writing and nuanced, relatable characters, this book is a must-read for anyone who has ever been both grateful and driven mad by the people they love most: their family."
—Allison Winn Scotch,
author of the *New York Times* bestselling *Time of My Life*

"Written with grace, passion, and insight, *Real Life & Liars* is a deeply felt novel that draws a vivid portrait of a family in transition, and examines the very real fear of leaving behind all you hold dear."
—Maggie Dana, author of *Beachcombing*

"In Kristina Riggle's moving debut, *Real Life & Liars,* she poignantly portrays the inner workings of a family faced by crisis. Funny, sad, and utterly believable, these are characters that seem like old friends."
—Elizabeth Letts, author of *Family Planning*

The Life You've Imagined

"*The Life You've Imagined* is a richly woven story laced with unforgettable characters. Cami, Maeve, Anna, and Amy will snag your heart as they explore the sometimes-wide chasm between hope and reality. A beautiful book."

—Therese Walsh, author of *The Last Will of Moira Leahy*

"In this engaging, companionable novel about family, expectations, and adversities overcome, Kristina Riggle performs the admirable feat of giving us characters who are somehow both familiar and wonderfully original. Unpredictable, touching, and true, The *Life You've Imagined* is a stand-out story; I devoured it and wanted more."

—Therese Fowler, author of *Reunion*

"Backed by Riggle's trademark unflinching honesty and imbued with heart and hope, *The Life You've Imagined* is a terrific novel about love and loss, letting go and holding on. A book to share with family and friends—I loved it."

—Melissa Senate, author of *The Secret of Joy*

Things We Didn't Say

by Kristina Riggle

The Life You've Imagined
Real Life & Liars

Things We Didn't Say

KRISTINA RIGGLE

wm

WILLIAM MORROW

An Imprint of HarperCollins*Publishers*

THINGS WE DIDN'T SAY. Copyright © 2011 by Kristina Ringstrom. All rights reserved. Printed in the United States of America. No part of this book may be used or reproduced in any manner whatsoever without written permission except in the case of brief quotations embodied in critical articles and reviews. For information address HarperCollins Publishers, 10 East 53rd Street, New York, NY 10022.

HarperCollins books may be purchased for educational, business, or sales promotional use. For information please write: Special Markets Department, HarperCollins Publishers, 10 East 53rd Street, New York, NY 10022.

FIRST EDITION

Designed by Diahann Sturge

Library of Congress Cataloging-in-Publication Data

Riggle, Kristina.
   Things we didn't say / by Kristina Riggle.—1st ed.
      p.   cm.
   ISBN 978-0-06-200304-1
   I. Title.

PS3618.I39387 T47 2001
813'.6—dc22

2010046346

11 12 13 14 15   OV/RRD   10 9 8 7 6 5 4 3 2 1

In memory of Donna Ringstrom, my "bonus mom" and leader of my fan club (Up North division). We miss you.

Acknowledgments

A deep, heartfelt thank you to my family for putting up with writing-distracted me, book-tour-traveling me, book-launch-stressed-out me, and still loving me as much as ever.

Thank you to the people at HarperCollins who lovingly tended my work from manuscript to finished book, then got those books into readers' hands: Esi Sogah; Stephanie Selah; Teresa Brady; my amazing editor, Lucia Macro; and more people than I know by name. It sure doesn't happen by accident or magic, and I'm grateful to have you on my side.

Much gratitude to the supportive and smart women from Nelson Literary Agency: Kristin Nelson, Lindsay Mergens, Sara Megibow, and Anita Mumm.

As ever, I'm indebted to Eliza Graham for her thoughtful and considerate reading of early drafts.

I received invaluable research assistance from Det. Pete Kemme of the Grand Rapids Police Department, Chris Byron of the Grand Rapids Public Library, and Thomas H. Logan, author of *Almost Lost: Building and Preserving Heritage Hill*.

I also consulted writings by Robert O. Friedel, M.D., and

Richard Moskowitz, M.D., and the Web site of the National Institute of Mental Health.

To the readers, booksellers, book clubs, librarians, bloggers, and journalists who have read, written about, and recommended my work: I'm humbled and grateful.

Chapter 1

Casey

My cigarette smoke twists through the predawn November air, until a gust breaks it apart. My hair whips across my face, so I turn into the wind, putting my cigarette behind my back to shelter it. The effect is like leaning off the prow of a ship.

The air is heavy with looming winter. Mornings like this, as a kid, I'd curse and groan, shivering at the bus stop in the cracking cold before the sun even came up. Now? I'd take this cold every day of the year if it always came with such exquisite quiet.

My boots crunch along the sidewalk in the gray stillness as I cast a glance back toward the drafty, narrow house where the children still sleep.

I thought one day they might be my children, or something like that. The day I first met them, Angel was doing up little Jewel's hair in crazy ponytails with pink glitter hair spray, then they moved on to me and wound ribbons into braids all over my head. I looked like a maypole. Dylan, though, reminded me of my family's half-wild outdoor cat, Patch. You had to earn his attention, and trying too hard was the worst thing to do. Dylan didn't say much that first day. He started peeking at me from under his dark, floppy bangs. By the time I left, I had earned a quick half-smile granted when no one else was looking.

A square of weak yellow light flicks to life from the second story. Even from a block away I can tell it's from Angel's room. I've got time; she'll be in the bathroom for an age, emerging in a puff of sweet-smelling bathroom steam when she imagines herself perfect.

My phone buzzes in the pocket of my parka, and I resume my daily trudge around the block, feeling my last free moments of the day burning down like my cigarette.

"Hi, Tony."

"Hey, Edna Leigh."

"I wish you wouldn't call me that."

"I'm just joshing with you."

"I'm not in the mood."

"Fine, *Casey.*" Though I've been short with him, his voice has a smile in it. I can always count on this, whatever else happens. "Does your husband get to say your real name, or do you make him use your last name, too? Shit, linebackers go by their last names."

"If your mother had named you after a great-grandparent, you wouldn't like it, either. How'd you like to be an Otis? Anyway, he calls me Casey, and he's not my husband."

"Yet?" he prompts.

"Right. Yet."

Michael must have already left for the gym to work off his worry about his job. Every day he comes home with more news of cutbacks and layoffs and buyouts.

"When do I get to meet him?"

"Not now."

"I'm beginning to think you're embarrassed about me. Least if we're going to sneak around we should screw around, too, make it fun."

I laugh, because Tony is twice my age and then some. He's a former neighbor but feels like my uncle, and these days is my only genuine friend. "It's not you I'm embarrassed about."

I step over a cracked piece of sidewalk without having to look. If they ever fix it, I'll probably fall and break my neck.

"How great can this guy be if he expects you never to have made a mistake in your life?"

"It's complicated."

"Ain't it always."

"Whatever. What's up with you, Tony?"

"Five hundred days sober today."

"You get a cake for that?"

"Come to AA with me, and I'll make you a double chocolate layer cake."

"Congratulations, anyway."

"C'mon, come with me. I promise to bake you a cake, or whatever you want. Name your price."

"I can't be bought with dessert."

"How very high-minded."

"I'm not going to stand there in some dreary church basement confessing to my past drunken sins, which, by the way, are two years old now. I'm doing just fine."

My voice startles me with its volume. An early-morning dog walker passing on the other side of the street jerks his head in my direction. It's Tom with his floppy-haired dog, Ted—named for the late senator Kennedy—and he gives me an uncertain wave.

"You sure sound fine."

I toss my cigarette down and stamp it with my boot heel. "Did you call just to hassle me?"

"Well, not *just*." Tony rattles off a cough and spits. "Talking to you is the highlight of my day. I wouldn't get up this early for anyone else."

"Then you have some sad days, my friend."

I'm already rounding the corner back to the house. Claustrophobic city blocks are like that, and I've unwittingly sped up my walk. My ego wants more time alone, my id wants out of the cold. The bare November trees lean over me, and I wish I could climb one and hide in its old branches.

The house's pitched roof and twin top-story windows create an air of surprise that I've returned.

"You there?" Tony asks.

"Yeah."

"You going to make it today, kid?"

I exhale a plume of white winter breath, considering. "I think so."

"Think?" His voice bears the strain of concern. He knows what stupidity I've survived. He knows about my old job, which I used to love—the only place I've ever excelled in spite of myself—the people I once considered friends, how I never see my family anymore because all of it comes braided together with booze.

"Okay. I will."

"That's my girl. Stay strong."

It's too corny for me, but I'm glad he says it all the same.

"Some days, I just—"

I have my hand on the rear storm door when the inside door jerks open. I yank the phone away from my head and hang up.

"Who was that?" asks Michael, rubbing his eyes, then his bare arms. He's still wearing what he wore to bed.

"My mother." I step into the kitchen's harsh yellow light and shrug out of my parka.

"She called early. And you hung up on her?"

The phone is buzzing in my hand with Tony's number showing on the display. I turn my phone over, his number toward my palm. I nod.

"You'll hear about that later."

"I expect I will. I thought you were at the gym."

"Headache."

"I'm sorry."

My phone chimes again, one brief tone, and I stuff it in my pocket. "Angel is up, I noticed. You talk to her yet?"

"Before her ladyship has come down the stairs? Heaven forbid."

I don't rise to this. I once joined in with his half-larky, half-serious use of this title for Angel, and the conversation fell to silence like a rock off a cliff.

"Going up to shave," he says, leaning in to plant a quick kiss on my forehead. I would usually seize up and treasure this small affection. Today, it stings.

When I've heard his steps go all the way up the stairs, I check my phone.

Tony didn't leave a voice mail. His text reads: *Caught by surprise?*

I send back one word—*sorry*—and delete both messages.

So Michael hasn't seen Angel. He doesn't know yet. Maybe she won't tell him at all, or maybe she's waiting. She's smart like that, knowing how to hold her cards until just the right moment.

Like mother, like daughter.

That's another thing I'm not allowed to say.

In the kitchen, pouring Jewel a bowl of Honeycombs as the older kids loll at the table, I offer Angel some breakfast, as casually as I can. "Want something to eat?" I fight to keep my voice level and mild, like I'm only the recorded voice on the phone, giving out the time.

"Do I ever?" she spits.

I laugh, as if this is an amusing joke. I do this partly to deflect her, partly for Jewel's benefit, since conflict gives her a tummyache.

I rinse my cereal bowl in the sink. Michael is to my left, pouring coffee. I don't know why I bother, but I cut my eyes over to him, searching for him to meet my gaze. He glances up at me, and I tip my head toward his daughter.

He sighs and turns around, flashing me a quick, shamefaced look as he does, knowing his admonition will be too mild, too late.

"Angel, you really should eat. And watch your tone."

Angel barely hears him and grunts at her phone, where she's texting. She pauses to push her white-blond hair behind one ear. There are candy-pink streaks in it at the moment, though she's promised the director of the school play she will bleach them out by dress rehearsal. She stretches out long in her chair, her body a graceful arcing swoop. She's gotten taller in the short time I've known her, more graceful, too. Truth be told, she's a stunner of a girl. Yet I've seen her scowl at herself in the mirror, caught her patting her stomach and fiddling with her waistband as if trying to check if she's thin enough yet, beautiful enough yet.

I try to ruffle Dylan's hair as I come back to the table, only he ducks my hand so I just swipe through the air above his head. I stuff that hand in my pocket.

"You've got music class today?" I ask Dylan.

"Yeah."

I should know better than to ask yes-or-no questions. "What songs are you working on?"

Dylan shifts in his chair, shrugging like his clothes are making him itch. His hair, dark like his dad's, flops over his light blue eyes, a combination that really should send the girls swooning. Maybe in a couple of years when his skin evens out and his voice smooths over again. "I don't . . . know." I note the pause. When he feels the stammer coming, he takes extra time to pronounce the word.

"You don't *know*?" Michael interjects.

"I haven't heard you practice in a long time," I say quickly, interrupting his dad. Dylan used to enjoy the company when he played his sax. We didn't talk, in fact most of the time I'd just work on my laptop, on the floor, propped up against his bedroom wall. He said it made him play better knowing there were "other ears in the room."

"It's okay," he says. "You don't have to."

The teen kiss-off. "You don't have to" equals "Please don't."

Jewel pushes her pink glasses up the bridge of her nose and

announces to the table in general: "Did you know that humans have 206 bones in the body? And we're born with more. Some of them fuse together, though."

I'm so grateful to her for cutting the tension with her factoid, I want to sweep her up in a hug. I cross my arms instead and smile. "Yeah?"

She's wearing a French braid today, which she must have conned Angel into doing. Apparently their mother was a whiz at complicated hairdos. I've never been good at that, and the first time Jewel asked me to fix her hair it took twenty minutes, and she cried all the way out the door with uneven pigtails.

"Yeah," she replies, and I'm hoping she'll continue her lecture but she refocuses on her cereal. She doesn't have to be up as early as her big siblings, but she likes to be, she says. She likes to watch everybody head off for the day. Plus, she gets the television to herself after they leave until it's her turn for the bus at eight thirty.

Dylan picks up his phone and reads a message, seeming to flinch. But then says casually, "Hey, Dad, Robert is sick today. Can you drive me?"

Robert is Dylan's ride to Excalibur Charter Academy. EXA, the kids call it, like *ecks-uh*. Angel takes the bus to the magnet school in town, having won entrance with good grades. Dylan's grades aren't bad, nor are they exceptional. He went to the regular public high school until that gun incident in the courtyard there, and then Michael's father arranged for him to attend his friend's charter school. In the tradition of communicative teenage boys everywhere, Dylan says EXA is "fine."

"Yeah, sure," Michael says, roused from his work trance where he was mentally rehearsing his day. "Angel, I'll take you, too, as long as I'm driving." With a nod but no words, Dylan trots up the stairs, probably to fetch his saxophone.

Angel hops up from her chair. "Thanks, Daddy."

In the bustle of bags and coats, I retreat to the corner of the kitchen. It's too small for all of us in here.

Michael sweeps by me and tries to land a kiss on my cheek. He misses, and is propelled out the door by the momentum of his kids coming up behind him. Dylan says nothing on his way by.

Angel says, "Bye, Casey. I hope you enjoy this nice quiet house today, all by yourself."

She's turned away from me as she says that, so I can't see her face.

How much did she read?

"Casey? Can I go watch cartoons now?"

"Sure, J. Go ahead."

I pick up her bowl and Dylan's Pop-Tart plate. Jewel wraps her arms around my waist, her nose buried in my belly. By the time I put the dishes back down to return the hug, she has fled to the living room to turn on *SpongeBob SquarePants*.

In the emptiness of the kitchen throbs the jagged emptiness in my chest, steadily growing in recent months, which I've tried to ignore but no longer can. It's where hope briefly flickered, in the days when Michael still kissed me before he left, without fail, busy morning be damned.

I take a two-minute shower because all the hot water is gone, and when I go back downstairs, Jewel's face is in a book called *A Kid's Guide to Positive Thinking*. She has pulled her glasses down to the tip of her nose to read, stretched out flat on the couch, the book propped on her chest. The TV still blares, but she won't turn it off, even while reading. Being the youngest in a house this full, she's been steeped in noise since the womb.

"Hey, Jewel?"

No response.

"Jewel!"

"Yeah?" she says into the pages of her book.

"Ally's mom is going to pick you up from Girl Scouts today."

"Why?"

"Something came up I have to do," I tell her, my voice catching a little, so I cough.

With no second car, I usually walk up to meet Jewel at the school cafeteria, where Girl Scouts meets. But if the weather's bad, or I'm sick, I impose on one of the other parents. And they do let me know that I impose.

I top off my coffee, and at the kitchen phone, I dial up Ally's mom, who agrees to bring Jewel home but advertises her annoyance with heavy sighs and a long pause to check her daily planner. Once while waiting to pick up Jewel I overhard her explaining to another mom: "She's not the stepmother. The father's *girlfriend*," with so much stress on *girl* you'd think I was fourteen years old instead of twenty-six. That's not so much younger than Michael, really. If we were forty and fifty, no one would even blink.

I could look older if I dressed more like the other mothers, but I'm comfortable in my baggy thrift-store Levi's with my hair in a ponytail.

Not that it will much matter after today.

I check the schedule, and Dylan and Angel both have practices today: sax for him, school play for her, and they both have rides. Michael should be home on time, unless there's breaking news, but in any case, Angel and Dylan will be home when Jewel gets dropped off from Girl Scouts.

So. They're all taken care of.

I put Jewel on the bus with a wave. She doesn't go for a hug this time, and I turn away quickly so she can't see the wetness in my lashes. I wait until I'm back inside the house to wipe it away.

I sit down at my desk and hesitate in front of the blank paper. From here, I can see the houses across the street: tall and narrow turn-of-the-century homes nestled together like children sharing a bed. Most are in muted colors, the occasional fanciful pastel. One, across and to my left, is electric green.

I used to so much admire these houses that I imagined their interiors filled with happy, harmonious families. It's not until these last few months I've become conscious of the assumption, and how ridiculous it was. We were all taught as children not to judge books by their covers, after all.

I recall Jewel's jaunty wave as she got on the bus. I can't imagine what she'll think. But then I remember also the "vision board" she's making in her room, the collage of pictures representing the things she wants to happen in her life. In the center of the board is a family picture. I'm not in it. It's a Christmas card portrait; the last holiday when Mallory and Michael were still married.

She likes me, Jewel does, but when she's really falling apart over something, she cries for her mother, as all children do, even the children of volatile Mallory.

Next to me is my journal. I haven't opened it again since before dawn this morning, when I saw scribbled in red ink on the first blank page: *You sure have a lot of secrets, CASEY!!!!!!*

For months I've been reminding myself how hard it is to be sixteen, and that for me to move in was a drastic change; maybe she feels supplanted as the reigning queen bee now that her mom lives somewhere else. That's the story I tell myself, anyway, to explain the hostility spreading like mold over our relationship. When I was just someone her father was seeing, we had fun shopping and drinking lattes together. But the weekend I moved in, she picked a dramatic fight over my inadequate laundry skills.

Each day since then has been more of a struggle not to see her mother in that haughty raised eyebrow and upturned lip.

I shake my hands out before I begin.

> *Dear Michael,*
> *I know I'm a coward for doing this in writing . . .*

I seal the letter in an envelope and put it on top of his dresser, where he empties his pocket change every day, changing from khaki pants into sweats or jeans. He'll see it as soon as he's home from work.

There's a picture on top of this dresser. It's of me. I'm wearing a baseball cap and my dark blond hair is hanging in a ponytail. I'm holding a baseball bat, glaring with mock concentration at the invisible pitcher, but my eyes are smiling and I know that the minute the shutter clicked I snorted with laughter. I don't remember the exact joke, but it didn't take much to get me started back then. I know I kissed him as soon as I put the bat down. Michael had added text to the picture before printing it out. It says, "Casey at the bat," in the blue sky behind me.

The ring snags on my knuckle, biting into the skin as I try

to pull it off. My hands are puffy. I yank again, letting it bang again into the existing scrape, which is now blooming with a line of red.

Against my will, my mind flashes to the moment Michael slid this ring on my finger, almost a year ago, on New Year's Eve. Mallory had the kids that night, and we sat on a rug in front of the living room fireplace. The house was then a place I only visited, a place we had to ourselves when Mallory managed to keep to her visitation days. I'd never seen its dustiest corners, never hauled the smelly trash to the curb. I knew but did not yet grasp this bit of history: it was not just a pretty house, but had been the Turner family home since Michael was a kid, and then the very home where Michael and Mallory had settled in as newlyweds. I still use the mixing bowls they got as a wedding gift to stir the pancake batter every Sunday.

That New Year's Eve, amber firelight wavering across his face, he whispered, "I never thought I'd do this again."

I gasped. He must have thought it was delight and surprise. It was more like a falling dream; a sickening plunge. *A stepmother? Me?* I thought of myself drunk at the bottom of a stairwell or puking my guts out in a smelly bar bathroom.

That wasn't the girl he wanted to marry. He never met that girl at all, never knew she existed.

It was me he wanted, the new me, the one who played board games with his kids and didn't even like the *taste* of alcohol. He made me chicken soup when I was sick and taught me to play euchre and told me dumb jokes until I laughed when I was having a bad day. He loves me, I thought. And that will be enough. So I said yes.

The ring still won't come off. I clench my bloody knuckle and resign myself to leaving it on, for now. An unwelcome loose end. I walk out of the room, no longer my room, and it wasn't ever, really.

I pause at the front door with my hand on the knob, holding my breath, allowing myself to feel this tearing away, doubting myself. If it hurts this much to walk out this door, does that mean I should stay?

But vaccinations hurt, too. Surgery hurts. Exercise hurts. Sometimes pain is necessary.

I yank on the knob. It comes open hard, as if resisting me, but that's just fancy. It's a sticky old wooden door, is all.

I almost sprint down the porch stairs, my bag slapping against my hip.

I'm halfway down the block when I realize I don't have my phone. Also, I should probably leave the key. I'll have to get my books and things later, but I'll do that at some appointed time, and Michael will open the door to let me in. Or maybe we can meet at a neutral location.

And I'll have to return the ring, once I get it off.

The house grows larger in my view, again with its surprised-looking front windows. It's disorienting to have turned around. Just minutes before when I crossed the threshold it had felt so final and momentous. For a moment I stand on the sidewalk in front of the house and consider leaving my phone there, too, maybe leaving it all there, forever.

The house already seems to me like it belongs to a stranger. A pretty wood house among other pretty wood houses, painted a soft gray-blue like a dawn sky before the sun has gathered full strength, a rounded, half-moon window and a wraparound porch morphing into mere details, as if I hadn't seen Dr. Turner and Michael carefully painting every spindle of that porch just last spring.

I can always get new books. I could turn around again.

But no. My mother will call, and then she'll worry, and that wouldn't be fair, considering what she's been through already.

I rush back up the porch, and suck in a sharp breath as I turn the key in the lock and shove the heavy wood door open with my shoulder.

My phone is in the kitchen, and I'm just picking it up when the house phone rings. I look at caller ID: the high school. I let it ring three times before I resign myself to picking up. After all, there could be something wrong.

Chapter 2

Michael
_____

I yank open the heavy metal employee entrance door at the *Grand Rapids Herald* newsroom, my head already full of yesterday's story and this morning's last-minute edits.

The scent of fresh ink clings to the building, though the presses moved to a facility miles away more than two years ago.

Every morning as I walk this hall, I recall a full, bustling office, the police scanner fizzing with static, the television on to the morning news, reporters already working the phones, editors squinting at their screens.

Reality hits me when I round the corner: half the seats are now empty, the computer terminals removed and redistributed to other papers in the company. Here and there a coffee mug sits, ringed with the brown remnants of mugs swilled on deadline. There still should be a buzz of activity. But a malaise has settled on the survivors. The loudest noise is the muted clacking of keys.

I sit down and punch the button to fire up my terminal, glancing about for Aaron. I see he's already busy with Tina, so I pull out my notes.

Gerald used to sit next to me. His computer is gone, as is his stuff. But there's still a photo print on his low workspace wall, snapped by one of our photogs during a candid moment. Gerald is scowling at his screen, his glasses on the end of his nose like something out of Dickens. The caption reads: "I *am* smiling, dammit," which became a famous Gerald-ism, uttered in response to an unbearable intern who exhorted him to smile. On deadline.

The terminal across from me, where Amanda works, has a note taped to the screen: *Just on vacation! Don't vulture my stuff.*

Now that my computer is awake, I pull up my story about local election reaction, most of which I wrote last night but will polish this morning for the afternoon paper. The city council just had its vote, and one of the more bombastic councilmen was unseated. Made for some fun quotes, but I couldn't get his city administrator nemesis to talk last night. He promised to call me this morning though, just squeaking under deadline.

Aaron has inserted a couple of editing questions easy enough to answer, so I set about doing just that.

That's when I hear his clomping cowboy boots coming up behind me. He's got a press release in his hand. I can see "For Immediate Release" from here.

"Hi, Michael, listen, I need you to get to a press conference at the university this morning, it starts at nine, sorry for the late notice."

I turn back to my screen. "I need to reach Henning for comment on the election. He said he'd talk to me this morning."

"We'll have to go without it. The university is making an announcement, potentially funding cuts, or maybe someone important is quitting."

Useless to argue. Our education reporter took the buyout last month. This might be an intern job, except the intern is already at the police station finding out who got killed overnight.

I sigh and hold out my hand for the release. As he gives it to me, Aaron says, "Oh, did you check out that rumor about a new strip club?"

"Yes, and it's officially bullshit, like I told you." I don't bother to conceal my irritation, and Aaron ignores it as he stomps back to his own desk. Now that anonymous online forums are part of the paper's Web site, some of the local cranks have taken to posting rumors, meaning I have to waste my time chasing them down, proving them wrong, wondering all the while how small-minded nameless trolls hiding behind keyboards became so important.

After polishing up my election story, I was supposed to spend the day analyzing building code enforcement violations for a series I want to do on housing blight and gentrification in the city.

I was supposed to do a lot of things.

I'm trying to read the release, but my snapshot of Casey distracts me. I don't have time to think about her now, so I turn my back to my desk, facing the center of the newsroom as I try to read between the lines of the press release and guess the announcement.

Still can't think. Angel's voice is in my head, telling me this morning something is "up" with Casey. Then she stared hard at me. I only caught a glimpse of her look, because I was watching the road, but I could feel her turned toward me for long moments. Can she detect the distance between Casey and me these days? If so, it's not a stretch to imagine that she'd be glad of it.

Last weekend Mallory took the kids, and we'd planned to cook a nice dinner for ourselves at home—going out costs too much, but I told her I'd light candles in the dining room and put on music. The conversation kept circling back to the kids, and Casey turned prickly and defensive at my gentle suggestion she was taking it all too personally. And in the midst of it all, Mallory found reasons to call me three times.

I'd hoped to fall into bed with Casey right after dinner and stay there, only she got up to clear the table and filled the sink with hot water and washed every dish. By hand, ignoring the dishwasher.

Watching her do that, her face locked in a resigned grimace, a look I recognized as Casey fighting back tears, twin geysers of sadness and anger erupted in me. I grieved for our vanished affectionate companionship, and was simply pissed that she chose to wash the fucking dishes instead of coming to bed with me.

My e-mail dings, and I reflexively look. It's a staffwide e-mail. Groans roll through the newsroom like a wave. Four o'clock staff meetings never bode well.

My cell phone goes off as I find the first blank page in a notebook, marking the spot with a paper clip. I scribble "Univ. press conf." on the top line.

"Hello."

"Michael, it's your father."

"I'm at work."

"We're having lunch today, are we not?"

I hadn't even looked at my planner yet. "Oh, we are. Though I have a press conference to attend."

"Surely you can manage to jot down some canned statements from a podium without too much strain."

"I realize it's not open-heart surgery," I reply to Henry Turner, M.D., but he ignores my remark. "However, they might have an important announcement, there might be reaction, analysis . . ."

"Analysis," he repeats, and I hear him huff through his gray mustache into the phone.

"I've gotta go. I'll call you."

I give up trying to make sense of the release and just take note of the location and parking.

Turning back to my screen, I decide to give last night's story one more read-through, double-checking the quotes and the vote totals from the precincts. I can't find it in the system at first, and I have a moment of queasy panic, thinking it vanished. Then I do find it, in a folder where I can't open it. It's already out of my hands, off to the copyeditors. Damn. Now I'll be anxious all day that I couldn't double-check. We never used to send the stories so early, but the copy desk is stretched so thin these days, they need more time. If I made a mistake on my late shift last night—I'm careful, but it's always possible to screw up—now I can't fix it, and it will be reprinted thousands of times, all over the city, with my byline.

There's nothing I hate more than a mistake with my name on it.

I set my phone to vibrate and put it in my pocket. It goes off immediately, but I don't even look. It's probably Henning calling with some terrific quote for the election story, and now I can't even use it.

I check my recorder for fresh batteries and head to my car to listen to some canned quotes from behind a podium.

The press conference is in the atrium of the administration building. They have arrayed many more chairs than necessary for just me, a radio reporter, a college kid in jeans and combat boots from the school paper, and a couple of TV cameras there sans reporters for the sound bite. I pick a seat close to the front, sharing nods with the handful of colleagues. I think I heard something on my way out of the office about a shooting at a nightclub last night, so that's probably where the TV reporters are, doing stand-ups in front of the building.

Casey reacted the same way most people do when I told her I was a newspaper reporter. Her eyes got big and she said, "Ooooh." She asked what I write and I told her, "I cover City Hall." Most people start to shut down right there, their minds shifting from fedoras and crime scenes to dreary ordinances and budget hearings. But she stayed interested, even when I did talk about the ordinances. Just as she was interested in my kids right off, and not just Jewel, the youngest and most cuddly.

Mallory—and now Angel—have so much scorn for the fact that she's young, but there's something infectious about that twentysomething enthusiasm. I haven't had that since, well, never. I had my kids too young for that and, anyway, I was old before I left the house for college.

I look at my watch. They're late to start. The radio guy looks like he might make small talk. He's trying to catch my eye. I leaf through my notebook—old notes from old stories, now in recycle bins and at the bottom of birdcages all over town—as if I'm doing something terribly important and shouldn't be interrupted.

My eye passes over a note in the margin, a note to myself that had nothing to do with whatever meeting I was in at the time. *Call Mallory re: weekend*, it reads. As I recall, she'd sent me a text that she didn't think she could take the kids. Another "headache," which had years before become code for her just not feeling up to mothering that day. At various times I'd feel compassion for her—I know what she's been through—and heated frustration. *Aren't you carrying this a bit far now?* I'd want to say. In any case, the approach of every weekend when Mallory has "parenting time" means a creeping anxiety about whether she might call it off, leaving me to smooth things over and stay positive, just like that pamphlet from Friend of the Court says to do.

People have asked me, my father loudest among them, why I stayed so long, as if getting divorced is like a Ferris-wheel ride. Who would gleefully dive into a world of lawyers and paperwork and "primary physical custody" and "parenting time" and negotiated exchanges of the children from one house to another?

Plus, divorce means the same income supporting two households. Dr. Turner didn't bother doing that math when he was telling me I should leave.

I was getting by. For a long time, I was getting by.

At least this weekend is our weekend. No explaining, no anxious pacing as we all hold our breath to see if Mallory will call and cancel. We can just pop some popcorn and watch a movie in front of the fire.

Men in suits spill out of the elevator, and all of us in the press corps, such as it is, straighten in our chairs.

Canned quotes about a new scholarship. The radio reporter asks, "What is the funding source?"

The suit behind the mic says, "Dr. Henry Turner's foundation."

My digital recorder clatters out of my hand, breaking off the battery door. It still seems to be running, which is fortunate because I can't even hear what they're saying. My own father, mocking my press conference task, and he's the one behind it all along. This means I'm not even supposed to be covering this; I can't write about my own dad. I'll end up typing up my notes and giving it to someone else, to be under some other byline, or maybe no byline, just "Herald Staff Writers."

He's not at the press conference, because he's not interested in the limelight. At least, that's what he'll tell whichever of my colleagues gets to call and interview him about this. Then he'll say something about the importance of education for underprivileged youth.

I note that the scholarships are for science and math. Fields he respects.

The press conference breaks up, and that's when I catch the quizzical glances thrown my way from the other reporters. Gus, from the radio station, sidles up. "Dude, I'm surprised you're here."

"I didn't know. Aaron just threw this release at me this morning."

I show it to Gus, who scowls at it. "Oh, that's old, they put that out on Monday. There was a fresh one this morning that told all about it, your dad and everything."

Jesus, Aaron. I fantasize about shoving one of his cowboy boots down his throat, pointy toe first.

Gus nods. "I know, dude. Sucks." He waves and walks off, his recorder bouncing along next to him.

I flip open my phone to check messages. A voice mail and three texts, all from Casey. Dammit, what now? The texts say, *Call home* and then *Where r u?* and *Call ASAP.*

The voice mail is similar. Casey telling me to call the minute I get the message.

I text back: *What? Busy here.*

I keep telling Casey she doesn't need to consult me about everything. If we're getting married, she has to learn to handle it herself when Dylan forgets his saxophone at home or Angel wants permission to go to a friend's house.

I drive back to the office, weighing how angry I can be with Aaron for the old press release. I decide I can be pretty fucking well mad because what's he going to do, fire me? We can barely run the paper with the staff we have now. Obviously.

And then, my dad. Good God.

At the office, I want to smash my watch on the desk, though it's not my watch's fault that so much of the morning has been wasted. Henning e-mailed me a great quote for the morning's story, too: "Maybe now the city council can leave behind the sandbox-level bickering and make progress on the tough issues facing us today." Won't make the paper now.

I managed to restrain myself from forcing Aaron to swallow his own boot, but I did curse freely when I explained the press conference problem. He told me to type up my notes and he'd get Kate to finish the story, as long as I finished getting quotes for Kate's holiday shopping feature.

"There, happy now?" Aaron had snapped.

"Ecstatic." Even better than a press conference. Interviewing store managers about holiday shopping! Hurrah! Enough to make me jealous of the intern covering the shooting. I never got to cover shootings when I was just starting. But then again, we had experienced reporters to spare, back then.

Casey had sent a new text: *It's important.*

"Fine," I mutter to myself, and dial the home phone.

"Hi," Casey says, and then right away, "Dylan's missing."

"What? No, he's not, I dropped him off at school myself."

"Well, he's not there now. The school called this morning to say he never showed up in class."

I suck in a deep breath. It's probably nothing. It almost always is nothing, just like a hot news tip usually fizzles upon investigation. I recall a time at the park when Dylan was five and Mallory lost sight of him and went screaming his name in the woods around the playground. Turns out he'd been sitting inside one of those plastic slide contraptions while Mallory and Angel had an argument, and had dozed off. The effect of that day had caused her to start drinking earlier than usual. She should have just checked the damn slide.

I sigh and pinch the bridge of my nose, where a headache is starting to throb. "He's probably being a rebel."

"What do you mean?"

"I mean he's fourteen years old. He's hiding in someone's car smoking pot or something. I'll ground him for life when he turns up."

"That doesn't sound like Dylan. And you don't sound worried."

"Case, it's only . . . 10:30. He's probably just cutting class."

"I don't know."

"Why, did he say something?"

"Not really, he's just seemed distant. I tried to ruffle his hair this morning, and he ducked me."

"He's a teenager, not a four-year-old."

"I know, but he never used to mind."

"Just when you get used to kids, they change."

"You don't have to tell me that, it's just—"

"Casey, look. I have to go. Call his cell and tell him to call us or he's grounded forever."

"I called it. Straight to voice mail."

"See, he shut off his phone, which means he's up to mischief. If he were dead in a ditch somewhere, it would ring. Anyway, he's not dead in a ditch, because I drove him to school."

"Not funny."

"I didn't say it was. Look, call me when he turns up, I really have to go."

"Okay. Well. Bye, I guess."

I guess. Casey's classic hint, leaving the door open a crack, wanting me to walk through it and get into a long conversation. *I guess* means, *Wait, don't hang up*, or *Don't walk away.*

"He's fine. He's a boy being a boy. We'll kill him later."

She says "Bye" in a small voice that makes her sound like she's twelve, a habit that sends a spark of irritation into my gut.

I've got ninety minutes to call mall managers before lunch with my father, the philanthropist, which means ninety minutes to figure out exactly what I'm going to say to his smug, mustached face about how he wasted my morning and embarrassed the hell out of me.

★ ★ ★

Dad always gets there first, always sits down first, every time we have lunch, and these days, since his semiretirement, he's always having a Manhattan.

He acts like everything is utterly normal, sitting there in his salmon pink dress shirt. "Mikey!" he says, rising to greet me, but not entirely standing up, before settling back in his chair and snapping the cloth napkin out. "I've already ordered. I'm sure you must be busy, so I didn't want to take up your time."

"Why the hell didn't you tell me that was your thing at the university?"

"I didn't know it was the same press conference. Anyway, with the *Herald* being so short-staffed, can they afford to care who's related to whom? It's not like it's much of a conflict of interest to type up quotes. I mean, really. What are you going to do? Make me sound heroic for giving a little money?"

He sips his Manhattan, a gleam in his eye, maybe imagining this hypothetical glowing article.

"You could have saved me a lot of grief."

"You didn't give me a chance, anyway, you rushed me off the phone so fast."

He leans back in his chair, his subtle smile nearly masked by his gray mustache. His full head of hair is showing signs of curling at the edges, which means it's been too long since his last haircut. He's really cutting loose, now.

I slump back in my chair, defeated as ever by his surpassing confidence that he's right.

"What's wrong, son?"

"Just having a busy day. This press conference messed up my morning, then I got handed a feature on holiday shopping, and frankly I'd rather chew broken glass then quote mall managers about their stupid sales. And now Dylan—" I slam the door on that, not wanting to show him a chink in my parental armor. Dylan will turn up and be grounded and Dad doesn't need the gory details. "Dylan is being sullen."

"Not unlike someone else I know," he says, stirring the cherry around in his drink with a plastic sword.

"He didn't used to clam up so much."

"Maybe it's your new family arrangement?"

"Don't blame this on Casey."

"Not saying it's her *fault*, Mike. But you have to consider what in his environment changed."

"Form a hypothesis and test it? Run a study with a control group? He's not a lab experiment."

My dad sighs and stares out the window. "Windy out today," he comments as a piece of trash careens down the sidewalk.

Our sandwiches arrive. Turkey, no mayo, side of fresh fruit, for both of us. Very heart-healthy from Dr. Henry. Usually I order this myself, but today I wanted a Reuben and greasy fries.

He waits until I have a giant mouthful of turkey to start in on my job.

"Sorry to hear you're having such a rough day. My offer still stands, you know."

I choke down my bite of sandwich and match his gaze. "If I want to pursue grad school, I'll pay for it myself."

"With what?" That smile again, at the worst of moments.

"I'm doing fine."

"Hmmm." He dabs at the corners of his mouth with his napkin.

With that one *hmmm*, he skewers my whole life, from my career choice to my disastrous marriage and the troubles between me and Casey he doesn't even know about, yet somehow he does. I haven't followed his advice, and as such he assumes my life is a train wreck.

The sickening thing is, he's more right than wrong.

"How's Mom?"

"Fine. Started a book club. Still swimming at the Y. This weekend she started winterizing the garden. How's young Casey?"

"Fine. Getting plenty of work, so that's good."

"Good to hear. She should keep herself busy while the kids are at school."

"She does. As I just said, she's got plenty of work coming in."

"Even in this economy? People still need computer programs, I guess. Well, good for her. And still plenty of time to help around the house."

"She works hard in her job. She's brilliant at it, in fact. She's a great girl."

"I didn't say otherwise, Michael."

I'm aware of the defensive edge in my voice, the paranoia even, that he's hinting anything negative about Casey, like that she doesn't really work. She's always on her computer, or on the phone to clients, or e-mailing pitches to new potential clients for Web development. We talked about her getting a full-time job, but she said she likes it at home. Less distracting than being in an office.

My dad switches to water now that his Manhattan is gone. Always in control, even of his vices, which are few and carefully chosen.

Considering my life with Mallory, I have to admire this about him.

I tuck back into my sandwich, and the rest of the lunch is spent largely in silence, except for my dad fielding a call on his cell phone. He makes arrangements to return the call, and I know it's a reporter. Kate, or someone from television.

The waiter puts the check diplomatically in the middle of the table. I don't even bother to grab for it, knowing he would win, and in the course of winning the bill, manage to denigrate once again my career choice.

He strides off to his SUV as I stand outside the restaurant in the biting wind, looking at my phone, noting with some surprise that Casey hasn't called to say that Dylan turned up. I swallow hard and clench my fist as I jam my phone back into my coat pocket.

I really will ground him for the whole year. I swear I will.

Chapter 3

Casey

I tap my pen on the kitchen counter as I wait for Marcy to answer her phone. Maybe Dylan is off making mischief as Michael believes, and maybe it's with his best friend.

As she answers, I hear a din of loud conversation.

"It's Casey, Dylan's—" I stumble over the lack of a word for what I am to him. "Hi. Is this a bad time?"

"Not really. I'm in line at the coffee shop."

Her words are rushed, her voice betraying impatience. It is in fact a bad time, but she'd rather get this over with than have to call me back. I don't have time to be offended at the slight just now.

"Is everything okay with Jake?"

"Of course. Why?"

"Well, Dylan's cutting class or something. He's not at school, though his dad dropped him off."

"Yes?"

I clench my fist until the nails burn crescents into my palm. "I was just wondering if you'd heard anything similar about Jacob. You know how those two are inseparable!" I laugh, making it light, not accusatory.

"Lately, not so much, actually. Grande nonfat latte please."

"What do you mean?"

"I mean—" She pauses, the noises changing as she shifts the phone, maybe pinning it between shoulder and ear. "I mean that they haven't been talking much lately. I thought you knew."

"No, I didn't have any idea . . . Did they have an argument?"

"Boys don't have arguments. They beat each other up or just quit talking. It was the latter."

"What was wrong?"

"Jacob didn't say. I was just making out the guest list for his birthday party, and he said he didn't want to include Dylan."

Jacob's been his friend since the sandbox. Since Dylan left the public school they hadn't seen each other daily, but with Facebook and cell phones, I figured they were still in touch.

"You didn't ask why?"

"He said it was 'nothing.' You know how boys are. Well, maybe you don't. Anyway, you can't pry things out of them if they're not ready to tell you. In any case, I wouldn't have any idea where Dylan is."

"Please call if you hear something."

"I'm sure I won't, but I'll call if I do. Have to dash now, bye."

I put my head in my hand and stare at the phone. My laptop, at my elbow, dings for new mail. I'm supposed to be working. I have deadlines for clients. Updates. Proposals. I had planned to be at the library today using the Wi-Fi until Tony got out of work, then I was going to crash on his couch until I found an apartment. That was the plan.

It still could be. I could take for granted Michael is right and Dylan is just misbehaving somewhere. The school has Michael's cell phone number on file. I could still go.

Except I can't. I imagine Jewel getting home from Scouts and finding only Angel here, the two of them wondering where their brother is, where I am.

Maybe Angel knows. I sit up straight at the counter.

She's not supposed to use her phone in class, but she could check it at lunch. I send a text: *Seen your brother? School sez not in class.*

The silence of the house presses in on me.

I feel achy, uncomfortable, and jittery.

I push away from the counter and start to pace through the first floor, in U-shaped loops through the connected living room, dining room, kitchen, around the curved open staircase and back.

Most days it's not that hard, not drinking. Michael doesn't often drink, himself. I don't go to parties, or restaurants. My old life feels like a dead skin I've shed along with the old boozy friends, and the small company where we all worked.

But there are times . . . when my palms start to itch and my heart feels tight and pinched. I can taste the velvety bite of it, and I can feel the uncoiling of my tension and hear my own carefree laughter, and I know that the liquor store is just blocks away and no one will be home for hours yet.

Tony's always telling me, "One drink is too many and a hundred's not enough."

I don't think it's like that for me. I bet I could have one, maybe even two. But then I think of all the energy I'd expend wondering, *Should I have this one? Is this one too many? But I'm feeling fine and not driving, but maybe I shouldn't . . .* Or the next day, *Did I have too many last night?* And then guilt would crash over me, I know it would. It was simpler, cleaner, simply to break off that piece of my life and set it adrift.

Then I met Michael, and he was so glad I didn't drink that I treasured up his gladness and decided that was worth more than any drop of Jack ever could be.

These days, though, Michael hasn't seemed glad about much of anything.

I try breathing from my gut. This attempt at breathing simply reminds me what I'm trying to avoid.

I seize my purse with its cigarettes and both the cordless house phone and my cell, and brave the snap of the November air on the back patio.

The first puff makes my head feel swimmy, and my heart slows down almost immediately.

Hurrah for self-medicating.

Michael's disapproving stare rises up in my memory. If he only knew what I've already given up. But he can't know, because he wouldn't love a woman like that. Never again, he said. But that "never again" speech came late, after I already loved him. Otherwise I might have saved us both the eventual agony.

It's like scratching at a scab to think of this now, our first meeting. But I'm too weary to keep pushing it out of my head. Here at the end, I can't help but think of the beginning.

I was sick that day. Feverish, pale, shaky. My head throbbed, and my sinuses were so backed up I thought I might suffocate in my own skull.

I had no friends anymore, because they were all drinkers and I was clinging to the fragile threads of a different life. So I dragged myself to the urgent care clinic alone. I actually perked up a bit in the cold, it being January, then. Nearly two years ago.

At the clinic, I saw a little girl curled up on her daddy's lap, her arm clutching a stuffed cat gone threadbare at its paws and belly. Her hair hung limp and tangled, and she wore Hannah Montana pajamas and bedroom slippers. She had round glasses with pink frames. She was asking, moaning, really: "Daddy? How long?"

Her father was rubbing circles on her back. "Soon, baby. As soon as they can see us."

"I don't want to blow up again," she moaned into his shoulder.

A wincing expression flashed on his face, something with shades of both pain and amusement. "I hope you won't throw up again, honey. But if it's going to happen, you tell me and we'll get you to the bathroom."

Her dad noticed me looking at her. He met my eyes and tightened his jaw. It was all there, right on his face. *I hate that I can't fix it.*

She was too old for peekaboo. I got out my phone, a fancy phone in those days before I completed my belt-tightening. I found a funny video of a monkey scratching his butt, sniffing his own finger, and falling off a tree branch.

I glanced at him, eyebrows up. *Do you mind?*

He shrugged.

I said to her, "Hey. Wanna see something funny?"

She raised her head a fraction of an inch off his shoulder. I leaned across the aisle separating us and showed her the short video. She smiled. I sat back, and she said, "Can I see it again?"

I sat on the chair next to them and found every G-rated silly video I could.

When they called "Jewel Turner," her father stood up and scooped her gently onto his shoulder. I stood up as if I belonged with them, forgetting myself. I sat back down, pretending to dust something off my pants.

The father looked back at me over his daughter's tangled hair, and mouthed, *Thank you.*

I was next. I didn't think about them again until I came back to the lobby with a prescription in my fist. Jewel's daddy was crouched, zipping up her coat. His coffee-dark hair was a mess, I noticed. I also saw a scar along his jawline.

"I hope you feel better soon, kiddo," I told her, ready to pass out of their lives.

"You, too," her father said, looking up at me, straightening her coat. "I'm Michael Turner."

"Casey," I replied, supplanting my last name instead of my given name, unthinking.

"I can call you and let you know how she's doing."

It was so transparent. I blushed, I think, or it might have been the fever.

Then he scooped her up and muttered, walking out the door. "Or not. She'll be fine, it's just a virus."

"Maybe you could just e-mail me an update," I said, walking with him through the door, and I rattled off my address, which was one of those that was easy to say and remember. I'd picked it brand-new, cutting off old ties in the process.

He disappeared into the night, and I dragged myself home, assuming the pleasant memory of his wide-open marble-blue eyes would be all I'd ever have of this really good dad I saw in a waiting room.

Maybe it should have stayed that way.

I grind out my cigarette, and the phone buzzes. Angel must have snuck me a text between classes.

Not there? Will call Mom.

Mallory. Oh, shit.

Dylan's room is not the smelly den one would expect from a teenager.

It's not what you'd call neat, but it's not filthy, either. No crumbs, no half-empty cans of pop. His dirty laundry is in the hamper, not stinking up his room. I almost wish it were disgusting, because I'm afraid Dylan is becoming a mini-Michael, that is to say, old before his time.

I value how responsible Michael is, truly, especially given what I went through with my brother. But Dylan is still a kid, even with a smudge of mustache on his upper lip.

I pull open the closet, holding my breath, bracing myself to see empty hangers as if he'd packed his things.

But no, it looks just as crowded as ever with his black T-shirts and oversize sweaters. Anyway, it's not like he could sneak a duffle bag into the car with his dad.

If Jewel had turned up missing, I'd be in a panic. She's vulnerable, small.

But Dylan is a teenager. And he got dropped off at school. This much we know.

My cell rings. Michael.

"Hi."

"Any sign of him?"

"Nothing. Angel hasn't seen him at school, either. I think she's going to call her mother."

"Well, maybe she had something to do with it."

"Like what?"

"Maybe she decided to take him to an amusement park, or the movies . . . you know how impulsive she is."

"But she could have signed him out of school, claimed he was sick or going to the dentist or something. Dylan would have wanted her to, rather than get detention for skipping, don't you think?"

"Maybe I should come home."

Yes, please. I don't know what to do. "I don't know. What would you be able to accomplish? Sit around and wait."

"I could call his friends."

"I already checked with Jacob's mom. She said they're not even friends anymore."

"Huh?"

"Yeah. His clothes are still here."

"Of course they are. He didn't just take off." The scorn is palpable. I know why; it sounds like I'm comparing him to Mallory.

"He went somewhere, didn't he? Did he walk right into the school?"

"I told you, I dropped him off."

"Don't snap at me, I'm trying to help."

A heavy, aggrieved sigh. "And I'm at work and my son is missing."

"I thought you weren't worried."

In the silence of his nonresponse, I can hear newsroom noise: a din of intense conversation, like a loud and disgruntled crowd.

"Michael?"

"I'm here. Just keep trying his cell, and call any other friends you can think of. Get the band parent list out of the junk drawer and try them. If a bunch of his friends are skipping school, then we know it's probably nothing. It'll be fine."

"I guess."

"What?"

"What if Mallory comes over here?"

"Well, we can't very well tell her not to. Dylan's her son, and if she wants to be at the house while we track him down—"

"By myself, though?"

"She's not going to eat your spleen."

I try to chuckle, and it comes out more like a cough. "Good to know she stops short of cannibalism."

"We'll find him, and I'll kick his ass, and everything will be fine. If Mallory turns up, just . . . play it cool. Stay breezy, relaxed. Don't hyper her up."

Relaxed. Right.

I hang up the phone and go out to the patio for another smoke. I'm going to need it. I check my watch after I light up. It's afternoon already, and all that I've consumed since one bowl of cereal at breakfast is nicotine and tar.

That means it's almost time for my mother to call. I call her instead to get it over with so I can go back inside and call Dylan's band friends.

"Hi, Mom."

"Edna! Hi, honey. How's your day going?"

I lie to her for the sake of simplicity. "Okay. Yours?"

"I ran into Petey at the store. You know he's still asking about you."

I know this, because he called me not long ago. "I'm engaged, Mom. And why did you give him my cell number?"

"I'm just saying. If you decide that raising someone else's kids is not your idea of fun . . ."

"I didn't sign up for fun. I love him." I prop my cigarette in my phone hand and cover my eyes with my free hand.

"Fun and love used to go together, you know."

"It wasn't always fun with Pete. We had plenty of not-fun times. Remember Billy's funeral?"

She gasps like she's been sliced. "Edna Leigh."

"I'm just saying, you only think he's a saint because we broke up. It's nostalgia."

"He just fit in so well."

"Did he ever."

"Don't you start with me. I know you're too good to even visit us anymore, but you don't have to criticize every move we make."

"I'm not criticizing. I was agreeing."

"How great can this Michael be if he doesn't even want to meet your family?"

"It's complicated," I say again, because it is.

"It doesn't have to be. Anyway, are you coming to Wanda's baby's party this weekend?"

My cousin's baby's first birthday. They'll even break out the beer for a toddler's party. By the end of the night, they'll be shooting cans off the back fence and having wrestling matches in the yard. They won't talk to me, either, instead whispering behind my back about how I blew town right after my brother's funeral, not even staying to support my grieving parents. Some of them outright blame me, I know.

My mother insists they don't, but I can feel their heavy stares, see it in the way they turn quickly away if they happen to meet my eyes.

"I can't. I'm swamped with work."

"I just bet."

"Can we not fight? I don't have it in me today."

"Me neither, honey. I ran across Billy's old hunting jacket today."

"Oh, Mom. I'm sorry. Are you okay?"

"Of course I'm not. But I'm standing up, so there ya go."

"I'll try to come to the party, okay?"

"Don't do me any favors."

"I'm trying to do the right thing, here."

"I know, baby. I'm sorry. It's not the best of days."

"I know the feeling."

"I'll call you later. I promised Wanda I'd babysit, and she'll be over soon. You know, I can't wait to be holding your own baby, darlin'."

"One step at a time. I guess I'm old-fashioned enough to get married first."

"Now don't you start in on Wanda."

"I'm not, I just don't need the pressure. I'm only twenty-six."

"I'm just saying. I love those baby cuddles, and when I get to be a grandma, I'll climb up on the roof and scream for joy! Oops, there's Wanda's car. Love ya bunches."

"Love you, too."

I've seen pictures of Wanda's baby. She's so deliciously chubby I want to stick my nose in her neck and blow raspberries. Her wispy hair looks like golden feathers, and with her pursed mouth she's like a pudgy little bird.

I used to fantasize about what my baby would look like, my baby with Michael. She'd have loads of thick black hair, just like her father, and hazel eyes, like me. Like my brother's.

At a furious, rapid pounding I nearly drop my phone. The doorbell broke a few months ago, and the front door is so thick you have to jackhammer it to be heard. I hurry inside and through the front room curtains I can see a tall stack of white-blond hair.

I yank open the door.

"Where's my son?" Mallory cries, gripping my arm like she's drowning.

Chapter 4

Michael

K ate startles me as she says in my ear, "Oh, the copy desk will love you for that."

Typing up the mall shopping story, I'd written, " 'It's a tough economy, but we're all hoping that with credit finally loosening up, the shopping season will give retailers a nice boost,' said Kenneth Delaney, spokesman for the Michigan Retailer Association, otherwise known as Captain Obvious."

I backspace past my sarcasm. "I wasn't really going to leave that in."

"Get your fun where you can, eh?" Kate flops into her chair at her desk, just to the right of me. "I had the fun of interviewing your father."

"Sorry. But then, I'm interviewing your mall managers, so I guess we're even."

"It was fine. He returns calls, knows how to spew a pithy

quote, doesn't nitpick the story after it's published. My idea of a perfect source." She stretches her arms over her head, tipping back in her chair. Her blouse rides up to reveal a sliver of skin, and I glance away.

"Yeah, he'd love to hear that. He loves to be perfect at anything."

"Tell us how you really feel, Mike."

"You know how family is."

Kate's cell goes off, singing, *"Since you've been gone . . ."* She mutes the phone and tosses it theatrically in her bottom desk drawer. "My ex. His own special ringtone."

"What now?"

"He thinks I owe him money. He's thinking of suing me. He thinks he's God. What else is new? I swear he invented crazy. And I married it. What the hell were we thinking, Mike?"

"Kate, I have to finish this up. I may have to get out of here early today, so—"

"Okay, sorry. Very diligent of you."

My dad's voice echoes across the years: *What the hell were you thinking?*

My mother was sobbing into her hands like I'd just told her I had incurable cancer.

"I hope she's going to get it taken care of," my father snapped, pacing in front of the brick fireplace, his shadow slicing across the floor.

My mother gasped. "Henry!"

"Marian, they are not equipped for this. How can he start a family and graduate at the same time? And then support a kid on a starting journalist's salary? He'll be lucky to support himself. We're still paying for his car. And who is this girl, anyway? We've never heard of her. What happened to Heather?"

"Another guy happened to Heather. And I told you, her name is Mallory."

"Mallory, the name tells me nothing. What is she studying? And why in God's name was she not on the Pill? This is the nineties, you have to be a mental defective to get pregnant accidentally."

"I will not let you talk about her that way!" My voice came out unnaturally high and reedy. Some big-talking man I was.

"Oh, great, now I suppose you're in love with her."

My mother wiped her eyes, her face shiny wet in the firelight. "Are you?"

There was hope in her face. Love would make it okay for her, because then it wasn't a terrible mistake, it could be welcomed instead of dreaded. I saw it all in her mouth slightly agape, her breath caught.

"I'm very . . . we're passionate about each other."

"Too bloody passionate," interjected my dad, who'd sunk into the club chair near the fire.

"We weren't thinking—"

"What else is new."

"Henry! That's enough." My mother drew herself up, her five-foot frame looking like a sliver compared to my dad's hulking form in the chair. "Michael needs our support. And this is a grandchild! Not a problem to be discarded! I'm not happy about the way it came about myself, but what's done is done."

My mother wrapped her thin arms around me. I rested my chin on top of her head.

"Mikey. We'll figure it out. And I think we'd better meet her, don't you think?"

My phone yanks me back to the present moment, alerting me to a text.

Mallory's here, no Dylan yet, reports Casey.

Poor Casey, having to fend her off alone. But there's this story, stupid as it is, and I have to get it done. Then I'll get home. And everything will be fine.

The words in my notebook swim in my vision. What was I thinking indeed?

But without Mallory, there's no Angel, no Dylan. And there was very nearly no Jewel because I'd finally packed my bags to go . . .

"Mike."

When I pull myself out of my thoughts, I notice I'd been tracing my scar.

Kate waves her hand in my direction. "Are you okay? You look pale."

"Just tired," I tell her, waving her off, forcing myself to stare again at the screen.

She lowers her voice and rolls her chair a little closer. "Is it Casey?"

I fight to keep from rolling my eyes. In an idiot-moment over a lunchtime Reuben, I'd told Kate that Casey is a terrific girl but she didn't seem up to the stepparenting gig. Kate had covered my hand with hers, and I let myself feel sad, and I let myself be comforted for a moment that stretched a little too long. Since then I've had to be vigilant about being professional, friendly, and no more.

Yes, Kate's gorgeous, and she's also full of sympathy and

sweet, understanding smiles. I also happen to know she's cunning and calculated, which is one reason she's such a goddamn good reporter.

"I can't talk right now," I tell Kate, and she finally rolls back to her screen.

I look at the computer clock. It's now 2:00 P.M. That means no one has seen or heard from Dylan in over six hours. He's not answering his phone or texts. This is not like him. In fact, he's the most dependable of all of them. Though he's been quiet lately, even by his standards. What have I missed?

I tell myself again it's probably nothing and buckle down to get the story done, so I can get home and make damn well sure it's nothing.

I'm just spell-checking the shopping story and removing all sarcastic asides when two e-mails arrive. One is from the publisher, reminding all of the four o'clock meeting. The other is from Kate.

> Hey Mike,
> I know you're not just tired. You have "ex stress." I can see it all over your face. Been there, done that. Oh, come to think of it, still doing that.
> Hang in there. I was going to say it will get better but it probably won't! Anyway, wouldn't want you to stick your head in an oven or something. This place would be boring without you.
> Want to get a drink after work? My treat.
>
> K.

I slide my eyes over to her. She looks sideways at me and smiles a little, one of those encouraging smiles, a silent "chin up!"

I e-mail her back, wishing I could move to an empty desk farther away from her without the gossip mill starting to churn.

Can't. Potential crisis at home. Report back to me about 4 o'clock meeting, though. I have to leave.

I file the story and go hover by Aaron to get his attention. He's on the phone with someone combative, based on his repetition of the phrase, "I understand what you're saying."

I can't take it anymore. I seize a piece of paper out of a notebook on Aaron's desk and scribble: *Home emergency. Have to leave. Story filed.*

I toss it in front of his face. Just as I turn to walk away, I catch a glimpse of him whirling around in his chair to say something to me, but I pretend I didn't see it and just go straight for my coat.

It's a struggle not to speed as I drive home. Mallory and Casey are not a good mix together, not on the best of days. I kept them apart for a long time, and discouraged the kids from talking about Casey. I didn't forbid it, exactly, I just told them that Casey was only a friend and their mother didn't have to hear every detail of my life.

Dylan and Angel got it, tragically fluent in the language of divorce.

Jewel, though, talked about Casey painting her toenails. When I picked the kids up, she screamed at me about this new "girl" dolling up Jewel like "a harlot."

My crazy hope to see Dylan sitting on the porch is dashed.

The porch is empty, and it's unsettling to be home now during the week, the sun still high.

Just inside the front door, I hesitate, listening.

I don't see Mallory until she's on top of me. She's hurtled herself at me, torpedo fashion, clinging to me and weeping. "Where is he, Mike? Where's our baby?"

"Where's Casey?"

"Do you think I care where she is? Where's our son?"

"I'm just trying to figure out what's going on."

Casey walks to the living room entryway from the kitchen, holding the phone to her ear and waving the band parent list at me.

I nod, and try to pry Mallory off of me long enough for me to take off my coat.

"Don't panic yet. He's probably just cutting school."

The more I've said this today, the less I believe it.

"Bullshit," Mallory spits, now pacing like a caged predator. "Dylan is a good kid, he doesn't pull stuff like this. He wouldn't make me worry."

Casey comes to the doorway. "I just talked to the music teacher, who asked his friends at EXA. No one has seen him at all. They all assumed he was home sick today. I also called the friends from his old school. Nothing. And for some reason, Jacob isn't talking to him anymore at all."

Mallory had stopped in the center of the room, but she resumed pacing. "Something terrible has happened. I know it. I know it in my heart."

Casey's cell phone buzzes, and we all stop to stare at her while she looks at the screen. She shakes her head and puts her phone back away without answering.

"What could have happened?" I mutter.

"How could you lose him!" Mallory shouts, and I've started to defend myself when I notice she's shouting at Casey.

"Hey, I'm the one who drove him to school. And I'm telling you, he walked right in the building."

"But something is going on, isn't it? You live with him every day. Don't you know what's on his mind?"

I step between them as Casey hugs her sweater around herself, shrinking against the archway to the kitchen. "If anyone would know, it would be me. Don't put this on her." I put my arm around Casey's shoulders. Her body feels tight and hard, like wire on a spool.

Mallory tosses her head. "Of course, I guess I shouldn't expect that of your girlfriend. It's not like she knows anything about raising kids."

Casey shouts from the archway, shrugging off my arm, "You're his mother, and you don't know!"

"He doesn't live with me every day. I'm only allowed to have him two weekends a month." Mallory turns away, her voice cracking over the words. "I can't believe this *girl* is allowed to see my son more than I am."

I want to yell that she agreed to that, and in fact if she hadn't pulled that stunt with Jewel in the car she would probably still have custody. And that this *girl* is the one holding her kids' hair back when they vomit in the middle of the night.

But the house phone rings, and I run across the room to seize it.

"Angel, honey, calm down."

"They're all saying Dylan is missing, that he's dead or something."

It's 2:40. She's between school and play practice. I can hear the chaos of kids shouting to be heard in the halls, lockers slammed.

"Who's saying such crazy things?"

"The kids. His old band friends. They say no one can find him, and Casey said he didn't show up to class, and—"

"They're just kids passing hysterical rumors. Casey was calling the band kids to see if anyone had seen him, or if one of his friends was also skipping school."

"He won't answer his phone."

"I know, we've been trying, too. Has he said anything to you lately? Anything that might help us?"

"I want to come home."

"Are you sure, sweetie? I'm sure he'll turn up soon. All there is to do here is sit around and worry."

Mallory has appeared at my elbow. "Of course she can come home if she wants." She grabs for the phone, and I shrug her off.

"Mom's there?"

"Yeah, she's worried, too."

"And you're home from work. I wanna come, too. I don't want to listen to all these kids talk about Dylan."

"Okay. Meet me by the auditorium then. I'll be there as soon as I can."

I hang up and pull my coat back on.

"I could go get her," Casey quickly offers.

Mallory, hand on hip, interjects, "She wants her parents right now."

Mallory can't get her because she doesn't have a license anymore. She must have taken a cab to the house.

"I'll be back soon." I cast a look at Casey. She seems washed

out and wan. I give her a small smile, the same "chin up" look
Kate gave me at the office.

I start up my car again and think of Dylan, only his face in my
mind's eye has regressed from a teenager to the mop-haired boy
honking notes into his first saxophone, to the first-grader missing a tooth, to the chubby toddler covered in spaghetti.

I press down hard on the gas, wondering if it's time to call
the police.

Chapter 5

Casey

Mallory perches on the barstool at the kitchen counter, drumming her nails, which are broken, jagged.

"How can you wash dishes at a time like this?" she asks.

"We're just waiting. The dishes are dirty."

She doesn't have to be on top of me. She has a whole house to hang out in. I'm under surveillance.

She points at the cupboard above and to my right. "That's a better place to keep the glasses. Close to the sink."

"We moved them to where Jewel can reach. So she can get a drink herself."

"Oh, we did, huh? Isn't that cozy."

I scrub the dish harder, though it's already clean.

She continues, "I thought you'd want your own house. One that didn't used to be mine."

My breathing is shallow so I have to will myself to take in enough oxygen, lest I pass out right here. "Less disruptive for the kids."

"Hmmm." Mallory gazes out the window. "No sense in moving yet, since you're not married or anything. Of course, Mike can't really afford to move anyway, seeing how the good Dr. Henry owns the place and rents it to him for a song." Mallory hops down off the barstool and comes close to me. I can smell her lunch from here. Something with onions.

"So, Dylan hasn't given you any clues to what's going on? Any at all?"

"I told you, I don't know." I turn to put the dish away, though there are plenty of other dishes left to wash, anything to give me a couple inches of space. "He didn't give you any clues, either, right?"

"If I had him with me, I would know what's going on."

I let the next dish fall into the water. "Easy for you to say when you're not at Ground Zero."

During the silent moment that passes, Mallory matches my glare.

She's won by goading me.

"Our differences aren't important now." She sighs, leaning one hip against the counter. "We'll have to be *mature* about this."

I feel a sneer creep across my face before I can stop it.

Mallory leans in again, crowding me so tightly against the kitchen counter that the edge pinches my back as I stretch away. "I know that might be hard for you, being so young and all."

I pull myself away and toss the dishrag in the sink. Banging the back door open into the cold, I notice I've forgotten my coat. I don't even need the cigarette, but I'm starting to think longingly of Jack Daniel's. I can just picture Mallory inside, chuck-ling at how she needled me into reacting.

The wind kicks up, and it takes four tries to flick my lighter, cupping my hand around it.

Despite my protests to Mallory, a cold strand of guilt starts to thread its way through my gut. He has indeed been more quiet lately. And now I remember he's been bringing in the mail every day, which at the time I thought was so thoughtful, but now I wonder what he was hoping to intercept.

Should I have grilled him?

Whatever bond I have with Dylan is built on respect. He tells me things in his own time, usually when I listen to him practice, between songs as he rearranges his sheet music. He'll just vol-unteer something, and I grab it like a coin tossed into the dirt at my feet.

I close my eyes as the smoke loosens the tension in my shoul-ders, as my head feels lighter. I review our last practice sessions, which were a few weeks ago now. Trying to remember what he might have said.

Something about Jacob? Or that girl flute player he likes? What was it?

The kitchen door bangs open. Through the storm door Mi-chael looks away quickly, like he's caught me doing something embarrassing. Masturbating, or picking my nose. I throw down the cigarette, though now I really want to finish it.

"Angel's back," he says, looking at the ground. "She's upset."

"Kids are so dramatic."

"Hey, her brother has been missing all day."

"I meant the other kids. The ones spreading rumors."

I go through the kitchen to find a tight knot of conversation on the living room couch. Angel is in the crook of Michael's arm, chewing her thumbnail. Sitting on his other side is Mallory, her knees together, pressed close to Michael's side. His arm is stretched out along the back of the couch.

Both Angel and Mallory have whitish-blond hair, bookending Michael's darker complexion. They all have those same bright marble-blue eyes, reminding me of their unbreakable bond, which I can never share.

They seem to notice me all at once. Angel folds her arms and looks away. Michael's eyes flit down to the floor. Only Mallory stares directly at me. "What?" she says.

"Nothing, I'm just . . . Back inside. What can I do to help?"

"Oh, because you've been so much help already."

Michael looks between Mallory and me, his brow wrinkled up, eyes questioning. Angel glares in my direction, jumping the gun on angry.

Mallory continues, never breaking her stare. "Here I am, upset about my missing child, and she picks a fight at the sink and throws a dishcloth at me." She gestures to her damp shirt. I must have splashed her.

"I didn't *throw* it." I know I should be cool about this, not hyper her up, as Michael says, but my anger leaches out in my words. "And not *at* her. I dropped it in the sink."

Michael pinches the bridge of his nose. "Please. Not now."

I don't know which one of us he's talking to.

Mallory points a long finger at me. "Threw, dropped, whatever. She's behaving like a pouty kid. When our child's life is at stake."

Michael squeezes Angel's shoulders as she gives a little gasp.

"His life is not at stake, we just don't know his exact location right this minute. Let's not borrow trouble, here."

"Yes, we've got plenty already," Mallory says, her voice pitching higher. She aims a long finger at me. "The lady of the house is with Dylan all this time and never bothers to find out what's going on in his head. She obviously doesn't understand what it's like to worry about your own children."

I retort, "I'm worried, too! But Dylan values his privacy."

"And so do you," spits out Angel.

The skin on my neck prickles, but then I remember my journal is stowed at the bottom of my duffle bag, which I threw in the back of the closet.

Michael rubs his temple with his free hand. "Mallory, I'm his father. If anyone should have known, it would be me. And if he trusted us so much, he wouldn't have disappeared without responding to our calls."

"Unless he didn't disappear of his own free will!" Mallory starts to shake in place, visibly. Her hands, in particular, seem like they have been struck by a palsy as she kneads her fingers.

Angel starts in again on her thumbnail. Michael squeezes her hand, then slowly stands up and crosses the room to Mallory. He holds her in his arms, and she falls onto his shoulder.

Trying not to react. I swear I can feel Angel watching me.

Michael says, but his voice sounds effortful, "He's not a helpless little boy. He can't be just . . . snatched off the street . . ."

Angel whimpers again, and Michael unwinds himself from Mallory, then pulls her along by the hand to the couch, where he tucks each of them in on either side of him.

"To me it's clear he went willingly. He shut off his phone. Not to silent mode, like he usually does at school, but completely off. That's deliberate."

"Maybe it's out of power," I say, struck by this sudden thought. Or he's not the one who shut it off. This part I'm smart enough to keep to myself.

Michael soldiers on. "It was on this morning, at breakfast, remember? Look, no one dragged an unwilling teenager from a small, crowded school without anyone noticing. So, as I said, he left the school on his own. He's not old enough to drive, and none of his friends have seen him who might have driven him someplace. So he's hiding out somewhere, for some reason. That's bad and upsetting, but it doesn't mean anything like what those kids have been saying at school, Angel."

He could have hitchhiked, it occurs to me. If he wanted to leave, he could have stuck out his thumb, and a trucker could have picked him up. With going on seven hours since this morning, he could be two states away by now.

I have a desperate urge to be valuable in this moment, to show Michael that I matter. "I remembered this: he's been religiously getting the mail every day. Maybe he was waiting for something."

Mallory leaps to a standing position, fists clenched. "And you didn't pursue that, did you?" She arranges her face in a parody of an empty-headed ninny. "You just went la-di-da, about your business being the happy homemaker." Back to sneering now, she advances on me. "I can't believe you would let this happen to my son!"

She seizes my arms, and her force surprises me so much that I don't realize for a moment or two that she's wheeling me backward, my feet scrambling under me.

Michael wrenches her away, yelling her name, yelling to stop. My shoulders sting from the dented impressions of her fingers and ragged nails. From the corner of my eye, Angel is balled up on the couch now, face hidden under a curtain of hair.

"Ouch!" Mallory cries, stroking her forearm where Michael must have grabbed her, but he's walking with me out of the room now, shouting something at her I don't quite hear.

Chapter 6

Michael

I guide Casey into the bedroom and sit her down on the edge of the unmade bed. She's massaging her right shoulder but seems otherwise intact.

"I'm sorry," I whisper, which seems wholly inadequate for having to pull my ex-wife off of her. I push a strand of hair back from her face, tucking it behind her ear, tracing her jaw with my fingers. "I'm sorry," I say, a little louder, because I really am sorry for so much.

She shrugs, not looking at me.

For years, married to Mallory, I apologized for her. *So sorry, she had a bit too much eggnog,* or *I know, Mrs. Martin, she didn't need to scream obscenities at you over the phone because your daughter pulled Jewel's hair,* and *No, my wife isn't coming to parent-teacher night, she has a headache.*

I thought when I divorced her, I'd get to stop doing that.

Casey is short, and perched on the edge of the bed, her feet don't quite touch the floor. She swings them slightly, like a kid waiting for a scolding. With her ponytail and blue jeans she looks very small and young indeed.

"It's not your fault."

She shrugs. "Small comfort, if . . ."

She doesn't finish the sentence, but I hear her anyway. If we don't find him at all.

"I think we should call the police."

Casey jerks to attention. "What about all those reassuring things you just said out there?"

"I'm trying to keep Angel from panicking. Mallory will panic if she wants to, I can't stop that, never could. But I'm telling you the truth now. My son has been missing for hours, and . . . I'm about a hair away from calling the police, but before I do that, I want to be able to tell them something useful. Can you get into his e-mail?"

Casey wrinkles her face. "I hate to pry."

"I know, but Case—"

She nods, cutting me off with a wave. "I'm not a magician, though, okay? I'm just a programmer, not a hacker or a spy." She rubs her arm where Mallory grabbed her, her gaze on the floor again, unfocused. "He's going to be mad about the snooping."

"I'm mad at him! He could get himself hurt doing God knows what with . . . who knows? What if he's on drugs? What if he's been . . ."

I trail off, unable to speak it aloud.

It's hereditary, so I've read. Mental illness. Not that Mallory has been officially diagnosed. I couldn't get her to attend therapy with any regularity. And anyway, she laughed in the face of the first shrink I dragged her to, after milking her for a Valium prescription.

My father once called her "a case study in crazy."

He said that the day after I found her white and groaning on the bathroom floor, her stomach full of Tylenol, after a particularly vicious fight. For months after that I laid awake debating if it was an attention-getting stunt or a suicide attempt, however halfhearted. Maybe both. Mallory herself likely wouldn't know.

That was the first time I left, packing the kids off to my parents' house in East Grand Rapids, just a few miles as the crow flies but a whole other world with its brick and ivy and leather furniture.

Dylan has always seemed to be on an even keel. Old before his time. But he is his mother's son, too.

Casey has remained silent, but now I can feel her watching me. She puts her hand on my knee and squeezes, her trademark gesture, started as a secret *I love you* under the table when we were still trying to be coy about our feelings in front of the kids.

I put my hand over hers, my secret gesture back.

"So how do we get Mallory out of here?" Casey asks.

I swallow hard at this. "Well . . ."

Casey stands up. "She attacked me just now! If you hadn't pulled her off me, she'd have yanked out my hair or God knows what! You're going to let her stay?"

"It's not that simple. She's Dylan's mother, and she's worried."

"Oh my God. You're not going to ask her to leave. What would she have to do, Michael? Break my nose? Send me to the hospital?"

"Don't you get hysterical, too."

"Don't you compare me to her." Casey's not shouting. Her voice is even, and cold like the air outside.

"That's not what I meant," I rush to say, though this is a lie and I'm sure she knows it. "But think about it. If I try to send her home it will be more fireworks, more drama. She will probably refuse, and then what? Do I physically throw her out and get arrested for assault? Do we really want to waste all that energy?"

Casey wilts from her ramrod angry posture, seeming to resign herself to the bitter reality of managing Mallory. "So, what, she gets to beat me up so we don't upset her?"

"I'll talk to her while you look for Dylan's computer, then we'll call the police."

"Fine." She walks past me without meeting my eyes. I reach out to her, but she doesn't see me try.

Downstairs, I tell Mallory and Angel that Casey is going to get into the e-mail, adding, "I guess he lost his right to privacy when he pulled this stunt."

"Assuming he did this himself," Mallory says, biting her lip and jiggling her knee, perched on the edge of the couch next to Angel.

"For God's sake. This is not the time for your melodrama. We've got quite enough regular drama, thanks."

"Oh, is it Pile On Mallory Day again? So soon, and I haven't even put up the decorations."

"Yeah, Dad," interjects Angel. "She's worried. Why aren't you?"

"I *am* worried!"

Angel leaps up from the couch. "You're never worried! You're always like, 'It'll be fine, don't worry about it.' It's like you don't even care!"

"Someone has to keep it together in this house! Do you want me to start wailing and beating my chest? What good is that going to do?"

Mallory stands up on the other side of the couch. "Stop yelling at her!"

"I'm not yelling!"

The house rings with the echo of my words. How many times has it been this way? Mallory, me, and a kid in a triangle, shouting, my resolve to stay calm crumbling like a burned-up coal at the slightest touch.

I close my eyes. My heart is still hammering along as I say quietly, "Angel, I'm sorry. Do you believe me now that I'm upset, too? I just don't show it the same way."

"Whatever." Angel flips her hair out of her face.

"Great, now I have a headache," Mallory growls, rooting around in her purse. "Angel honey, will you get me some water?"

I turn away from them, heading up the stairs two at a time to go check on Casey's progress in Dylan's room.

Chapter 7

Casey
_____

Rummaging in Dylan's room feels wrong, like I'm some kind of shady criminal ransacking his space.

I poke my head under his bed. No old socks, and no laptop, either.

This makes me think of Angel finding my journal in my desk—why was she even in my desk?—and reading it. While trying to focus on Dylan, all I can think is how far back she read, and what she's going to tell Michael. I thought I'd be gone by now, the fallout happening in my absence.

She probably read about Tony, and though he's just a friend, it wouldn't look good from Michael's view, since he knows nothing about him. Even worse, in my journal I've off-loaded so much that I can't say out loud. Memories of a life that's years old and yet a bottle of whiskey away. Memories of my brother, whom Michael doesn't even know ever existed.

I've recorded frustrations about my life now, too, including the issues with the children. Hurtful things I would never say out loud, but if I don't let it out, I will explode. Explode, then drink.

The weak afternoon light already fades as I crawl under his bed. Jewel will be home from Scouts soon, and I'd give my left arm to be able to solve this mystery before she comes in the door. If only I could do it without invading Dylan's private spaces.

If only he had talked to us. At least his dad. Didn't fathers and sons have a bond? Billy and our dad did. They didn't have deep discussions about feelings, or life lessons—not in front of me, anyway—but they were so in sync, right down to their loping gait and their way of sitting in a chair and tipping back, balancing on the rear legs. If they needed to talk, I'm sure they would have. I'm sure they did.

But Michael is so busy all the time. Even at home, half his brain is at work. And now that he can get his work e-mail at home, he's constantly plugged in, not to mention double-checking his stories, terrified of a blunder. As if the world will spin off its axis because he misquoted somebody.

Nothing under the bed but dust and some old sheet music. I scuttle backward out from under there, brushing dust bunnies off my shirt. I look at Dylan's sock and underwear drawer. That's where I used to hide things, way toward the back of my deep old-fashioned dresser. Dylan puts away his own laundry. It's one of the kid's chores.

I can't see in the back of the drawer, but my hand crawls among the socks, and I hope I don't find anything lurid in there, the kinds of things a pubescent boy would hide in his room. My hand lands on something smooth, cool, and plastic.

His phone.

There's a folded piece of paper inside the case, with the light blue lines and ragged edges of a spiral notebook. I unfold it— other than the sharp creases the paper is flat and even, so it looks fresh—and read this in Dylan's precise printing: *Don't worry about me. I'll be fine.*

Michael comes in to see me holding it. Before I can protest, he snatches it and the phone out of my hand. He reads the note, then throws it down on the floor. "Fuck."

I bend to get it as Michael rubs his temples. "That's good, right? That means he left of his own will. Better than . . ."

"I guess. Yeah. But . . . What the hell, Casey? Why would he leave? I mean, all the crazy times we had when Mallory lived with us, and now?"

I step forward to try to embrace him. Michael returns the hug, but stiffly, his air distracted, as of course he would be. With his other hand he's turned on Dylan's phone. "Empty," he says. "Nothing in his address book. Looks like he's got a bunch of voice mail, but I'm sure that's all us. He purged it. Where's his laptop?"

I shake my head. "Can't find it. Why didn't he take his phone?"

"Cell phones can be traced. Shit."

Michael picks up the note again and turns away, running down the stairs. I trail after him until he reaches the file cabinet in the home office, what must have once been a sort of parlor or sitting room at the front of the house. He riffles through the file cabinet. "Cell phone bills," he says by way of general announcement. He looks up at Mallory and Angel.

"We found a note. He ran away."

They both gasp, trading looks. Angel allows a hesitant smile, but Mallory seems to be not at all mollified.

Angel goes to her father's side, helping him look for the bills. We never bothered investigating Dylan's calling habits before. As long as he stayed under his allotted minutes, we didn't have any reason to care.

"Shit," Michael mutters. He shows me the most recent bill. No phone numbers on it, just the basics. It does, however, show a big spike in his calling activity from what we're used to seeing.

He seizes the desk phone and starts to dial.

"What did you find out? Did you hack in?" demands Mallory.

I shake my head. "His laptop is gone. He either took it with him or hid it somewhere besides his room."

Mallory shakes her head. "No. He wouldn't do this on purpose. He wouldn't just . . . leave. It doesn't make sense. Unless . . ."

Mallory advances on me, and I can smell her perfume, a tangy citrus that tickles my nose. The emerging wrinkles around her eyes are cakey with makeup. "Unless it's you. We never had any trouble with Dylan before, and suddenly you're here and he's gone all secretive and now he's run away."

Michael is behind me, on the phone to the cell phone company, demanding a detailed copy of their bill, phone numbers and all. He's getting transferred. Angel hovers near his shoulder, but she keeps glancing our way.

"What are you trying to say?" I ask her.

"I'm trying to say he's obviously not happy with his new little family here, is he?"

"Nor is he happy with the old one, because he didn't run to you."

"Yes, please, kick me while I'm down, while my son is gone."

"He's gone from me, too! He's my stepson!"

"He is *not*. He is the son of your fiancé, who happens to have primary physical custody. For now, anyway."

I will not take the bait. I will not.

Mallory ignores my nonresponse. She gets closer yet, until I can see her pores. Her voice drops in pitch and volume. "He ran away from here, so your record as a not-even-stepmother is not exactly perfect. But mine?" She takes a step back and smiles. "I haven't been in a lick of trouble since the separation. I've been a regular sweetheart, in fact. I took anger management classes, and I barely even drink anymore. Did you know that? My lawyer is very proud."

I half turn toward Michael, and Mallory hisses in my ear: "I will not let you raise my children."

Mallory steps back, leans on my desk, and examines her nails, chipping at a piece of flaked polish.

I look at Angel. She is next to Michael on the other side of the office, not looking our way.

Michael bangs the phone down. "Stupid phone company. They claim they can't do it for, like, weeks. Such bullshit." He drops into his desk chair and tips his head back like he's sunning himself. "Christ, we're out of milk, too. I was going to get some on the way home today."

"Let me do it," I say. "Jewel will be home soon, you should be here for her. It's just an errand, no reason you should have to leave."

Michael's shoulders droop. "Thanks, babe. That would be a big help."

I go looking for my keys and remember they're in the duffle bag. The one I packed when I was walking out this morning.

With a sickening crunch it all comes back, the recent months of coldness from Michael, the hostility from Angel and distance from Dylan, the fact that we haven't set a wedding date and he shuts down all talk of a baby between us.

One little *babe* in the face of all that, because I'm going out for milk, changes nothing, after all.

I retrieve my keys from the duffle bag and go out the back door, away from Michael, his daughter, her mother. I glance back through the office window and see Michael's arm around Mallory again, stroking her shoulder, just like he always used to do for me.

I remain in the Honda in the tiny parking lot of the corner store, smoking my cigarette and letting my hand dangle out the open window. The cold air is painful in my lungs, but I don't care. I wouldn't be comfortable in warm air, either.

I don't know if Mallory can win back custody. She gave up quickly in the divorce, Michael said, and he was relieved about that. He didn't want to tear apart his children's mother in a public courtroom, or even in paperwork, and anyway, he always said, so much of her behavior seemed beyond her control. So there was much he held back. He could bring it all out again to fight her, but the kids are older, more aware. Angel in particular is defensive of her mother, lately. I think as Angel gets older she starts to feel more protective, more adult and maternal. I've seen it in the way she hovers over Jewel, and nitpicks her father's eating habits when he's tempted by greasy food. Mallory must seem vulnerable to her. I want to cry for her, for all of the kids, to imagine them at the center of a courtroom battle.

My presence would hardly help such a battle. I could even

weaken his case for custody, if Mallory's lawyers start investigating me. My own past would invalidate any argument Michael hoped to use about past bad behavior serving as an indicator of poor mothering skills.

Michael can't lose his children, and not to her. He'd be torn apart daily, wondering whether Mallory was drunk behind the wheel again, or unconscious on the bathroom floor. His kids fill him up, even on their bad days. He'd be eaten up from the inside out to be without them. Not fair that people think that only happens to mothers.

He might even get back together with her, rather than risk turning them over to her care.

My eyes are going swimmy as I stare at the graffitied side wall of the store. With my free hand I wipe under my lashes, flicking the damp off my fingers.

The sun is already dipping low in the November sky. Where is Dylan going to spend the cold night?

I grind my cigarette out on the outside of the car door and flick it down into the parking lot as my phone rings. It's Mom.

"Hi." Suddenly so tired the word comes out more breath than speech.

"You okay?"

"Just a headache."

"Have some tea, that always helps. Or Motrin, do you have Motrin?"

"Yes, Mom, I have Motrin. What's going on?"

"Just wanted to hear your voice. Wanda's darling little baby is so adorable, and I forgot how good that baby smell is."

"That's nice, Mom."

"What is it, Edna?"

"I'm just distracted. I had to run an errand and I have to get back to the house."

"Well. I'll let you go then. Sorry to have bothered you." She sounds affronted. I can almost picture her shrinking back into her chair.

"No, it's not that, just . . . ."

"No, no, I understand. You've got a busy life with all those kids, don't you? I'll just go watch some TV."

She gets off the line before I have a chance to rally myself to be talkative. As her one remaining child I should be able to do this for her, just talk on the phone, is that so hard?

I heave myself out of the car to go get the milk, considering that maybe the mundane chores of housekeeping are all I can manage, and perhaps I should leave the emotional work of being a family to someone else, someone equal to the task.

Chapter 8

Jewel

B ye, Mrs. Morton," I say, hopping out of her great big car with my backpack. I can't wait to tell Dad about school today. We studied alligators, which are as old as dinosaurs. I didn't even know that. And I know a lot about dinosaurs.

"Bye, Jewel," Mrs. Morton says. "Have a nice night."

Something's weird, though. I can tell right away. Something about the house. In this book I read there's a whole part about trusting your gut, and right now my gut says, "Uh-oh."

My mom is here? She gives me a hard hug, and her belt buckle presses into my chest. After she lets go I see Angel behind her, who's supposed to be at play practice, and Dad's home early, too.

"Dad? What's going on?"

"Come here, honey, there's something I have to tell you. Let's talk upstairs."

Mom turns to Dad. "What's wrong with talking right here? With both her parents?"

My stomach is pinching me. That's how it feels when something is going wrong. I wonder where Casey is.

"What, Dad?" My dad sits me down on the sofa, and my mom sits on the other side. "Did my other grandma die?"

"No, J.," says my mom. "Dylan's missing."

"What?"

My dad looks over the top of my head, giving my mom his mean-face look. "Try not to worry, Jewel. He skipped school today and didn't take his phone, that's all. We're having trouble tracking him down."

"That's the same as missing, Dad. I'm not an ignoramus."

I just learned that word. I like the sound of it.

"But there's missing and then there's *missing*, like being on the news and with the police looking for him. He's not *missing*."

"Yet," says my mom.

I look up at her and her arms are folded, but her whole body is jiggling, like she's on one of those massage chairs in the mall. Uh-oh. This is one of the warning signs, like a volcano. I saw on PBS one time a special about volcanoes, and there was this machine—I forgot the name, but it was *something-graph* and it detected tremors before a blow. I don't need a something-graph because I can see it right in front of me.

"Where's Casey?" I ask Dad.

My mom makes a little disgusted snorty noise, and my stomach pinches harder. Angel rolls her eyes. She's slouched in a chair, texting on her phone.

Dad answers, "Casey had to run out for some milk. She'll be back soon."

I shrug, to show I don't really care.

My mom pulls me close to her, and the stomach pinching re-laxes a little because her breath doesn't smell like drunk.

"I want to go lay down a minute," I tell them. I stand up, and my mom's hands cling to me for a bit, like when you walk through a spiderweb and all those little threads hang on.

I go upstairs to my room and curl up on my bed, still wearing my shoes.

For a while I liked the funny smell of Mom's breath—though sometimes she chewed a lot of mints, which covered it up—because my mom was calmer when I smelled it. She wasn't so likely to yell. I didn't know what it was.

Then there was that day at school. My stomach started pinch-ing me because I couldn't remember to write my numbers not-backward. It was only kindergarten, and I wasn't good at school yet. I guess I made my tummy sound worse than it really was and got sent to the school nurse. So they called my mom to come get me.

I couldn't smell her breath, but I could tell she was feeling pretty good. She joked with the school secretary. I do remember she wasn't wearing a coat for some reason, even though it was winter. And she forgot to wait for me to buckle my seat belt, because I was still fiddling around with it when the car went spinning all crazy.

The memory of it still makes me dizzy.

I hear the front door downstairs open and close and I sit up in my bed, listening for Dylan. Must be Casey, though, because everyone would be real happy if Dylan was down there. I can only hear some quiet talking.

I turn over to face the other wall, where my "vision board" is, which I read about in a book that the librarian said had too many big words for me, but she's new and doesn't know that I'm a very good reader. Everyone says so. I have a certificate and everything.

When the car stopped spinning that day I ended up on the floor of the backseat, and I think something bopped my head because I touched my head and I was bleeding. This scared me, but what scared me worse was that Mom was leaning back on the seat like dead people do on the TV shows she likes to watch. The air bag was all empty in front of her like a pillowcase. People were already running up, though, and pretty soon there were sirens and Mom was sitting up in the front seat and talking and holding me in her lap. She called my grandpa because my dad didn't answer his phone.

Then the police officer and my mom had an argument. Then she blew into a little machine and by then Grandpa Turner was there and he's a doctor so he looked at my head and told me it wasn't deep and I'd be fine, but I didn't care about that.

On my bed, I wrap my arms around my stomach and curl up tighter. I kinda wish I'd been hurt bad in the crash so that I'd been at the hospital and not there to see the next part. It's the part I keep thinking of when I can't sleep.

I saw the policeman put handcuffs on my mom, and put her in the back of the police car. She was cussing him. She didn't even look back at me. My grandpa said the police just had to talk to my mom, but I've watched enough shows to know that she got arrested. I shouted "Mommy!" but she didn't hear me, and my grandpa told me it would be okay and not to worry.

But every time grown-ups say that, there's always reason to worry. Always.

My grandpa took me back to his house, where Grandma

made me cookies and let me watch all the *SpongeBob* I wanted until Daddy got there, and he looked like a zombie, he was so greeny-white.

And there were lots of grown-ups whispering. And I learned what "drunk" meant.

And then Mommy moved out, and we don't see her very much.

I used to wish really hard to rewind time back to that kindergarten day. And in the movie that plays in my head, this time I just write my numbers backward, and maybe the teacher frowns at me but my mom is still home and everyone's together.

But I know that can't really happen. So instead I put our family picture on the vision board and maybe if I hope really hard, "put it out to the universe" like the book says, then my mom will come home.

She didn't smell like drunk today, so that's good. That's really good.

But if Dylan doesn't come home, it doesn't count.

I stretch out my hand and touch his face in the picture, and think of him giving me a horsey ride, so I go ahead and cry on my pillow.

Someone's shaking my arm.

I open my eyes, and it's dark in my room and it feels like night. But it can't be. I'm not in pajamas. My dad is there, and the hallway light is on. He's still wearing his work clothes. I must have been napping.

"Hey, babe. Come down and get something to eat."

"Where's Dylan?" I stretch. My neck is all kinked up because I slept weird. "And what time is it?"

"It's six o'clock. He's not home yet."

"Why isn't he home?"

"I don't know, baby. Did he . . . Did he say anything to you? About school, or anything?"

I shake my head. I know Dylan loves me and stuff because he's my brother, but it's not like he tells me secrets. He's way older than me.

I put my hand on Dad's arm before he gets off the bed. "Are you worried about him?"

He stops, and he's got his thinking face on for when he's trying to think how to answer me. I hate that. But then he drops that face and he sighs. "Yeah," he says, and he pulls me in for a hug. "Yeah. I am."

He stands up and takes my hand and I let him hold it even though I'm a big girl and I don't need his hand to get down the steps. "We got pizza," he says. "No one wanted to cook."

"Do you have any leads?"

He stops on the steps and gives me this funny half-smile. "Leads? Where did you pick that up? You're not reading murder mysteries, are you?"

"Not yet. I saw it on *CSI*."

"*CSI*? Your mother lets you watch—"

He interrupts himself and bites his lip, looking away, and my stomach pinches up because I did it again, tattled on Mom, but I didn't mean to. He starts back down the steps. "Anyway. No, not yet."

My mom rushes up to hug me when I get downstairs. She tries to smooth down my hair. "Baby, are you okay? Are you feeling sick?"

I shake my head. I've learned my lesson about admitting to stomachaches.

"Hi, kiddo," says Casey.

I almost didn't see her because she's sitting on a high bar-stool in the corner of the kitchen, balancing a paper plate on her knees. She looks like she could be as young as Angel, especially with her hair in a ponytail. And I'm not sure exactly why, but that really makes my mom mad, and Angel, too.

Well, I do know why it bugs Angel. She's told me before that Casey tries to be her friend and she doesn't want to be Casey's friend. That just because she wears high-top Converse doesn't make her "cool," and it's embarrassing to think that Casey might be our stepmom when she looks like a kid instead of like the other moms. One time at the mall a lady thought Casey was our big sister, and I thought Angel was going to barf.

I sneak Casey a little smile, then look quick at my mom, who was talking to my dad and didn't see it.

The adults are talking again, so I pretend to be invisible so maybe they'll forget I'm here and stop changing what they say around me.

My dad is talking about how he must have some other friends they don't know about, someone who knows what's going on, maybe he's sneaking around with a bad crowd or something, since none of his band friends know anything, and since his best friend Jacob isn't his friend anymore. That's news to me, and it's a bummer. I liked Jacob.

They all look at Angel, and she goes, What? Stop looking at me, I told you I don't know anything about it. Angel is ripping apart the pizza with her fingers, pretending to eat it. She'll throw it away, later, when none of the adults are looking.

My mom starts talking to my dad about why he doesn't know all his friends and we need to break into his Facebook account and they turn to Casey and she just looks down at her pizza and starts picking at it.

"I made him give me the password when he started Face-book," Dad says, "just so I'd know, but that was a long time ago and he changed it."

"Girl Genius can figure it out, though. Right?" says Mom, pointing at Casey, her hand making like a gun, like she's playing cops and robbers.

They don't allow that at my school, not even pretend-finger guns.

"I can try," Casey says, still picking at the pizza. "But it's not like the movies where anyone who knows a little code can punch buttons and break into anything. It would be just me, guessing the password. Anyway, didn't you make him take you as a Face-book friend? Look at his profile. You might not have to break into anything."

My dad looks down at his feet. "I tried that already, at work. I think he put me on restricted view of his profile because there's pretty much nothing on it. Angel, what about you?"

She tosses her hair behind her shoulder. "No. Not since he wrote on this guy's wall and told him he was being a jerk to me. I defriended him."

My dad stands up straight, his eyes wide all of a sudden. "Wait! Casey, you set up a network backup. It automatically backs up our computers over the network, right? Even e-mail."

All the grown-ups and Angel start looking at each other, and they all stare at Casey.

"Well, that's true—"

"Why didn't you say something?" my dad shouts, slapping his hand so hard on the table it rattles his water glass. Everyone jumps at this, and Casey gasps out loud. "It's dark out, and he's been missing for almost twelve hours! Jesus, Casey!"

Her hands fly up to her face. "I just . . . I didn't think of it right away . . ."

"Yeah, right," my mom whispers loudly. I can tell by the look on Casey's face that she heard.

My dad goes over to Casey immediately, saying, "I didn't mean to shout . . . I just . . . I'm getting desperate, here." He tries to reach out to her shoulder, tries to pull her in for a hug, but she's all rigid, like a flagpole.

Then Casey nods, and whispers something like "fine" or "okay" but I can't tell. She walks around the table and away from Dad, out of the room, down the hall to the basement steps, where all her computer stuff is.

I could see the look on her face when she went by. I bet Casey has a stomachache, too.

Chapter 9

Michael

Mallory puts her hand on my shoulder and rubs lightly. I feel myself sag and realize how tense I've been.

"She just doesn't get it. When you're not a parent it's hard to understand what it's like to be afraid for your child."

I shrug off Mallory's hand. It wasn't fair to explode at Casey, and from the look on her face, I might as well have punched her.

She'll forgive me when it's over. Mallory is right—it's impossible to understand what it's like to be a parent until you are a parent yourself.

Mallory strokes my hair above my ear, where it goes curly because I haven't bothered with a haircut. I resist the urge to bat her hand away and instead just stand up.

"I think it's time to call the police."

I immediately wish I hadn't said this in front of Jewel, whose face puckers into a snarl of worry. Angel's eyes are round.

Mallory exhales. "Yes, I think we'd better."

"Kids. I don't think anything bad has happened to Dylan. He's a smart guy. Obviously, since he's covered his tracks. He'll be okay," I say, rushing past this because I'm not sure I believe it, "but because it seems he doesn't want to be found and none of the friends we know about can find him, we have to get help. I'll give Casey a little time to investigate his e-mail to see if we can give the police something useful to go on, and then I'll call."

Mallory seems refreshed, somehow, as if she'd just had a nap. She starts bustling in the kitchen, picking up the plates, packing away the leftover pizza, going instinctively to where our trash can is, since it hasn't moved since she lived here.

I say, "Angel and Jewel, if you have any homework you should probably do it."

"What?" shrieks Angel. "My brother is missing, and you're making me do homework? Are you out of your mind?"

"Watch your tone. You still have school in the morning. All we're doing is sitting around waiting here."

"I am *not* going to school tomorrow."

I open my mouth to object, and Mallory jumps in. "Honey, you can stay home." She turns to me, one hand on her hip. "Really, Mike, what harm does it do for her to miss one day? It's Friday tomorrow, she has the whole weekend to catch up. Do you honestly expect her to concentrate right now? And Jewel, too? Good grief, she's only eight."

In a flash I see myself as they see me. The Mean Dad, insisting on homework and school as important above all else, even now.

But it is important, so goes my internal dialogue.

But you sound just like your father.

My father. I suppose I'd better clue in the grandparents. They have a right to know what's going on with their grandson. And maybe it's possible Dylan confided in them, if he couldn't talk to me.

I rub my temple, hating to cave in to Mallory, but hating worse the looks on my kids' faces. "Okay. Fine. Both of you can stay home tomorrow, but we'll pick up your homework and you'll do it over the weekend. We'll have found him by then. Life can't stop because Dylan pulled this—"

I was going to say "stunt," but that doesn't seem right. A stunt is something you'd expect from a hothead, a rebel. Dylan is considerate and serious. I have to confess he's run away, but he must have felt like he had a damn good reason.

This has to be true. Because otherwise I don't know my son at all.

I leave Mallory in the family room watching crap TV with the girls, trying not to care they are watching a reality TV show about Playboy bunnies. I'd almost forgotten this side effect of living with Mallory: the constant feeling of my best parental intentions being eroded, so gradually I hardly notice, until they're eating frozen pizza four nights a week and staying up as late as they want and doing homework in front of the television.

So then I come down harder to make up for her slack, and become the Mean Dad. It's a wonder the kids were willing to live with me.

Though Mallory is not always a ball of fun, and we never know which version we'll get.

I go up to my own room to call my parents. Regrettably, my father answers.

"Dr. Turner," he says, as if he's still working and on call for cardiac surgery.

"Hi, Dad."

"Hi, son. How goes the battle?" as he always asks, because he knows my life seems to be filled with mortar rounds broken by tenuous cease-fires. Less so since my divorce, but still.

"I have to tell you something."

He mutes the TV, where he'd likely been watching the History Channel, his favorite.

"Go on."

"We can't find Dylan. I dropped him off at school this morning and he went in the building, but no one has seen him since and he hasn't come home."

"Why didn't you tell me this at lunch? My God, he's been gone twelve hours now!"

"I thought he'd turn up."

"What difference would that have made? I deserved to know this."

"Right, because the number-one thing on my mind is how *you* feel."

"Don't attack me. It's not my fault he's gone."

"Didn't say it was."

I brief my father on what's happened, and he listens quietly.

"So, it's clear what you do now."

"Is it?" I ask, rubbing the bridge of my nose because my father is always clear about everything.

"Yes, of course. You go to the media, seeing as you're a member of the media."

"Dad. The media doesn't do runaways. There are no Amber alerts for runaways, for example. It's not news."

"So *you* say."

"Don't you think I'd know?"

"I can't believe you won't try."

"I'm telling you, the newspaper is not going to give me special treatment because I work there. Probably the opposite, so they don't look like they're doing favors. Just last week Aaron had to tell this hysterical mother that we weren't going to do a story about her kid who ran away, and they can't very well turn around and put Dylan's face in the paper."

"Hmmm. Maybe I'll see what I can do."

"Look, can I talk to Mom?"

Without preamble my father hands over the phone. I brief Mom about it, and she gasps in all the right places. Thank God she understands. Of course she would.

"And Mom, please tell Dad not to bother with the media. I don't think they'll do a thing, even for Dr. Henry Turner."

"I'll see what I can do, dear," my mother replies. "Although you know that when your father makes up his mind, there's little even I can do to change it."

"Can't you slip him a mickey?" I say, laughing weakly.

She ignores the joke. "Just call me the minute you know something and tell me if there's anything I can do. Do you need me to come over?"

"No, it's a little crowded already. Mallory's here."

"Oh, dear."

"It's all right, actually. She's in good form."

"I'll pray for him. Let me know, honey. He'll be okay. I'm sure it's just a boy thing and he'll come home soon."

"I never did anything like this."

"Well, you had . . . Things were different for you."

We say our good-byes, and I slump back on my bed. I listen for sounds of mayhem in the house. Everything sounds normal.

It's an understatement to say things were different for me, an only child of a driven, ambitious doctor. Though I certainly knew other children of ambitious, successful parents who did their share of screwing up.

I grimace now to think of the furious desperation with which I studied, only barely aware that I was doing it for attention. I told myself that I wanted good grades so I could get into the college I wanted. I was staying in on Saturday nights because I didn't want to end up sloppy drunk and knocking up a girl in high school like Mitch Donnelly.

And all I got for it was a nod and a twitch of mustache.

Now Mom, on the other hand, lavished me with praise. That should have helped, and I did—I do—feel glad she's proud of me, but I always knew the reason her praise was so voluminous, so effusive, was because Dad's was so lacking.

There's a soft knock at the door. Casey must have some news. "Yeah, come in."

Mallory slides in through the door, her head down, peeking up at me through her white-blond hair. She's got a beer in her hand, and my stomach drops. Great. She's going to start drinking, here, now, of all times. I didn't even know we had beer in the house. I sit up on the edge of the bed.

"Thought you might need this." She holds it out to me. I accept it warily, and look back at her.

She reads my expression and smiles, but there's no light in her eyes. Rueful. A look I seldom see from her. "Yes, you're wondering where my drink is, no doubt. Nope, I'm not drinking these days. I don't suppose you knew that."

I didn't. She could have told me she'd sawed off one of her own legs and I'd have sooner believed it. Yet she's standing before me in arm's reach of a beer and hasn't taken a sip. "I didn't know we had any."

She shrugged. "I found one way in the back when I was looking for a Diet Coke."

I take a sip, and it's cold, but otherwise tastes like nothing to me. I set it down carefully on the nightstand.

I put my elbows on my knees and hold my head in my hands. "Jesus, Mal. Why would he do this? And where is he sleeping tonight?"

I'm not looking at her, but I can hear a thread of a crack in her voice. "I know. I thought I'd always know where he was sleeping. That's silly, I guess, eventually I knew he'd grow up, but . . . And actually for me it's been over two years since I tucked him in every night. I never would have guessed that at twelve years old he'd be living somewhere else."

"Not now."

"No, I know. I made that bed, didn't I?"

My second shock in the past few minutes. I look up to see if it's still really Mallory standing there. She's holding her own arms like she's cold. She might be; she's only wearing a thin cotton shirt, and this place is drafty, especially upstairs.

"You look like you're freezing. Let me grab you a sweater." I stand up and go to my closet, selecting a navy blue wool sweater my dad bought me for Christmas that I rarely wear. I hand it to Mallory and she slips it over her head, stretching up as she does so, arching her back so that her breasts push against her shirt before pulling down the sweater. I wonder if that was for me, or if it's just part of her general habit of pulling attention her way, like a planet pulls its moon.

She looks out the window at the dark evening. She bites her

lip. She walks over to me and stands close, meeting my eyes. "Why won't he call?"

Tears well up in her lashes, and I pull her to me. She turns her head to the side and rests her face on my shirt, her nose against my neck. We fit like puzzle pieces this way.

The door is still open, and when I hear a noise I look up to see Casey, holding on to a notebook. Her face is pale except for two dots of pink on her cheeks. She, too, looks cold, because her hands seem to be shaking.

"I found something," she says.

Chapter 10

Casey

It took time to sort through all the e-mail this house generates: between my job and Michael's, the older kids, it's quite a soup.

Until I found a name I didn't recognize, responding to Dylan. A girl we've never heard of.

I'd shut myself down, as soon as Michael shouted at me. I was leaving anyway, as of just this morning. For all I know Dylan ran away because he hates me now.

And I thought it had worked. I thought I'd turned my feelings off like a spigot, and I was something like proud because this was an effect I used to only achieve with the aid of Jack on the rocks, or in desperate times, Jack straight out of the bottle.

But when I walked up the stairs to Michael's room—what just last night was *our* room—and saw him embracing Mallory through the open door, saw her wearing his sweater . . .

I won't be right until I get out of here.

My voice quavers despite my best efforts. "I found something."

Mallory steps away from Michael, adjusts his sweater, plays with the sleeves. Michael says, "What is it?"

"There are e-mails. Several of them, from a girl named Tiffany Harper. I've never heard of her."

"Me, neither. What did they say?"

"I didn't read them. But I brought them up on-screen so that you could."

Mallory brushes past me and is halfway down the stairs before she calls out, "Where is the computer?"

"To the right once you get to the bottom of the basement steps," I tell her.

Michael starts to walk past, too, but he stops just before me. I study the divots in the old, scarred floorboards.

"Thank you," he says. "Casey, look at me."

I turn farther away and notice an open beer sweating on the nightstand and wonder what it's doing there.

Michael continues. "I'm under stress here. I didn't mean to shout."

Swallowing hard, I say, "Go read the e-mails. See what you can find out."

I feel him standing in front of me for another long moment. *Just go!* I want to scream. I also want to step into his arms and let him hold me, too, but it's time to find Dylan.

And anyway, my time has clearly passed.

He finally turns to go, and it's like something's been snapped away. I hear his feet hurrying down the stairs.

I walk over to the bed and sit down on the edge. The bottle

sweats invitingly just like in a commercial full of mountains and rushing rivers and people having fun. People relaxed and unwinding.

I brush my fingers over the cold glass. It comes back in a rush, how the happy hours always started with beer, that good-time end-of-day drink, a round purchased by someone and then by someone else, until we were all throwing money into a pile at the center and bottles kept coming.

It feels as natural in my hand as a pencil, a toothbrush.

I nearly run down the stairs, stepping lightly as I can in the rickety old house, until I reach the kitchen, where I turn the beer upside down and watch it glug out in explosions of amber foam.

The smell of it nearly does me in and I almost tip the bottle right up again to save some, but the last drips come out and I sigh, shaking it briefly before setting it on the counter where we always put empty pop cans and such.

The girls are still watching TV, numbing themselves to the absence of their brother with insipid shows, but at least this vice won't kill brain cells. Not literally. Anyway, they're smart enough, and today is a rough day.

I shrug into my parka and step onto the front porch for a smoke. I sit down in the porch swing and prop my feet up on the railing. The cigarette flickers to life, and I sigh deeply after the first lightly dizzying puff. This causes me to cough.

The homes are close to each other here, with big picture windows in front rooms. The street is narrow, too, so it's not hard to look across the road into the duplex across the way, with a Middle Eastern family living downstairs and two college guys upstairs. There's a miniature porch off an upstairs dormer window, where the guys like to sit on balmy nights, drinking beer and smoking. Sometimes one of them plays his acoustic guitar, and we share a wave across the road as renegade smokers, an endangered breed.

Tonight it's cold and the porch is quiet. Through the downstairs window I can see the flashing of a television program in the darkness of the room. Maybe the kids watching a movie, or maybe they're in bed already. Just toddlers, they are. I've seen them walking as a family with the little ones in a double stroller.

Quitting smoking was next on my list. I wasn't about to smell like an ashtray in my wedding finery, and besides, soon after that there would be a baby, and I wouldn't smoke pregnant. Also, in my daily battle to stay away from the liquor store, I'd have a tiny, unwitting ally growing inside. I wouldn't need to hold on to any vices anymore. At least, that's how I imagined it.

I consider a call or a text to Tony. I'd like to tell him about my close call just now. He'd be proud, and I'll admit it, I need the praise, I need someone to tell me I done good because today I'm finding it harder and harder to remember why I ever gave it up.

I close my eyes to try and conjure up my rock-bottom moment. But it seems hazy, like something you only wished were true.

What does come clearly to mind is happy hour.

Chuck led the parade out the door. "Come one, come all!" he shouted. Our productivity had tailed off through the afternoon. It was a sunny spring day, and had been a helluva week. We were coding a major project for a client and had finally made some headway. When Chuck, even as our boss, started an improvised game of charades in the meeting room at two o'clock, we'd all started to wrap up anything serious.

We'd been shouting bar names all afternoon, trying to come up with a consensus. The patio at the Black Rose won the day, and at four o'clock when Chuck grabbed his bag and his jacket, we all filed out behind him like rats behind the pied piper. He bought the first pitcher.

Pitchers were wonderful. Our glasses just kept filling with so little effort. Our laughter got more raucous. We looked out to the sidewalk with pity on the drones trudging to their cars to drive home on packed highways to things like Little League games and excruciating kiddie band concerts whereas we, all of us, were free as eagles.

There were seven of us at JinxCorp, back before I had to quit, when I threw away my old life to stay home and do contract work. Alone.

We were all single, or at the most coupled. Not a child among the bunch. This was probably by Chuck's design because no one squawked too loud about overtime, especially when he'd sometimes spring us at four o'clock and buy rounds at the Black Rose.

The sun dropped a little lower and the Michigan April was cool, so we stepped inside to listen to the band belting out classic rock. I danced with my hands in the air, belting out with the band: *"Ride, Sally, ride!"* And when I came back to the table one of the seats had disappeared, so I sat on Kevin's lap, and he put his hand on the small of my back, then wrapped it over my hipbone, and I didn't mind a damn bit.

He drove me home—I'd taken the bus to work—and crushed up against me in the apartment building stairwell, kissing and biting my neck and cupping my breasts until I decided, Oh what the hell, I'm on the Pill, and let him in.

It worked out pretty well, because then I had a ride into work the next day.

Everyone smirked over their computer screens as we walked in at the exact same time, Kevin showered but wearing clothes that stank of the bar.

As with many mornings there, I popped an Advil, drank about a gallon of water alternated with mugs of strong bitter coffee, and by 10:00 A.M. I was right as rain.

Kevin and I never dated. It was a mutually pleasurable arrangement. No one ever frowned at me over it, made me feel guilty, or in any way cared about what I did.

At the time this felt like a good thing.

My cigarette is down to a nub. I grind it out on my shoe and keep the butt in my hand since there's no can out here and I'm too tired to walk over and flick it into the street.

Now, with the three kids watching every move, and Mallory waiting for me to screw up, and Michael's disapproving gaze when I so much as smoke a half-pack in a day . . .

"Chuck says fuck it!" was my boss's favorite saying when he wanted to dismiss something as irrelevant.

If only I could feel that cavalier again. Was being numb really so bad?

My phone rings, and my heart leaps with the hope it might be Dylan before I realize at the same instant I see her number I haven't talked to my mother in hours.

"Hi, Mom."

"What's wrong? You never called back."

"It's been crazy here."

"Are those kids giving you a hard time again?"

If she only knew. "No, Mom. I don't want to talk about it."

"You know it makes me nervous when you don't check in."

"I know."

"So I heard from Julie, and she says she hopes you come to the baby's party."

"Oh, does she now? Interesting turnaround."

Julie, my dad's sister, and her husband Rick always had a special connection with Billy, never having had any sons of their own. Rick, Dad, and Billy went hunting every November as soon as Billy could hold a rifle.

At the funeral she managed a limp condolence hug for me, and the rest of the time glared and whispered. Rick couldn't even look me in the eye.

"They were grieving, too," Mom says now, as if that makes it all fine. "They know it's not really your fault."

"Not *really* but kind of? Thanks for the ringing endorsement."

"Edna, honey, that's not what I meant, of course we don't blame you."

They may not have blamed me, but I do remember my mother grilling me for every detail of that night, and how she focused an awful lot on the fact that I talked my brother into coming to the party, and the reason he started fighting in the first place.

"Whatever, they could barely look at me back then, and now they want me to show up? Why, so they can gossip about me some more?"

"Maybe they want to make it right."

"Sure they do. Well, tell them—"

The front door swings open. It's Angel.

"*If you care*, Dad has some clues about Dylan."

"I gotta run," I say, and "Love you, Mom" because even when we fight I say it, considering. You just never know what the future brings.

I walk back in, and Jewel wrinkles her nose. I know I've come in with waves of stench. I can't smell it myself, I'm immune, I think, but I see it in other people's faces.

"Go ahead," I say, while I dampen my cigarette with water before I drop it in the kitchen trash, hurrying back to the front room.

Michael looks like a schoolteacher, still in his work clothes, standing up in front of the fireplace while everyone else sits. Jewel is cross-legged on the floor. Angel and Mallory sit like double vision on the couch. I take the uncomfortable wooden rocking chair.

"Well. This is what we've found. He's been writing this Tiffany girl for months now. From what I can tell, they met on Facebook. They think they're in love, and they decided to run away together."

I sneak a look at Mallory. She's staring with intensity at Michael, and worrying a thumbnail in her teeth.

Michael goes on: "It would seem they picked today to run away, and they're trying to get to New York City."

"And how did they think they were going to get there?" Mallory asks now, prompting, since she must already know the answer herself.

"They're taking a bus. I think they dealt with specifics over the phone, though, because the messages get more vague as they get more recent."

"Her number's disconnected now, though," Mallory says with a wave of her hand as I open my mouth to ask if they've tried to call it.

"So our next step," Michael says, "is to call the police, because it seems that two minor children are alone somewhere out there on buses trying to get to a huge, dangerous city."

Mallory leans back on the couch, pulling her knees up to her chest, toying with the sleeves of Michael's big sweater. "He was smart enough not to hitchhike, I'll give him that."

Jewel pipes up. "So he's okay, then."

Mallory answers, "You bet, J. The cops will find him at a bus station somewhere, and then we'll tar his butt as soon as he gets back home."

Michael swallows hard and then folds the printouts carefully, running over the crease with his fingers again and again. "I hope you feel better now, kids. It's getting late, Jewel, you should probably get ready for bed."

"Awwwww, Dad!"

"Mike, you told them they didn't have to go to school tomorrow. What difference does it really make?"

Michael's jaw goes tight, and he walks out abruptly. "I'm going upstairs to call the police station."

"Mom?" Jewel asks. "Can we make popcorn? The old way, on the stove, with butter?"

"Sure, baby! You got it." Mallory bounces off the couch and takes command in the kitchen. Jewel trails after her, talking to her about dinosaurs and alligators.

Angel remains on the couch, eyes fixed on the floor. She looks washed-out, her face blending into her pale hair.

I sit down on the couch, close enough to be considered next to her, but far enough not to be invasive, so I hope. I've never gotten good at this dance with her, this push-pull of too close, too far.

"Are you okay?" I ask.

"Fine." She tries to say it forcefully, but her voice breaks.

"You can tell me."

"If you can have secrets, so can I."

The first time we've been alone since she read my diary. "It's not what you think."

"Oh? You lied in your own diary?"

"I mean, you read things out of context."

"Yeah. Context makes it all better."

"Why were you even in my desk?"

At this she flops herself back on the couch, folding her arms tight across her. "None of your fucking business. Now go run along and tattle to my dad about how I read your diary and said 'fucking.'"

"I'm not going to tell him."

"Oh, so he won't ask me what's in it?"

"That's not why." *Because I'm leaving.* "Anyway, it doesn't matter. I was asking about Dylan, and about you."

"He's fine, isn't he?"

"Probably."

"Thanks for being so reassuring."

"It won't help him if you hide things from us."

"Hypocrite."

She stands up and whirls on me, and for a moment I think she might hit me, with her hands balled up into fists, the memory of Mallory grabbing me by the arms so fresh in my mind.

She stomps off to her room and slams the door in such a way that would normally earn at least a mild reproof from Michael, but today nothing is as it should be.

I venture upstairs to Michael's room again. This time when I crack the door he's alone.

He's on the phone, clearly with the police. In one hand he's clenching the receiver. The other hand is wrapped tightly around a piece of bedsheet, which he keeps unwinding and winding again as he talks.

"Look, I tell you, this isn't like him. He's a good kid, he's hardly ever been in trouble before . . . What good will that do in the morning? Do you know how far away he could be by then? Dammit, he's fourteen years old! . . . It just doesn't feel right to me . . . What happens if you're wrong, then, huh? What happens if—"

Michael's voice cracks. He lets go of the sheet, cradles his head in that hand.

He nods a few times, and then punches the hang-up button without saying good-bye. He tosses the phone down, and it slides off the edge of the bed, landing with a plunk on the floor.

"All the times as a reporter I've spent on the phone with upset, grieving people, trying to be calm and professional. I never realized how much they must have hated me."

I sit down on the bed and pick up the phone, putting it on the nightstand after checking for serious damage.

"What's happening?" I prompt, as Michael remains silent, staring at the floor between his feet.

"They'll put a *report* in some database. The desk lieutenant said he'd have an officer check the bus station if I e-mail him a picture of Dylan to show around. And if he still hasn't checked in by morning, they will have a detective check it out. By morning!"

"What did you mean by 'doesn't feel right'?"

He raises his face to look at me. "I don't think he's meeting a girl at all."

Chapter 11

Angel

Stupid Casey and her stupid questions.

I get a text from Hannah.

Dylan OK?

I hate how all these kids are making my drama into theirs to get attention. Like, if he totally disappeared for real, by next week they'd be on to the next thing, like that kid whose brother died of cancer and everyone was acting like their own brother died and then within a week it was all, whatever.

I don't even think Hannah likes me. Last week, I came up to her and the girls at play practice, and the minute I walked up, everyone stopped talking and they all stared at me, and I swear Emma was smirking. So it's not like she really cares. It's not like any of them do.

I shut my phone off and put in my earbuds, cranking it up so loud that Dad would say I'm ruining my hearing.

Who gave Casey the right to come into my house and start acting like she knows so much? And getting on me for having secrets when she's the one writing about Tony. Calling Tony. Tony said this, Tony said that.

And she used to drink herself stupid all the time, too. Bet Dad doesn't know that. He thinks she doesn't drink because she doesn't like the taste.

For a reporter he can be pretty stupid sometimes.

My stomach rumbles, and I grab a bottled water that's sitting on my dresser and take a swig. It helps a little. I couldn't eat that greasy, nasty pizza for dinner. And I didn't eat much for lunch today. Later, I'll go back down and get an apple or something.

I pick up my script for *The Miracle Worker*. I should practice some of my lines, especially because I skipped rehearsal and we're supposed to be off-book by next week, but they'd hear me and someone would stick their face in here and try to "help." Like Casey, putting on a supportive, sweet act when I know what she really thinks of me.

I can't remember the exact words, but it was something like, *can be such a bitch.*

I wanted to rip her journal in half and in fact I gave it a try, but that's harder than it looks, so instead I found this red marker and let her know that her secrets aren't so secret anymore.

"Why were you even in my desk?" she asked, like she's the poor victim here. I just needed a piece of paper. I didn't expect to find out my dad's girlfriend secretly hates me. I mean, I knew we didn't always get along, but "bitch"?

How many other people hate me in secret? Hannah, Emma, their friends, and now Casey, too?

I know that Eleanor hates me out loud, already. Everyone

thought she'd get the part of Anne Sullivan in *The Miracle Worker*. She's pretty much the best actress in school and she's always in community theater, too, and I heard she even has head shots and almost got an agent once when she went out to L.A. She's so beautiful the guys all cling to her like they're metal and she's a magnet.

But then I got it, and Eleanor is my understudy, which means she's loving today because she did the part at rehearsal. She's probably already off-book for my part, too. She's got a freaky ability to memorize lines.

I was so shocked when I saw the cast list, I thought Mrs. Nelson made a misprint, so I asked her. But she said no, she thought my audition had been "earnest and soulful" and she knew I had it in me.

So she might as well have put a target on my back. I mean, some people think that Eleanor is overrated and a ham and that she waves her arms like she's a cheerleader every time she reads a line.

But mostly they're all waiting for me to fuck it up.

Maybe if Dylan stays gone I can quit the play.

Oh, that's terrible. I curl up on my bed and scrunch my eyes. *I didn't mean it I didn't mean it I didn't mean it*, I say in my head, in case I somehow jinxed him.

I don't know what to do with myself now. I don't feel like reading lines. I have permission to blow off homework.

My big plan for the evening had been to tell my dad all about the diary, and then he could promise not to marry her and I'd know at least I wouldn't be having a stepmother who hated me. But I can't really do that now.

I sent Dylan a text earlier that said "WTF? Where r u?" And

then I sent some more that were nicer and more concerned, but now I find out he didn't even take his phone.

I should probably tell my dad what Dylan told me last week about hating his new school, but he swore me to secrecy. And that's different than reading Casey's diary, because I didn't mean to do that, I just stumbled on it.

But Dylan's my brother, and I promised.

Anyway, it's probably not related. It sounds like my brother thinks he's in love, the idiot.

My door opens and it's my dad, and he's got this big frown. I can't hear him, but I can read his lips. I sigh and take out my earbuds and sit up cross-legged. He sits on the edge of my bed.

"Angel, I've got to ask you something."

"What?"

"You know something's up with Dylan. Casey said you were looking really guilty when I was talking, and you were evasive just now."

"I didn't realize I was being *interrogated*."

"You need to tell us what's going on."

"I don't *know*. Anyway, you guys know that he's going to New York by bus. The cops will find him, right?"

" Look . . ." My dad runs his fingers over his hair and pulls at his tie. He's never gotten out of his work clothes. "You can't tell Jewel this, okay?"

"Tell her what?"

"Promise me."

"Okay, fine, I promise. What?"

"I'm worried that he's not really meeting a girl."

"Who else could he be meeting?"

While my dad tries to figure out what to say, suddenly it hits me. He thinks it's like the *Dateline NBC* show where they catch perverts trying to meet up with young kids.

"No, it's not like that," I say. "He's not that dumb to fall for some sweaty pervert pretending to be a girl."

Without saying anything else, my dad pulls out a printed photograph. I take it in my hand, and it looks like a fashion model. The girl's hair is windswept, and she's gazing off to the side. There's a beach behind her.

"This girl doesn't look fourteen, and she doesn't look like an ordinary girl. This looks like the kind of picture you'd download off the Internet if you wanted to impress a teenage boy. If you wanted to lure him somewhere."

Now I start to feel kinda light-headed.

"Angel, please."

"I don't know anything about the girl."

"What *do* you know about?"

"Nothing. Honest."

My dad looks like he might cry. I've only seen him cry once before, when Mom and Jewel had that wreck.

"Dad?"

He swallows hard before he answers me. "Yeah."

"Do you really think it might be a . . . guy?"

"I know it's a Gmail address, which could be from anywhere. And this picture doesn't look right. And in the e-mails it sounds like she's the one trying to convince him to run away. He had to be talked into it."

"Did you tell the cops this?"

My dad nods and sighs hard. "It's after hours. They said they'd check the bus station, and Casey is e-mailing a photo. They think he's just a lovesick runaway."

"Isn't that bad enough?"

My dad stands up and kneads his neck with his hand. "They had fifteen runaway reports last week. And running away is not against the law. Honey, I told you the whole story because you're the oldest. But you can't tell Jewel. I don't want her to know anything about what we suspect unless—"

Dad can't finish what he's saying, but he doesn't have to. He bends over for a hug. It's an awkward angle, but I let him do it, and in fact I hug him back, hard.

Chapter 12

Michael

I come into the kitchen to see my ex-wife at the stove popping popcorn with Jewel, both of them laughing, Jewel on a chair with her arm around her mother's waist. It's like a peek into a parallel dimension where we never got divorced and she got the help she needed and straightened herself out.

We could still have been married, which I guess would be good for the kids.

But then I wouldn't have met Casey.

Mallory turns from the stove to see me, and her laughter falters a little over our common concern.

Mallory is having one of her pretty good days, back like she used to after each child was born. Something about pregnancy and newborns seemed to level her out—maybe the intensive work that a young child requires would crowd out whatever else was going on in there. But eventually they get older, they play alone, they don't want to be rocked and coddled, they're in school all day. If we'd stayed married, I would have had to get a vasectomy or I might have ended up parenting a litter.

I walk back upstairs into the bathroom to splash cold water on my face. In the sharp glare of the light in here, my scar stands out quite a bit. I remember the young nurse practitioner at the after-hours clinic slipping me a little card with a number for domestic violence victims to call.

I actually laughed. I was dizzy with the dissipated adrenaline from the fight and disbelief that I was actually there at all. Then I apologized. The young man had looked so earnest. He was actually biting his lip, his face creased with concern.

Oh, I'm sure the domestic violence people would have taken me very seriously, probably advised me to leave. But men don't get to run away and keep their kids.

I suppose I could have made a case for her unpredictable and volatile nature and taken the children with me, but the truth is, she had never hurt the children. Not physically, at least. And she could have plausibly argued that my injury was an accident.

Mallory's ability to persuade goes far beyond simple charm. I think that's why Angel has a talent for acting, because she sinks into a part and lives in a character's skin. Fiction becomes truth while she's onstage.

Mallory has always had interesting notions of fiction and truth.

In that tiny clinic room, an image came to mind as the nurse adjusted the bandage: Mallory in a doctor's office, a bruise on her arm, tearfully clutching the card and nodding, yes, yes, she should call.

Not that I ever touched her in anger—if I didn't trust myself, I would walk out to the porch—but I realized then I'd have to be twice as careful. Even if that meant she clawed my face to ribbons with her nails, I would have to let her without raising a finger in my own physical defense, or risk losing everything.

I scrub my face dry on a crusty towel, and then I hear something in the kitchen. The phone?

Mallory grabs it before I can get there, clutching it with both hands. She shoots me a look that I can read as *It's the police*, and she's nodding.

"Okay. Yes, thank you. Yes, please."

She hangs up. "Dylan got on a bus to Cleveland."

"What?"

Casey had come down the stairs behind me at the ring of the phone. She hovers, mute, in the bend of the open staircase. Angel rushes past her and all the way down the steps, her iPod in her hand. "I heard the phone," she says. "Cleveland?"

"That's what the cop said," Mallory continues. "That they showed his picture at the bus station and the staff remembered him. Because of his stammer. But they said he must have ordered the tickets online and had them mailed because he already had them. He was confused about which bus, though, so he asked for help."

That solves the mystery of him always getting the mail. "Was he alone?"

"Yes."

"Well, the girl did write that they were meeting up in Cleveland and going together from there."

"So they're going to have the Cleveland police check the station there," Mallory says.

Jewel had been munching on the finished popcorn. "Good! Then they'll bring him home, right?"

I teeter on the brink between protective lying and gentle truth. "He's been gone a while, hon. He's probably not in Cleveland anymore. He's probably on another bus."

"They said his ticket was only to Cleveland," Mallory says. "Why wouldn't he go straight through if he's supposed to be going to New York?"

Mallory and I lock our eyes. If "Tiffany" is really a pervert from Cleveland, there's no reason to buy a ticket all the way through.

In the silence, Jewel gobbles more popcorn, then yawns.

"Babe, you need some sleep," I say, as much to dispel the frightening quiet as anything.

Jewel shovels in another handful, then nods.

I start to step forward, but Mallory waves me off. "Let me tuck her in. I don't get to every night."

"Make sure she flosses," I say. "The popcorn."

I walk over to where Casey still stands as if she's afraid to come into the room. I speak quietly, so Angel won't hear.

"I can try to get her to go home . . ."

Casey shakes her head. "She'd just blow up. We don't need that. Anyway, I can see why she'd want to stay."

"Thank you."

Casey flinches away as if I've said something wrong.

"You've really been a champ about this."

She gulps hard and still won't meet my eyes. I venture, "I said I was sorry about before. Why don't you get some rest, it's been a long day."

"Don't talk to me like I'm one of the kids."

I open my mouth to argue then realize she's right, of course, that's exactly what I'd been doing. Right down to my soothing voice.

Casey then says, "Maybe I should go. Give you guys some space."

"No!"

I glance back over my shoulder, and Angel is staring at us. I nudge Casey back up the stairs to our room.

"I don't want Mallory to feel like she's replacing you."

She closes her eyes and sags in the shoulders. "I'm tired of everything we do viewed as how it affects Mallory. That's why you don't want me to leave? Some strategic gambit?"

I pull her in for a hug. "I need you."

I hugged Mallory so recently that my animal mind compares before I can tell it to shut up. Casey is shorter, more slight. Her head rests on my chest, not my shoulder.

But she doesn't cling as tight.

"Please stay here."

"I don't think the kids want me here," she says, her voice muffled by my chest.

"It's just a bad day."

"I'm not talking about just today."

I take her shoulders and gently push back to look at her face. "The kids love you."

"Jewel puts up with me. Dylan . . . He's been acting like I'm invisible now for weeks. And you're not blind. You know how Angel feels."

"She's a teenage girl. If she behaved perfectly, there'd be

something wrong with her. And she's been through hell with her mom, she's really sensitive. Every time I say anything even lightly critical, Angel flips out."

Casey rubs her face under her eyes, then asks me, her stare hard, "What if Mallory tries to get the kids back?"

"She won't."

"Why are you so sure? What if she goes after me as unfit to be in the house?"

"That's ludicrous, plus the biggest case of pot calling the kettle black, my God. She's steady tonight but believe me, she's all kinds of crazy. And manipulative. You've been . . . I can't think of a wrong step you've made. And believe me, after what I went through with Mallory . . ." I try a smile.

"Not a wrong step, huh?" she says, but she's not looking at me, and has the strangest expression on her face. "I need to step outside."

Oh, she's feeling guilty about the smoking. "Case, smoking doesn't make you an unfit stepmom. It just makes you stink."

"Ha," she says weakly, and heads out the door.

I bump into Mallory coming out of Jewel's bedroom. "Put on your pajamas, sweetie, I'll be right back up," she calls over her shoulder. "I think we should call the police back," she whispers to me as we descend the stairs.

"They said a detective would call in the morning. I tried, but they think he's just another runaway."

We're in the kitchen now, and Mallory puts her hands on her hips. Angel is back in the front room, watching TV. I can hear canned laughter and see the flickering light. Out of reflex I wonder what Dylan is doing in his room, and this is like a punch.

"I will call him back," Mallory continues. "And *I* will convince them that my son is not some hoodlum runaway, and that we think he's meeting a sexual predator."

"We don't know that for sure—"

"Goddamn you and your calm! You think you're so great because you keep it together for everyone, but guess what, sometimes you need to panic, and this is one of those times. Our son is out there, at night, meeting someone with a fake picture, a disconnected phone, and an e-mail address that could be anywhere. Where do you suppose he's staying the night if his ticket was only to Cleveland?"

I have no answer. Possibilities flash through my mind from a bus station bench to highway overpass to . . .

I did a story about a missing girl once, on a weekend cop shift. They found her weeks later, strangled and naked in the woods.

But Dylan is a boy, a young man in fact. He's smart, too.

Apparently, he's also easily led.

Mallory is not waiting for my answer, because she never waited for my blessing to do anything, even when we were married.

"Yes. Yes, this is Mallory Turner, I talked to you a few minutes ago about Dylan. We have significant reason to believe this is not just a simple runaway . . . Well, first of all, he's never done this before. He's a good kid, plays in the band, very respectful. This is very odd behavior. The picture that this supposed girl sent, it's obviously some model head shot. And it's a Gmail address—anyone can sign up for those with any kind of name. But here's the thing, in the actual message? Whoever this is had to talk him into this. Lure him, you might say . . . He's a good kid, but he's naive. Trusting. I'm really afraid, and now we know he's left the state . . . Please, you've got to help me!"

She's crying now, clutching her fist as if he can see her through the phone, pausing for a moment to listen.

"Then call one in from home! I mean, heaven forbid we inconvenience the police with a possible crime being committed against our child! If he turns up dead, this is on your conscience, do you realize that? How will you sleep at night?"

Her shrieking has drawn Angel in from the other room. Now I'm worried Jewel will hear, so I approach Mallory and tap her arm, shushing her. She bats my hand away with surprising force.

I'm not sure if she's acting or she has convinced herself. In any case, she pauses for a few moments, and then, more calmly, says, "Okay. Thank you. Thank you so much. We're desperate here. Okay, someone will call. Okay."

She hangs up. Her voice trembles, but her smile is wide. I recognize that face. It's Mallory Triumphant.

"They're calling in a detective from home. Can you believe they don't have detectives scheduled all night? He got all snotty and said, 'Ma'am, this isn't New York City.' Whatever. They're going to do something kind of like a subpoena but not technically, but anyway they're going to do that to the e-mail and cell phone companies to see who owns the phone and address."

We all whirl around at the sound of sniffling on the stairs. Jewel is standing behind us, has been for how long I don't know.

"Honey, don't cry."

"I thought he was just meeting some girl! Something happened to him?"

"No, honey, look, we were just trying to get the police to help us find him, he's probably fine."

"But not definitely?"

"We . . . we don't know what's going on."

"And we still wouldn't know if you had *your* way, Dad." Angel sounds so much like her mother. They stand together, both of them with their arms folded.

"Hey, I said I tried, too."

Mallory tosses her hair. "Well, I *convinced* them that we're worried. And I am! And why weren't you monitoring his online stuff! You've got the computer geek right here in the house and you didn't keep tabs on him! You should have known he was talking to some . . . person in Ohio or something, you could have dug deeper and found out if this Tiffany even existed, and now he's gone! Our boy is *gone*! And to think I'm supposed to be the unfit parent here!"

"Enough in front of the kids!"

"Oh yes, we can't have a fight in front of the children, oh no. Heaven forbid."

The front door opens. Casey, back in from the porch. She blanches at the sight of Mallory with her fists balled up, stance wide, like a boxer.

"And you! You're the one home all day, sitting in on his band practices. You should have known! A mother would have known!"

"*You* didn't know!"

"Only because I didn't have the chance. Remember last weekend when my visitation was interrupted by his band festival trip?"

"And the weekend before that you were *ill*," Casey shoots back, advancing into the kitchen. She sheds her parka and throws it on a chair.

"Yes, I was! And that makes four weeks since I've even seen my baby! And maybe I won't ever again!"

Jewel gasps, and I turn around to carry her back upstairs. The shouting continues, but I can't deal with it, I'll have to let the women in my life tear each other apart for now.

Once she's tucked under the covers, Jewel creases her forehead, and tears shine in the corners of her eyes. I tell her to pray hard for Dylan and try to sleep and that maybe we'll have good news by morning, and that he might even call us, and remind her that her mother gets really worked up sometimes and sometimes there's no reason to be. At this I can see Jewel thinking hard; she looks up at the ceiling, and I can see her running through her memory for times Mallory flew off the handle over nothing.

Her nod to me is false, though. She's not a good liar like her mother, and I hug her in gratitude for that.

"Do you want me to stay with you until you sleep?"

"Yes."

"Okay, baby."

I finally take off my necktie and rest on top of the covers next to her, where she's curled around her teddy bear like a little kidney bean.

Chapter 13

Casey

H ow dare you put this on me?" I shout, sinking into the futility, in fact knowing that every time I shout at Mallory, Angel hates me just that much more.

"I just can't believe that I was supposedly such a terrible parent that I couldn't have my children and yet here you are, someone I don't even know, getting to live with them, and then my son gets involved with some stranger on the Internet and runs off, and you! You're a computer person even, and you just sat back and let it happen! Because you're an *idiot* who knows nothing about children!"

"I was respecting his privacy!"

"He'll have all the privacy he wants if we never see him again!"

I clench my fists. It's not my fault. It's not. "Stop with the melodrama, you're scaring the kids."

"I didn't know Jewel was on the steps. And Angel is not a child anymore, she deserves to know what's going on. And listen to you: *melodrama.* My child is missing, and you call this melodrama? I'll show you drama." She picks up a candy bowl from the counter, an earthenware thing that Angel had made in school years ago when she was young enough to be doing arts and crafts. She heaves it up over her head and stares me down.

I'm lifting my arm to protect my face when the phone rings. She plunks down the bowl and seizes the phone.

"Yes! Yes, Detective, this is Mallory Turner. Thank you so much for calling. I'm really worried."

Angel stares at me as she backs away toward the stairs. "Just what we needed right now. A fight with the girlfriend."

She turns and stomps her way up.

Mallory takes the cordless phone downstairs to the computer, and I'm all alone in the kitchen as fear wells up in my chest that Mallory might be right, that I respected him right out of the house and out into the dangerous world.

But it's the only way I could connect with him. I learned quickly not to ask him how school was. He'd say "Fine," or not reply at all. But in the evening, in breaks from practicing his sax, he'd volunteer an anecdote. And if I limited my responses to neutral signs that I was listening—*Really? Huh, weird, wow*—he'd tell me more. From this I learned about his first crush, a flute player named Emily who'd just gotten promoted to first chair in her section. But if I sounded too interested, he'd turn his eyes back to his music and bring the sax back to his lips and let the music do the talking.

Maybe this is what comes from living with a reporter for a

father and Mallory for a mother. I get the impression that when they all lived together, Mallory wanted to know every detail of their lives, down to which snack they bought from the vending machine. I sensed something like relief from him when we were together. He gradually laughed more often. Smiled at me.

These things meant more to me than any gooey declaration of affection. It was his way of skywriting "I like you." I even imagined he might love me, in a certain way.

Until he stopped asking me to join him during his practice. About the same time he started getting the mail every day.

Maybe I am stupid about kids.

My phone rings in my pocket, and I almost shut it off, but the area code is unfamiliar, so I answer.

"Hi," is all he says.

"Dylan?" I try to keep myself from shouting, screaming. I grip the kitchen counter for support as I tremble where I stand. "We're worried about you, pal. What's going on?"

"I'm okay. I wanted to tell you."

There's a loudspeaker. What's it saying? I can't make it out. Voices, shuffling. "Are you okay?"

I bite my lip so I don't pepper him with questions.

"Yeah, that's what I s-said." He's testy. I can almost see him tensing on the phone, getting ready to hang up.

"Where are you, buddy?"

"I'm . . . I'm . . ."

A blur from my peripheral vision becomes Mallory inches from my face, shouting, "Gimme that phone!"

I hunch my shoulders and turn away, trying to listen for clues, to his voice, for his answer.

Her fingers dig into my shoulders as she whips me back around to face her. One hand seizes my phone and the other shoves me down hard.

"Dylan!" she shrieks into the phone. "Dylan?"

Then she starts sobbing his name over and over, slumped on the kitchen counter and mumbling about the dropped call.

I pick myself up off the floor as Michael comes running down the stairs. I wipe the blood from my face from where I bit my lip hard in the fall, and allow myself a bittersweet recognition that when Dylan decided to call home, he called me.

Chapter 14

Michael

Mallory sobs on the counter and Casey is on the floor with blood on her face but what draws my attention is that Mallory is sobbing our son's name. Casey picks herself up so I go to my ex-wife shouting, "What? What happened?"

"She wouldn't give me the phone," wails Mallory, and that's when I notice she's holding Casey's cell. "And now he won't answer."

I look questioningly at Casey, who's applying a damp paper towel to her lip. A circle of pink spreads.

"Dylan called," she says, examining the towel. Her voice is steady. "I couldn't make out where he was, but he says he's fine. He was somewhere with a loudspeaker."

Mallory tenses. I've seen that look. I grab her wrist and pry her fingers off the phone.

If Dylan called this number, this phone has become the most important thing in the house.

"What the hell is wrong with you?" I demand of Mallory. "Keep your hands off Casey, or you can get your ass home."

"Oh please, she just *fell*. It's not like I punched her. Trust me, if I wanted to do some damage, I'd do better than that."

"And I suppose her falling had nothing to do with you."

"I was just trying to get to the phone! That *girl* was standing between me and my son!"

Casey looks pale, but answers evenly, looking again at the paper towel pink with her blood. "He called me. I was just trying to hear where he was."

"And then the call dropped!"

Casey stares back at her, throwing the damp towel in the sink. "Dropped my ass, he hung up because you were screaming at him."

"How dare you, you silly little bitch!" shrieks Mallory, and I seize her upper arms, anticipating her. I'd started to forget how strong she is when she's mad.

"Let go of her!" hisses Angel, who has come down the stairs. She's wearing her pajamas, and without her makeup, her hair brushed smooth, she looks so much younger. I open my hands from her mother's arms, wanting to explain but knowing in the same instant she won't care.

Mallory rubs her arms as if I'd wounded her, and she calms with the appearance of her daughter, an ally. In fact I might have hurt her a little. It wasn't until I let go that I realized how tight I'd clenched.

"What the hell?" says Angel. "Stop with all the fighting down here, J. is asleep."

"Dylan was on the phone," I tell her. "He said he was fine."

Angel forgets her umbrage over the fight and relief blooms on her face. "So he's coming home?"

I turn to Casey, but Mallory answers. "He didn't say that. We got disconnected, so we don't know much. But he seems okay."

Angel's shoulders sag, and she sighs. "I'm going to try and sleep now, I guess. If I can trust you guys not to tear each other apart like a pack of hyenas." She cocks an eyebrow. "Wake me if he calls again, though."

Casey has remained silent, dabbing her lip now with a dry towel. The blood on the towel is down to a few specks. There's a divot in her lower lip. I approach Casey to get a better look at her face, reach for her cheek. She jerks away from me, strands of her hair falling between us, blocking my view of her eyes.

Casey clears her throat once Angel has gone back up the stairs. "Could I have my phone back, please?"

I'd pocketed it, without realizing it.

Taking it out, I find myself staring at it. Dylan called this number. Not the house, not my phone. He could try again, especially if the call really did drop.

"Michael." Casey's voice has a note of pleading.

"Can't I hang on to it? I'm not going anywhere."

Her coolness crumbles before my eyes. "My mother might call. I promise to let you talk to him if he calls again, but please, it's my phone."

I hand it over to her, and Casey snatches it from me, burying it deep in her jeans pocket. I hear a disgusted snort from Mallory, and when I glance at her, she's glaring, slit-eyed, at Casey.

I can't count the number of times Mallory paged through my cell phone records or my personal e-mail, grilling me about this or that conversation with a woman, usually a source, sometimes a coworker. Sometimes Kate, until I told her not to call me at home. I stopped trying to hide my password, that very act being enough to set her off, and accepted my lack of privacy.

So I'm well used to paranoia.

But I do wonder . . . why won't Casey let me hold her phone? When so much is at stake?

"I'm going to see if he updated his Facebook page," Casey says.

She heads for her desk in the office at the other end of the house.

"Stop beating up my girlfriend," I say to Mallory, in a half-joking tone, trying to keep things light, keep her away from her personal red zone.

She sinks into a kitchen chair. "Oh, please. *Beating up.* She tripped when I grabbed the phone. She bit her own lip. Not my fault she's clumsy."

I take the chair opposite her. Most of the lights are off in the house but the one over the kitchen table, and this makes me feel like a TV cop interrogating a suspect.

"She's not clumsy."

"Michael, I did not try to hurt her. I wanted the phone, and she kept it from me."

"Couldn't you wait for your turn?"

"Jesus, what am I, six years old? That was my least favorite thing about being married to you, when you talked to me like one of the children. And anyway, she had no right. She should have given me that phone the very instant she knew it was him. I gave birth to him." At this she hits the table hard with her index finger. "I nursed him, I sat by him in the oxygen tent when he was two, I took him to speech therapy."

"When you could get out of bed."

"I was going through a rough time then."

"When are you not?"

She tosses her hair back over her shoulder. "Oh yes, the rich doctor's son is going to lecture me again about how long I'm allowed to have a rough time."

"At the expense of the kids."

"Fuck off. You don't know what it's like to be me."

I have no retort for this, never had. Though the story has changed often enough I'm not sure which parts are real, it's clear she didn't have an easy time of it. One doesn't get to be like Mallory without some damage of some kind.

"I'm still their mother," she says, her voice strained, as if trying to hold something in, an unusual effort for her.

I see her love for them in her face, and this breaks down my fortress. She loves them and they love her back despite it all, and this is why I can't hate her.

"I should have spent more time with him." Her hand traces circles on the table, over and over. She's stroking it, almost lovingly. "I've been trying lately, Michael. I need to be better, I know. I'm going to be more involved, I am. That is"—she slides her eyes over to me, turning her head only slightly in my direction—"if you'll let me."

"Of course," I tell her, grasping her hand, stopping it from its circling. The closeness startles me, and I let go. "That's all I've wanted, I want you to see the kids, I want you to keep to the parenting time."

" 'Parenting time.' 'Visitation,' " she says, her face puckered. "I don't want to just pick them up at appointed hours when the court says so. I mean, I want to come over more often, take the kids out even if it's not 'my time' on the schedule."

It sounds like a reasonable request. But I feel that little *ping* in my gut, same as I get at the newspaper when a source tells me something that *feels* wrong. So I'll have to check it out, dig deeper.

But now is not the time.

"We'll talk later," I say, pulling my hand back. "I can't think about it right now."

She nods, and her hand resumes the slow circles on the table.

Chapter 15

Casey

My eyes fail to focus on the glowing computer screen in front of me. I have not turned on the rest of the lights, preferring the shroud of darkness for the illusion of walls and privacy. I doubt Dylan put anything on Facebook. I just needed to get away from them.

Past my computer screen I can see the porch and the street outside. Under the streetlight, a couple stands close together. I think they're arguing, based on their posture. The man gestures broadly, limbs flying fast in the air. The woman stands straight, her arms wrapped so tightly around her you almost can't tell she has any. Her head is bent toward the ground like a shriveled flower in the frost.

It makes me want to rush out and defend her, though perhaps she's the guilty party.

It's not so easy to tell, looking from the outside in. I mean, one would think that my fiancé would rush to my side when he came in to find me bleeding on the floor and his ex-wife carrying on.

I shake my head a little, refocusing on the screen. I'm not important now. It's Dylan, and that's why Michael went to her, because she was crying about Dylan.

How much time will the police invest in a teenage kid who willingly left home? I heard on the radio on the way home from the store that there was a shooting last night. And I'm sure Cleveland has its own share of crime and urgency.

My brother ran away once, though he didn't run away so much as go on a bender with friends and forget to come home. Billy was sixteen then, thinking of himself as a man. I thought of him that way, too, though now I know Dylan and Angel, and those years seem fragile. In a way, teenagers are more vulnerable than Jewel, because Jewel at least knows her limits.

My mom had been panicking the whole time Billy was gone, my dad raging about the house about how he'd "beat his ass" when Billy showed up. When Billy finally did, my dad yelled at him, and Billy just turned right around and got back in his car. By then Billy was a head taller than Dad, taking after my grandfather in the height department, and nothing our parents said seemed to do more than annoy him.

It was me, in the end, who got him to apologize to our mother. I explained to him, once his hangover had receded, how Mom was sobbing through the house and couldn't even cook dinner, she was so upset, and so we were eating TV dinners and pizza rolls. That got his attention; nothing stops my mother from cooking.

He never did promise to keep to a curfew, but he did call home if he wasn't coming back for the night.

He also quit going to school. It was like he felt he deserved a trade-off for that one concession.

I told him that he was a dumbfuck.

We'd been sitting in a clearing in a patch of woods behind our property. It belonged to someone else, but no one ever seemed to care that we used it. I think it's a subdivision now.

There were a few stumps, arranged almost as if they were chairs around a table. Sometimes if it wasn't too windy we'd play cards out there, the ants coming out of the dead stump to walk across our clubs and diamonds. Didn't bother me. We were country kids, and a few ants were nothing to fuss about.

This particular day Billy was having a beer. I wasn't. I hadn't joined in yet, being only fourteen and in some ways timid. I hadn't yet understood that parents are powerless against a willful teenager.

"Why should I go back? Do you know they put me in freakin' algebra? Like I'm going to college." He pointed at me with the beer bottle. "They're the dumbfucks."

"You got a B on your last test. And you didn't even try."

He shrugged and took a deep gulp.

"Don't you want to get out of here?" I gestured to the woods, but I meant our small town outside of Lansing. Michigan State University was close by, and although it had a fair share of hicks—Moo U was its nickname, after all—to me it was like a beacon. I'd swallowed the college education party line as a ticket to a different, broader life. Plus, maybe I could live in a house that wasn't falling down around me. One of the shutters had fallen off just that morning.

"I like it here," Billy said, shrugging. "I'll earn some money.

I can work in a shop or something. Down at the Olds plant or whatever. I'm a simple man with simple needs."

Billy laughed hard at this, tipping back his head and roaring at the sky. Then he finished off his beer and wiped his mouth with the back of his hand. "But you know, Sprite. You go to school. Take algebra, take honors English, and you go make us a fortune. And like you said, get out of here. Cuz you're smart and you'll do fine."

He leaned forward to ruffle my hair, then for a moment he cupped my chin in his hand, which smelled of beer and smoke. "Yeah. You'll do fine."

I curl over in the desk chair and press the heels of my hands into my eyeballs. It's been a long time since I've let myself think of Billy this long, and thoughts like this would come followed by a long swig of Jack.

I bet a normal girl would confide in her fiancé about such a huge loss. I was all set to try and be normal and tell him, a year ago when it was opening day of hunting season. I kept thinking of Billy every time I saw hunter orange and camo. But the words jammed up in my throat like a logjam on a river, and one of the kids distracted us, and then it was on to the next thing. And Michael always looked so worried, as it was, about everyone else.

Michael's touch on my shoulder jars me nearly out of my chair.

"Hey. Did you find . . . Are you okay? Are you hurt?"

I sniff hard. "I'm okay."

"You don't look okay."

"I'm just tired."

Michael leaves it alone, as I knew he would. He used to chase down my evasions, but lately he gives up the chase quickly. I used to think that's what I wanted.

I answer his aborted question. "No, I didn't find anything, sorry."

He leans against my desk, staring at his feet. "You know Mallory's spending the night, right?"

"I figured as much."

"You okay with that?"

"How can I not be? I mean, what am I going to say?"

He says, looking down as if addressing the floorboards, "You could have just handed her the phone."

I stand up out of my chair so quickly it rolls across the wood floor and catches on a rug.

"I'm going for a walk."

"Casey . . ."

I'm shrugging into my coat and pulling on my boots. "What?"

"Can you leave the phone? In case . . ."

I take the phone out of my pocket with a trembling hand and rest it with care on the top of the desk, using up all my willpower not to smash it into Michael's chest or slam it to the ground.

Outside, I notice the arguing couple is gone. I wonder if they split up, or are somewhere having makeup sex.

I have to smoke the cigarette out of the uninjured side of my mouth, like a gangster. Even so, the puffing is painful. I don't stop, though. It's not as simple as stopping something that hurts just because it does.

I'm not going around the block this time. I'm walking toward downtown, where there are stores, lights, people. Something other than old houses and naked trees. As I get closer, I see couples and groups walking together, laughing and talking.

I pass by the Meyer May House, a long, flat Frank Lloyd Wright design in muted brick that sprawls along the block in sharp, deliberate contrast to the vertical, flamboyant Victorian homes all around. I toured that house once, with Mrs. Turner as the docent guiding us.

When I finally go, I need to move far enough away that there won't be landmines everywhere, explosions of memory.

This thought swells my chest with fresh agony. I don't want to go. This morning I thought I wanted to, thought I'd be free despite the sadness, but now I know that was bravado talking. Like that old song goes: freedom only means you've got nothing left to lose.

Now that we're losing Dylan I don't want to lose any of them, even Angel, who hates me. Even Dr. and Mrs. Turner, who just think I'm a nice young girl; even the Meyer May House and Heritage Hill; the family I was supposed to have here with Michael, pushing the baby in a stroller along the leafy, narrow streets, the bigger kids all around us.

An icy wind kicks up and pricks my ears. I should have brought my hat. It's cold even for November, now, and I'm noticing white flakes in the air. Is there snow coming? Usually Michael watches the local news with fanatic attention, making sure he's not getting scooped. Today we didn't even turn it on.

I duck into a store to get warm.

It's a liquor store.

I smirk, looking down at my own shoes. I can't even pretend to myself this is an accident. I know this neighborhood well enough, having lived here for almost a year now and taken numerous solitary walks.

I hang back from the counter, staring up at the selection. Jack is my favorite, of course, but I won't say no to vodka, and Seagram's 7 in a pinch will do. I used to pretend I was fancy and even have wine, with a cork and everything, though I could put away a whole bottle and only feel buzzed so it wasn't cost-effective.

I turn to the back of the store, where the coolers are. Maybe just a beer. Not much alcohol in that, really. More alcohol in NyQuil. Even Michael opened a beer today. It's been a stressful day. People use alcohol to relax and why not? If it's okay to take a Valium for nerves, why not a drink?

I could handle this all better if only I could calm down.

Ah. Killian's Red. My college drink of choice. Cheap, but it has flavor. It will do just fine.

I can already feel my heart lift at the prospect of that foam touching my lips, the cool tang of the beer, the unwinding of my shoulders that will begin. I'll give one to Michael, hell, even to Mallory, and we can sit together and feel less crazy while we await word. It'll be like a peace offering.

I'm smiling to myself at the register, and when the guy asks me for ID I start rooting through my pockets.

My wallet is not in my coat pocket.

The man stares at me, tapping the counter with his fingers, drumming out his impatience. Someone behind me readjusts his purchases in his arms. I start rooting around in my pants pockets, even the back pockets, which I never use. My fingers touch a bill, and I hope it's a twenty or at least a ten, but now I have to convince him I'm twenty-one because . . .

As I look up to think of an excuse for not having ID, I catch sight of myself in a huge distorted mirror above the counter, the kind meant to spot thieves in every corner of the store. My head is huge in the center, the store disproportionately wide around me. I'm hemmed in by bottles.

"Sorry," I tell the guy, and I run out the door.

I sprint down the block, away from the store, all stores, all bars, back to the neighborhood, panting with the unfamiliar exertion. I round a corner and slip; my feet fly away from the ground, and I come down hard on my side.

That's when I notice the sleet has started. The sidewalks are collecting shiny pools of ice, nearly invisible in the dark. I pick myself up, and for a moment I lean against a tree, until I stop shaking.

I resume my walk back to the house carefully now, so it takes a good deal longer to return. I can't feel my lips now that the wind has kicked up. My hair is damp with snow and sleet.

When I get to the porch I'm trembling again, though exactly why I can no longer say. I fish through my pockets, only to find I left not only without my wallet but without my keys. And my phone is inside.

I press the doorbell before I remember it's broken. I knock as loudly as I dare, but there's no answer. I peer in the front window, over my desk. The lights are off in the whole down-stairs.

I knock once more, then curl up, shivering, in the chair on the porch, waiting for someone to wonder where I am.

Chapter 16

Michael

I hand Mallory a pair of my sweats out of the laundry basket on the floor of the bedroom. With the drawstring waist she should manage okay.

She accepts them and glances at the bed.

It's the same bed we had, the one we purchased together just before we moved into this house. Casey and I did buy some new sheets, but that's the same bed, the same mattress.

I see Mallory still staring at it and wonder what exactly she's remembering.

"You can't sleep in here," I blurt out.

"I wasn't going to ask. What, you think I came here to seduce you?" She smirks now. "You wish."

Despite this, she pulls off both my old wool sweater and her T-shirt in one swipe, not bothering to turn around or leave the room, exposing her lacy red bra.

I turn my back to her. "Jesus, Mal."

"Oh, like you haven't seen them before."

I hear a soft fall of fabric, and I know she's dropped the bra to the floor.

Oh, dammit.

I sit down on the other side of the bed, facing away from her, not just because she's undressing in front of me, but because my stupid penis is springing up like it's party time.

It's been a while for Casey and me. A hungry man is not picky about his meal.

And if I'm honest, sex was one way in which Mallory and I were very, very compatible.

I think of the unsexiest things I can imagine. I think about work, that always does the trick at the worst possible times.

But work makes me think of Kate.

"It's safe now," Mallory says, chuckling.

Not hardly. I say, without standing up, "Go on downstairs, I'll get you some blankets for the couch."

She doesn't move, and for a moment I'm terrified she's going to come around to my side of the bed.

Mallory walks out, though, closing the door with a soft click behind her.

I ponder taking a cold shower, but the thought of Casey walking in this room just now seems to have done the job. I wait a few more moments to be sure, then go in search of blankets and a spare pillow.

Where is Casey, anyway? Maybe I should have let her take her phone. I could have called to check on her.

Downstairs, Mallory is mercifully clothed and not very sexy

in my bulky gray sweats. She's tossing back a pill with a glass of water. Headache, she tells me, after she gulps it down. She then stretches out, and it seems rude to just throw a folded blanket at her, so I snap it out and drape it across her.

Mallory stretches her arms and catches me around the neck. I freeze there.

Her hands are clasped snugly. Not tight exactly, but resisting my pull upward.

"Thank you," she says.

I use my own hands to unclasp her arms, and stand up fully. "For what?"

"For being so kind."

"What did you think I would do? Make you sleep on the porch? Make you go home and worry alone?"

"How do you know I'd be alone?"

I frown at her. Has she got a boyfriend again? God, that last one . . .

"I'm kidding, Mike. Yes, I am alone at the moment, if you must know."

"Good night. I'll wake you if I hear anything."

I'd already called the police just after Casey left for her walk. They were sending the paperwork to the cell phone and e-mail companies and said they'd call when they knew more.

They were neutral and businesslike, and I know that's how they should be, professional. In fact, that's how I always act when I have to report on a tragedy. But now, on the other side of trauma, their coolness is infuriating.

"Mike?"

"Yeah."

"You ever going to bed?"

I'd forgotten I was just standing there, hovering over Mallory. I give her a halfhearted wave and go upstairs.

Where the hell is Casey? I don't want her tromping into the house late at night and waking everyone up.

The light is still on in Dylan's room, from our earlier rummaging.

I should be telling him to turn out the light, close his laptop, and go to bed. I should be talking to him about band practice.

I try to imagine where he is. I picture him someplace relatively safe. Maybe he somehow got a motel room with this girl—with no credit card? Underage? Well, he got on a bus—and he's warm and sleeping.

I can see him in his bed now as clearly as if he really were there. I can smell Dove soap on his skin. He takes a shower at night because it's impossible to get in there around Angel in the morning, so every night he smells of Dove. We always used that on him, back to his toddler days when we were doing the scrubbing. It was good for his sensitive skin, which always seemed to break out red with the slightest dryness.

I bet he didn't take his Eucerin. He's going to be itchy.

I run lightly down the steps and grab my sneakers out of my gym bag. My hands buzz with unused energy. If I could run to Cleveland now, I would. I'll drive there right now. When the police find him I'll be partway there, then, and we won't have to wait as long to be reunited. If Cleveland doesn't pan out, I'll drive to New York by the likeliest route and stop in every hotel lobby and show his picture. I'll visit every bus station.

Casey and Mallory can watch the kids. Or not, my parents can, whatever.

My shoelace breaks. "Fuck." I try to knot it, but one side is too short.

I slump over, leaning against the back door, defeated by a shoelace.

As my blood rush slows, reason resumes its seat. At the very least I need Casey here. I can't dash off while she's still out walking, or whatever the hell she's doing.

I look at the clock. Nearly midnight. I should be worried about Casey, too. A young woman—a small, slight woman, at that—alone walking in the dark city, and I went and confiscated her cell phone.

I ignore my loose sneaker and grab my coat off the hook, slipping out the back door so I don't wake Mallory.

My plan is to go around the block, her favorite walk route—and a route that would never take this long—when I happen to glance at the house and see something on our porch. Human-size, like some derelict has snuck up onto our porch swing to sleep.

I approach slowly, because if someone is nuts or high enough to sleep on a stranger's porch . . .

"Casey?"

She rolls herself up to sitting in the porch swing. She's shivering hard, her wet hair plastered to her head. From here her lips look blue, where they're not red with the blood from her lip, which has split again.

"What are you doing?"

Her words are clumsy, like she's been at the dentist and her mouth is numb.

"I'm l-l-locked out."

I pull her up off the chair and get my own keys out of my pocket. "Didn't you knock?"

"No one heard me."

When I get her inside the warmth, she shivers harder. I wonder, with Mallory right there on the couch, why she didn't hear the knocking. But I look over, and she seems to be snoring already.

"Go upstairs and take a bath. I'll make you some tea."

She nods and walks hunched, as if she's frozen so stiff her joints won't stretch.

After I make Casey some tea, I'm going to the computer to map a route to Cleveland. I'm not going to sleep until I know he's safe.

I bring up Casey's tea, and she's wrapped in her bathrobe, the running tub steaming up the small bathroom. She nods her thanks.

Before I go, I take out her phone and rest it on the bathroom counter.

Our eyes lock for a moment, her face passive, watchful, before I close the door. I'm weary, and my sleepiness causes me to prop up for a moment against the hallway wall and close my eyes.

I'm a caretaker again, still, always.

Chapter 17

Mallory, 1995

Not until I heard Angel squeal "Daddy!" did I even notice Michael was in the house. I'd been concentrating so hard on Dylan's little forehead. He'd been staring at me as he sucked away on his bottle like he was trying to figure me out and I was thinking, Join the club, kid, and my stitches hurt and Angel was jostling me as she pretended to read me *Goodnight Moon* and said good night to all the things in our living room.

I wondered how long he'd been standing there, staring at us. I imagined how we looked sitting there, how very domestic, and found myself amazed again at how normal things were.

He swung Angel up and nuzzled her neck, then as Angel wrapped her arms and legs around him to hold on like a barnacle told me, "Guess what I found out today?"

"Yeah?"

"I got the job!"

I hadn't meant to startle Dylan, but I couldn't help but shout with joy. He'd been slaving at that internship for too long, with a little money but no benefits, while his dad had been paying all our hospital bills.

Dylan shrieked fit to make my ears bleed, ignoring the plastic nipple. I teased his lips with it, and a shivery panic started to creep up my spine. But Michael untangled from Angel and scooped up his baby in his big hands, and I swear Dylan took one look at those clear blue eyes and settled right down.

"You're amazing," I told him, ignoring the whispering thought in my head, *He loves his daddy better than you.* "Professional reporter and father of the year, too."

I rose gingerly, wincing at the stitches pulling, and gave him a peck on the cheek. "How are you today?" he asked me.

"Fine," I answered breezily.

He didn't answer, and when I met his eyes, he was staring hard at me. "Better," I answered. "Pretty good." And it was true.

Michael interrupted my thoughts by suggesting we go out and celebrate. I told him yes please, as long as I could shower.

I should have known dinner wouldn't go well. Angel had missed her nap and Dylan was fussy, but I didn't mind taking off early with doggie bags, since it made Michael so happy to take his family out at all. He was celebrating being a provider for us, with a steady income and everything.

On the way home now, with our still-warm food in Styrofoam containers in our laps and the kids dozing in their car seats, I stole a glance at Michael, the early autumn sun glowing in the car. I found myself stunned nearly every day that he loved me, was still with me, even knowing my sordid past, how I'd buried myself in sex with half strangers as a way to forget, maybe punish myself.

He always insisted it didn't matter. He also insisted—the ever-practical doctor's son—that we both get tested.

For this I bit down my impulse to be insulted and hurt, and made myself think differently and so far I'd been rewarded with a loving, attentive husband, if a bit stuffy at times, with a tendency to be critical.

Forcing myself to think differently was exhausting, though, and that's how I thought of those dark periods. I needed to hibernate sometimes, to recover from that effort. When I felt the darkness creeping up—like in that old horror movie, *The Blob*, it would rise from the ground and gradually swallow me—I would call Michael to tell him I needed rest and crawl into bed for a few days.

That was better than the alternative, because if I ignored the Blob, it would go the other way, and soon I'd be throwing things, screaming, and this would make Angel cry.

It was easier to be different when pregnant, so that's why I convinced Michael to have another baby, even before graduation. For one thing, *he* was different when I was carrying a child: even more careful and solicitous, treating me like blown glass.

Maybe now, I thought, tipping my head back on the headrest, the warm pasta heating my thighs, NPR softly on the radio, maybe now it will stick better, the even-keel feeling, because I'll have so much to do. Two children, and a whole house to clean and maintain.

The Blob was so much more common when I was bored. Like it wanted to fill the emptiness.

Michael had been talking about his new job at the *Herald*, so I tuned back in.

I squeezed his thigh. "I'm so proud of you."

He blushed a little, and shifted uncomfortably in his seat. He always reacted that way to praise, having gotten so little from that stuffed-shirt father of his.

In the house, after we slurped down our leftover meals, I gratefully let Michael take over with the kids. I stretched out on the couch, on my side, the only way I could rest that didn't seem to hurt somewhere. I flipped channels and listened to him read to Angel, taking breaks to coo at Dylan in his bouncy seat . . .

The next thing I knew the house was quiet, and Michael was nudging me to make room on the couch. Dylan was dozing in his car seat at our feet, sucking on a pacifier.

I shifted slightly to make room for him, and then rested my head in his lap, facing the television. He stroked my hair back from my face.

He reported to me about all he'd done for the bedtime routine, as if I were going to grade his report card. I just murmured, still in the fog of dinner and my doze.

The telephone shrilling made me jump. Michael leaned forward to answer the cordless, sighing, both of us hoping it wasn't the newspaper.

"Oh, hi Kate," he said.

I felt my body go stiff. I pulled myself up, away from him, and listened to his side of the conversation.

"I can't now," he said. "I'm with my wife and kids."

Oh yes, he's twenty-two years old and already tied down with me, the fat, bloated cow, and the babies. Little Katie—I'd met her, she had round perky boobs and wore the shortest skirts I'd ever seen in an office—was practically shouting, so I could hear her just fine as she said, Oh, come on, he was allowed to go out and celebrate a new job, wasn't he? The wife could watch the kids?

Michael flicked his eyes over at me. Was that guilt? It sure wasn't a loving gaze.

"I should go," he said. "I'll see you at work." He hung up and turned to me, and I could see him searching for explanations.

"Go then," I spat. "Go have a drink with your little slut."

"She's not a slut, she just—"

"Oh, it's perfectly normal for a single girl to call up a married man while his wife's stitches are still healing from labor to ask him out for a drink? Go then, don't let the ball and chain stop you."

"She just doesn't know how it works, she's practically a kid."

"She wouldn't have called here if she didn't think you might go. So is that who you have lunch with every day? And a drink? Is that why when I call you at the office I can't reach you?"

"No! I'm not interested in her, okay? Not in the least."

"Bullshit, you're not. You'd have to be blind or gay not to be."

He scooted closer to me. "I don't want you to be upset. I will tell her not to call here ever again. I love you, Mal."

"No matter what?" I asked, feeling the tears spill over then, my fear of his answer loud like drumbeats in my head.

"No matter what," he said, pulling me back to him, tucking me in the crook of his arm.

He let me cry on his shirt, and he kissed the top of my head.

Then he said quietly, almost murmuring, as if he thought I wouldn't hear, "I wish I knew how to make you believe me."

I wish I did, too.

Chapter 18

Michael

Casey and I passed the night together in the kitchen, neither of us willing or able to sleep.

While Casey was still thawing out in the tub, I'd abandoned the idea of driving all night toward Cleveland, feeling too tired and scattered to focus, afraid I'd end up crashed on the side of the road, compounding tragedy with rash, pointless action. The Cleveland police were looking, the Grand Rapids police checking out the phone and e-mail records. That was their job.

Yet the idea of sleeping in my warm bed felt like a betrayal, not knowing where my son was, whether he was safe and warm himself. I kept returning to the missing children stories I've reported and read over the years, and wondered anew how the parents survived it. At least Dylan checked in once, at least we're pretty sure he left on his own.

How could you ever go on with your life, the mundane things

like eating, showering, mowing the lawn? Yet people do, especially if they have other kids depending on them. Birthday parties, school plays. All the while, not knowing.

We didn't speak, Casey and I, the whole night. What else was there to say?

We moved in restless circles like hummingbirds from the kitchen chair, to the office chair, to the counter by the phone, steering clear of Mallory on the living room couch.

I eventually changed out of my work clothes, grabbing some sweatpants in the dark of the room.

The sun rising behind the cloudy sky provided no beautiful views, just a gradual erasure of darkness.

The phone shrills at 7:30, and I run for it.

"Mr. Turner? It's Detective Wilson."

My throat is frozen. I cough out, "Yes."

"We got the information from the cell phone and e-mail companies. The phone and e-mail are both registered to a Harper household in Cleveland. We called the number and also talked to the Cleveland police."

I grip the countertop. "And?"

"Ed Harper, the owner of the phone and computer in question, has also reported his daughter, Tiffany, missing. This should be some sort of relief for you, sir, as we're satisfied that he is indeed with a girl as he believes."

I let out a shaky breath. "Okay. Thank you. What now?"

"Mr. Turner, we've alerted Cleveland police to be on the lookout for your son and the girl, but I'm afraid that's all we can do at this time."

I close my eyes, put my head in my hand. "Running away is not illegal," I mumble.

"Sir, may I suggest you contact the National Center for the Missing? They are set up to help parents in your situation. I'm sorry, I wish we could help you, but we simply don't have the manpower to chase runaways."

I hang up, forgetting to say good-bye to the officer.

The wood floor creaks as Mallory comes into the kitchen, wrapped in a blanket. Casey stands just where she was when the phone rang. She's wrapped her sweater tight around her, and her eyes are big as she watches me. She bites her knuckle.

"Well?" shrills Mallory, her hair matted from sleeping, a jagged sleep wrinkle down the side of her face.

"The good news is, he apparently is meeting a girl. A real girl, who is also missing. The bad news is, now that the police are satisfied they are runaways, they're not going to chase them anymore."

"Oh, my God," moans Mallory, sinking into a kitchen chair. "He's never coming home."

"We don't know that," I hasten to say, back to the exhausting job of reassuring, propping up.

Casey moves around in my peripheral vision, and as I join Mallory at the table, Casey plunks a coffee down in front of her.

"I need some cream," Mallory says, taking the cup without looking at Casey. Like she's a waitress.

I remember suddenly that it's Friday. I'm supposed to be at work. Late at night I'd let a call from Kate go to voice mail and never did listen to it. I should have, it was probably about that staffwide meeting.

I bring a coffee with me to the office desk and dial up Aaron.

"Aaron, I'm not coming in today."

"Shit," he replies, his fingers clacking on the keys as he talks

to me. "I'm shorthanded already. And listen, you should probably call Evelyn."

Another round of layoffs, just like the last time they called an
all-hands meeting.

"Oh, great. I'm toast, aren't I?"

The clacking pauses. "We don't know that. They're talking to
everyone individually."

"I can't deal with it now. I'm having a crisis at home."

"I know, I'm sorry."

"How?"

"Your dad called this morning already."

"Dammit."

"Don't worry about it, I know the drill. I ended up transfer-
ring him to Evelyn. She'll say no, too, but I didn't have time to
argue with him. But listen, I am sorry. I wish we could help—"

"No, I know. Dylan's not in town anyway, it seems."

"Hey, I've gotta go, but listen, when you hear something, let
us know, okay? Meanwhile, when you can, call Evelyn. About
the meeting you missed."

A voice interrupts us.

"Gotta run, Mike."

I barely get out a "good-bye" when he hangs up. I don't mind.
The paper still has to come out. Life goes on and all that.

I glance out at the blowing snow whirling in the gunmetal
sky. It's daylight now, I could risk the drive more easily. Except
my little Honda wouldn't be of much use in a wreck. It would
crumple like tinfoil.

I hear footfalls on the steps and turn to see Angel. She comes
right to me, and I just shake my head. She throws herself into
my arms, burying her face. When she steps back I can see from

the pale blue hollows under her eyes that she's slept very little.

"The good news is," I tell her, smudging a tear away with my thumb, "is that they have confirmed that Tiffany really is a girl."

I see her relax a few degrees. "Oh, good. Well, that's good. Can I have some coffee, Dad?"

"We don't have any lattes or anything, kiddo. Just the boring Maxwell House stuff."

She shrugs. "I'm so tired."

"Well, fine. Go ahead, if you can stand it."

Angel rummages for a cup, and as she's pouring coffee from the machine, the sight of her performing this simple, adult action thunks me in the chest like an arrow. My girl, my first child, who was a baby when we were still in college and babes ourselves.

Jewel emerges now, her hair knotted from her usual crazy sleeping. She's rubbing her eyes beneath her glasses, skewing them as she does so they end up crooked on her face.

She looks at the kitchen clock and gasps. "Oh, no! We'll be late for school!"

For a moment she stares around at everyone in pajamas, none of us hurrying, no one packing lunches. Then her face crumples in. "I forgot!" she cries, and flees back upstairs, wailing. "I forgot!"

Mallory is faster, and closer, so she gets there first. I follow them up the stairs.

Jewel sobs on her bed, burying her face in her blankie. She still keeps the blankie around, but I haven't seen it much since the first weeks after Mallory and I split. Actually, I'd thought it was put away somewhere by now.

"Baby," Mallory says, stroking Jewel's hair, but her hand is shaking. "He's okay. I'm sure he is. Don't you ever get so mad sometimes you want to leave?"

Jewel shakes her head into her blanket.

"Well, teenagers do. And you know what? Pretty soon he'll get hungry and cold and miss his own bed and he'll decide to come home."

At this Jewel picks her head up and looks at Mallory, her face puckered as if with confusion. "But doesn't he miss me?"

I interject, "It's complicated. Teenagers are confusing people, and they don't always think very clearly."

Jewel's eyes dart between us, one hand already on her stomach.

I sit down with them on the bed, putting my hand on her mother's shoulder, and my other hand on Jewel's knee. "It's okay. I'm sure he misses us and that's when he'll decide to come home. He's a good kid, isn't he? He'll realize that we're worried and he'll come home."

Jewel nods, but there's no light in her eyes.

A moment passes, all of us ringed together, our hands on each other, joined by worry. In my line of sight is that picture on her bulletin board, the last picture taken of us as an intact family. It's tacked up next to a magazine cutout of a pony.

Jewel breaks the silence. "Can I watch cartoons while I eat?"

"Sure," answers Mallory, and I sigh but don't protest.

Jewel runs downstairs at this, leaving Mallory and me alone in her room.

"Thanks," I say.

She's rubbing her own hands, threading the fingers through each other, twisting her turquoise silver rings. She stops suddenly, shaking her hands out.

"For what?" Now she starts playing with her hair. I've seen

this before. It's restless Mallory, usually followed by Mallory filling up a plastic cup with boxed wine.

"For . . ."

She smirks. "For not being crazy. Yeah. You bet. At your service." She gives me a mocking bow, tipping an invisible hat.

"You're not the only one upset."

"Could have fooled me."

"Would throwing things make you feel better?"

"A little emotion never killed anybody."

We slip right into the worn grooves on the record of our marriage. She's too unstable, I'm cold.

I turn away from her and stomp back down the stairs, once again hearing a ringing phone, the sound sparking a mosaic of frightening and ecstatic possibilities.

Chapter 19

Casey

ngel taps her fingers on her coffee mug, her eyes unfocused on the center of the table. Every time she sips, she grimaces. I'd offer her more cream and sugar, but I don't want to draw attention to my presence.

Lately it's like she's sunburned. I can't so much as brush up against her. And that was before she read my journal.

It was a year ago in May that I first met them. Angel turned fifteen that summer, and I took her and some girlfriends to the mall one summer Saturday. I lagged behind them most of the time, enjoying their chirpy laughter and their habit of bursting into song, heedless of—or maybe because of—the stares. They were sharing earbuds from their mp3 players, and I tried not to make faces thinking about the ear germs.

We sat at the food court eating greasy egg rolls and I was still mostly ignored, but then Angel said, "Oh, Casey! Listen to this!" and she launched into an incomprehensible story about some romantic triangle involving a girl named Tessa. I didn't know any of the kids involved and could barely follow her disjointed tale, especially when the other girls kept throwing in more details about other people I didn't know.

But I leaned in anyway, my elbows on the table, making faces and gasps of shock to match theirs, glowing with pleasure at my inclusion into the circle.

After I moved in, Angel had the same girls over for a study date, which was really a pretense for gossip. I popped them some popcorn, and as I brought it in, I heard one of them mention Tessa.

I said, "Oh, the one who was dating a football player and a marching band guy at the same time?"

In the cold silence that followed, one of them stage-whispered, "*Awkward* . . . ," drawing the word out, marking the moment. The girls then all looked at Angel, who stared at me with an unguarded fury.

"Do you *mind*?" she hissed. "This is supposed to be a *private conversation*."

I backpedaled. I'd only made it to the first step down from the landing when I felt the door slam reverberate through the floor.

At the table now, hunched over her coffee, Angel sighs and kneads her temples. Jewel comes down the stairs, her face wet, but composed, and doesn't look at us as she heads for the living room to flip on the television.

"I should have gone to school. Now they'll have to rehearse without me. That's irresponsible of me, to affect everyone else because Dylan decided to be a jerk."

I say nothing, listening for Michael to come down.

She continues, "I need the practice, too. I'm supposed to be off-book by Monday."

I venture, not looking directly at her, "I could run lines with you."

"Shut up and go call your boyfriend." She stands up and adds, "Then go write about what a bitch I am."

We hear Michael's heavy step on the stairs at the same time the sound of the ringing phone jerks us to attention. Angel gets there first, seizing the phone hard, then immediately relaxing. "Oh, hi, Grandpa. No, nothing. Here, I'll let you talk to Dad."

She hands the phone to her father, saying she's going to take a shower.

"Hi, Dad," says Michael, closing his eyes and kneading the bridge of his nose. "Yes, I figured as much . . . Well, we shouldn't get special treatment and I wouldn't want it . . . We did hear that he really is meeting a girl . . . No, I don't . . ."

Michael's shoulders sag as he talks more to Dr. Turner, a man I've found as scary as any I've ever known, and I've known some characters. Oh, he's benevolent enough, but he feels he has great power. I've seen it in the way his eyes dance when things are going his way, and it's as if he thinks he made it happen through force of will or intellectual manipulation.

Only, his son hasn't done what he wanted. For a doctor who has watched hearts beat inside open chests, who has held life in his hand and crafted a modest fortune and a foundation to do good works, it must be infuriating that his own son hasn't fallen into line.

So Dr. Turner relishes the small victories of control. Like owning this house we live in.

I want to walk over and hang up. Just click the button down

and free Michael of whatever lecture he's hearing. It's not that simple, though, as I'm well aware.

I approach Michael and circle his waist from behind, resting my cheek on his back, listening to his heart thrum beneath my ear. His voice sounds low and rumbly like this as he murmurs, "Mmm-hmm."

Then his free hand untangles my fingers and he steps slightly away.

I slip into my parka and pick up my cigarettes, this time adding a hat because it looks like the wind is whipping up outside.

Outside on the sidewalk, I dial up Tony, having already received a voice mail I didn't listen to, and two texts asking if I'm okay.

"Can you meet me?" I ask, as soon as he's picked up.

"What's wrong?"

"I can't say it all on the phone, it's too much."

"Just say where."

We agree to meet at "the Castle," a chateau-esque granite building once a home, later a restaurant, now a dentist's office. Fifteen minutes later, I'm leaning on a tree in front of it, staring at the garish magenta sculpture on the front lawn, when Tony pulls up in his ancient Monte Carlo.

I hop into the car, warming my hands at the heater vents. Inside I'm overheated from my walk and my anxiety; my exposed skin is almost numb.

Tony scratches his chin through his red beard, now threaded with more gray than I remember from our days as neighbors.

"What's going on, Edna Leigh?"

I ignore his use of my given name and explain about Dylan,

the presence of Mallory. As I finish up my story, I notice I've been twisting my engagement ring, which would now slide off easily, should I choose to remove it.

"I used to run away all the time," he says, and because I know what kind of life he's lived, I laugh.

"Oh, that's supposed to make me feel better?"

"I've turned out okay."

"Yeah, finally at age, what, fifty-five? I'd like Dylan to be spared some of your more colorful adventures. Besides, he's not—"

"Not what?"

"He's not worldly. He's quiet, a little awkward around new people. He has this stammer that comes out sometimes—"

"Yeah. I get it." Tony taps his steering wheel. "So what are you going to do? Anything I can do to help?"

I tip my head back on the seat. "I don't know. I'm not sure why I wanted you to come, even. I just had to get out of there for a bit."

"Yeah. Oh, hey, why don't you send me a picture? I can send it to some of my trucker friends. They can keep an eye out. Rest stops and whatever. Hell, maybe he'll stick out a thumb and one of my friends'll pick him up. You never know."

I smile at him, and just then my head feels swimmy with cigarettes and lack of sleep and food. I pull out my phone. "I'm sending you a cell phone pic I've got. It's not the best, but it will help." I send it to Tony's phone, and he looks to make sure he got it.

"Great. Need a lift back?"

I shake my head, hard. Tony doesn't know that Angel read my journal, that a sighting of him now would be almost the worst possible thing.

"Stay warm, kiddo," he tells me as I get out of the car, before I shut the door. "They say there's a blizzard coming." He squeezes my hand before I step back into the cold.

I wonder if the blizzard will hit Ohio. I don't think Dylan has his warm coat.

I hurry back to the house, because I've been gone too long for a walk around the block. No one seems to have noticed my absence.

Michael is at the computer, the Web site of the National Center for the Missing open in front of him.

Three small pictures on the screen have the mottled blue backgrounds and strained smiles of school photos. They have "missing" dates and cities attached.

One day these kids were posing for a photographer, having greasy school lunch pizza, getting scraped knees on the playground. Now they're gone.

How would we know where to find a girl from Greeley, Colorado?

And how would anyone else know how to find Dylan?

"Time to call the hotline," Michael murmurs, and picks up his phone.

From my end of the conversation, it's clear the person on the other end is well trained in reassurance and warmth. Michael repeats, "Yes, exactly," and "We're very worried," and keeps pinching the bridge of his nose.

He lets go of his nose long enough to grab a narrow spiral notebook out of his desk drawer and starts writing in pencil. But he shoots me a look, shaking his head slowly. I walk around him to look at what he's writing. There are things that we've already done, like break into his computer, search his room, call his friends. There are things the police already said they cannot do for us. We can't use GPS to track down his cell, because he didn't take it.

Michael has written, *Missing poster—(like for lost cat?!)*.

Now Michael is nodding as if the other person can see him. He seems to be holding his breath.

He drops the pencil and crumples down to the desk, putting his head on his arms. He lets the phone receiver roll out of his hand.

I wrap my arms around him, feeling his body heave with the effort of holding everything in. This close I can hear the woman on the phone saying, "Hello? Mr. Turner? Are you there? Hello?"

Chapter 20

Michael

Casey doesn't understand that her attempt at soothing me is making this worse. I don't want soothing, I want answers. Action. Results.

I swallow hard, exhale, shake off Casey like a dog shaking off the rain and pick up the phone again, finishing up my conversation with the well-meaning woman on the other end who won't stop expressing sympathy.

The phone rings again. It's not a hopeful sound anymore.

"Hello."

"Are you the father of Dylan Turner?"

"Yes." I sit up straight at this, my ears pricked, my hand reaching by rote for the notebook.

"Your goddamn son has run off with my daughter. I'm pressing charges on him when they find that sonofabitch."

"My son did not coerce your daughter anywhere. In fact, we have e-mails that show this whole stunt was her idea."

"I'll just bet. I know what horny boys are like. He just wanted to get her alone and vulnerable, away from her parents and their strong moral values!"

My hand grips the phone so hard I might break it.

"We need to help each other. Two families looking betters the odds. And last I heard they were in Cleveland. Are you in Cleveland?"

There's a beat of silence. I can feel the anger wafting from him and I feel it, too, both of us hurt and furious.

"Yeah."

"Then you can put up posters. Let me send you a picture of Dylan, and you can put your daughter on the poster, too."

He huffs into the phone. "Fine. But this isn't done. When we find them, it sure isn't done."

This guy is an asshole, but I appreciate that confident "when" in that sentence.

It takes me a moment to identify that rumbling in my gut as hunger. I haven't eaten breakfast and only picked at last night's pizza. Not that I feel like eating—can't help but wonder, Is Dylan eating?—but it's something to do, once I send the picture of Dylan to Tiffany's father.

Angel comes down the stairs with her damp hair making dark circles on her purple T-shirt. The shirt's neck scoops low, and her collarbone juts sharply from her upper chest. As she walks into the kitchen, I notice her grab a belt loop and hike up her pants.

"Angel, have you eaten today?"

"Yes."

"What?"

"A bagel." She scowls as she pours more coffee.

"We're out of bagels."

"I don't know, whatever. I don't remember."

She's not yet gaunt, but there's less of her than I remember.

I grit my teeth, considering. I could let it go, today. But how many times in the last weeks have I wondered about Dylan—when his stammer showed up again, when he quit inviting Casey to hear him practice—but something else came up, swept me along in the tide of everyday busywork, and I never asked? And now he's gone.

"You have to eat something."

Angel sighs, tosses her head. "I'm not hungry."

"Eat something small."

"I don't feel well."

"Then don't drink that coffee. It's acidic."

She pours out the coffee and slams the mug down on the counter. For a moment I remember her mother, hurling another mug from that same set. They look so very much alike, and I recognize the expression on Angel's face now, as Mallory Furious.

"I don't want to see you starving yourself."

"God." She leans hard on the kitchen counter, folds her arms. "Is this what it's going to be like now? Dylan acts like an idiot and runs away and I'm under surveillance?"

"Can't you see that I love you? And I don't want you making yourself sick?"

She looks at me sideways now, a wet strand of hair hanging over one eye. In the silence there's a sad awareness of how rarely I've said out loud, "I love you."

"I'm fine," she says, narrowing her eyes. "Don't take Dylan's problems out on me."

Mallory approaches from behind me. I'd almost forgotten she

was here, she'd been so quiet with Jewel in the living room, no sound but the racket of commercials and dopey Nickelodeon shows.

"What's your problem now, Mike?"

"I'm worried. She's not eating."

"Of course she's not! I'm not eating today, either."

Mallory walks to Angel and folds her in a hug, and together they walk out, arm in arm, looking even more alike from the back, as they retreat from me.

Does she think I don't love her? How could she think that? I stayed with their mother years longer than I should have, because I couldn't bear to be apart from my children. I kept them with me after the split instead of surrendering them to Mallory's unpredictability, I have given up any life outside of work, home, and one hour at the gym . . .

Not true, I correct myself, sinking down into a kitchen chair, my bones so tired they have a will of their own. Not true because I dated Casey, fell in love, and moved her in.

And now Casey and Angel spark up against each other like flint and tinder, have been for weeks, and it's only been worse of late. And yet still Casey is here. Maybe Angel thinks I'm choosing Casey over her.

Why should I have to choose? I tighten my fist and clench my jaw until my molars hurt.

"Should" is meaningless. Reality is all I've got.

Chapter 21

Dylan

Tiffany's head is in my lap.

This is not really so great.

Because we're in a mall and she's asleep and my leg is going to sleep and we've been up all night and we're not in New York City but Cleveland. I'm tired of dragging my sax case around, which is heavy enough even when I haven't stuffed clothes in it, like it's a suitcase.

Also? I'm hungry.

I wonder if this is how my dad felt when he married my mom, realizing he'd just made a huge mistake but it's not like he can just erase it and start over.

My dad would never say it like that; even when they split up, he was always careful to not say anything bad about her, and to say that he never regretted a thing because he's glad to have us. I bet some days he wishes he could wave a magic wand and have us, and Casey, too, but not our mom. I see what his face looks like when he talks to Mom, like he's fifteen years older.

I look down at Tiffany and her hair has fallen over her face, so I brush it back. A security guard from the mall walks by, and he glares at us. He's been by here, like, three times. I should wake her up.

I jiggle my leg a little, but she doesn't move.

She started out kinda mad at me because I didn't run into her arms and swing her around like something in a movie when I first saw her, but it wasn't my fault I was surprised. She didn't look anything like her picture, and I can't be blamed for that because it isn't her, and she admitted it right away. She didn't think I'd like the real her.

I'm not gonna lie, the picture she sent was prettier. She's a little heavy, for one thing, and she's got some pimples that she covers up with this orangey makeup. But that's not her fault, and anyway, I like her because we talk and the things we say, and that's what I told her. And I hugged her and it was nice.

It was just a shock, you know? I can't help being shocked. You get an idea in your head of somebody . . . Lucky for me I've learned to tell people just what they want to hear, so it's mostly okay now.

Well, obviously it would be perfect if she looked super-hot in addition to being witty and funny and nice.

Trouble is, in person? In real time? She's not as funny as she was over the computer.

Or maybe I'm just being an asshat because she doesn't look like her picture.

I shake her awake by the shoulder before the security guard comes back to ask why we're not in school. She sits back up, and I tell her we should walk like we have somewhere to go or we're going to get hassled.

She nods, and we stand up and start walking, having to swing around the moms pushing kids in strollers and the old people walking with their white sneakers. I'm starting to feel like a neon sign is over our heads going, TEENAGERS NOT IN SCHOOL! RUN-AWAYS!

"We should go somewhere else," I say to her.

She slips her hand into mine. It feels clammy. I resist the urge to pull my hand away and wipe my palm off on my jeans.

"Where are we going to go? We're out of money." She pouts, like it's my fault or something.

The bus station people wouldn't sell us tickets, being under-age, and I remember feeling annoyed with Tiffany because I thought she was going to plan ahead and buy them through the mail, like I did, where they can't check ID.

We hung around until the bus station people started to look at us weird, and then we just started walking. We walked until we were so tired we couldn't stand up and it got really cold and started snowing so we found a sheltered bus station bench and snuggled up as best we could, using my sax case as kind of a pillow, mostly so it wouldn't get stolen. We had loads of time to study the bus lines and enough change for bus fare, so in the morning, we took a bus to the mall so we could eat at the food court and have somewhere warm to be.

But then we found out her wallet was missing, probably stolen on the bus, and I was going to ask her why she had it in her backpack where it was really easy to get into, instead of, say, in her front pocket.

But then I saw her lip was puckered out and her eyes were all teary.

I don't think she's actually sixteen, either. That's what she said on Facebook, that she just turned sixteen. But she seems pretty young.

I spent my own cash already—I never had much, but Tiffany made it sound like she had tons. Now we have no money and no ride and it's snowing really hard out there, too.

After the wallet got stolen I decided to call home with a calling card I bought for emergencies, since I wasn't taking my phone. Tiffany was in the bathroom, and I called the first number that came to mind, Casey's cell, the number I call if I need something during the day when Dad's at work. But somehow my mom grabbed the phone and started screaming and then Tiffany came out of the bathroom and I didn't want her to think I was chickening out so I hung up.

"I think we should hitch," Tiffany says, now swinging my hand in hers, which annoys me. I stiffen my arm so she has to stop and she gives me this little hurt look through her hair.

"Yeah, and then we get hacked up into bits by some maniac. Good plan."

"C'mon, there are two of us. We won't get in someone's car if they look crazy."

"Not all psychopaths wander around drooling and rolling their eyes."

"Okay, no droolers. That will narrow the choices."

I allow a smile at this. "No, serious, Tiffany, we can't. Have you seen the weather out there? W-w-w-we didn't dress for standing by the side of the road sticking out a thumb. Someone would probably call the cops on us, an-n-n-yway."

We walk a few more steps, and I test the waters with something. "You know, we could call your parents."

She stops dead, forcing me to stop, too, by yanking on my hand.

"We can't do that! It's horrible, I can never go anywhere or do anything, I'm like a prisoner in that house. I had to escape."

I look around to see if anyone heard that. A mother wheeling a stroller by gives us a long look.

"S-s-someone will hear you."

Tiffany had told me all kinds of stories about how she was never allowed to go anywhere but school, the library, and church, and couldn't even use the phone unless her dad was in the same room listening, and her only Internet access was taken away when he found out she was talking to me. She had to change her e-mail address and send me messages through Facebook and Gmail at the library when she was supposed to be studying. He took away her phone, too, when he found out she'd been sneaking calls to me.

She said she had actual bars on the windows, and a lock on the outside of her room that he threatened to use if she disobeyed.

This all sounded pretty bad.

And she talked about running away alone, and I didn't want her to do that and get abducted and murdered. So she said I could come with her. At first I thought that was a bad idea, but then school every day was awful, and I had no friends at my old school anymore either, then Angel and my dad and Casey started fighting all the time. I couldn't even breathe, it felt like. My stammer got worse, and some kids at EXA started mocking it.

Tiffany started talking about freedom, and it all sounded so . . . free.

But she also sent me a picture of a model instead of her face, and told me she was older than I think she really is.

"I'm hungry, anyway," I tell her, stalling. "Let's try to find something to eat."

"With what?"

I sigh. I hadn't wanted to do this, but I'm running out of options. "I've got my dad's credit card."

She lights up like fireworks. "You do! That's great! Let's go to T.G.I. Friday's!"

I shake my head. "We can't go anywhere where they have time to really look at the card and ask for ID and stuff. We should probably, like, walk to a convenience store and just buy some food where I can just swipe the card and scribble something on the paper. A gas station, someplace like that where they won't care."

She nods. "Okay, fine, a gas station. Then we'll hitch. Really, it'll be fine. My cousin used to do this all the time, my mom's cousin I mean?" She says that last part in a rush because she'd already talked about not having cousins, back in our first days writing to each other. "He said a *couple* can get away with it, no problem."

Outside the mall doors, through the blowing snow, I see the glowing sign of a gas station across the busy street.

"Well," I tell her as we turn to walk into the storm. "I guess. But I think we should go someplace warmer than New York. Florida or something."

"Oooooh!" she exclaims, skipping across rows of snow in the parking lot, raising her voice to be heard over the wind. "Disney World!"

Yeah, right. *Hey, kid, you just ran away from home with no money and no car, where are you gonna go now?*

Whatever, I'm freezing. Maybe hitching isn't so bad, if we're careful.

Chapter 22

Michael

O f course I'll drive," my father says when I tell him I want to go to Cleveland, if nothing else so that when the police find him, I'll be halfway there. Yet I dare not brave these wintry roads in my little Honda.

"I was thinking I could just borrow your SUV."

"Have you slept all night? Certainly not. Driving sleepless is like driving drunk. I'll be over as soon as I can."

"I can bring Casey, we'll take turns driving."

"I'm sure she didn't sleep, either."

I can't refute this. Neither of us suggests I bring Mallory along. For one thing, she doesn't have a license anymore.

"I will drive you," my dad says, hanging up the phone before I have time to argue.

"I'm going to shovel the drive," I announce to the house in general, though Jewel is reading in her room, Angel is upstairs on her phone, and Casey is on her computer downstairs forwarding Dylan's picture to anyone and everyone she can think of.

I need air. Plus, I'd feel bad if Dad broke his neck on our front walk.

I sip in the cold outside. Mallory must have turned up the thermostat, because it's gotten warmer than usual in there. I watch it carefully because heat costs a fortune and the house is old and drafty. That was one of our classic fights. What started as "Stop turning up the heat" would result in her shouting, "You don't care about me!" and would usually veer into crazy territory from there, about how I obviously didn't care about her because I was having an affair.

The snow is wet and heavy, the kind that causes heart attacks when old folks try to clear their own driveways.

Early in my career we had a huge morning snowstorm, and some photographers went out to shoot a photo for the standard front-page weather story. One of them took an ordinary shot of "man shovels driveway," with the snow flying dramatically off the shovel. Later in the morning, I fielded a strange call.

It was the man's neighbor. Just minutes after that picture, the man had dropped to the ground with a heart attack and was not expected to live. The neighbor had seen the photographer taking the picture and had the presence of mind to call and beg us not to run it.

We replaced the picture, and the man died later that day, in the hospital.

I stop to lean on my shovel, panting with effort, and remember watching Dylan as he got swallowed up by the school doors.

"Mike!"

Mallory is on the porch, wearing one of my old heavy coats.

As I look up, she picks her way down the slick steps. "Mike, I hate to bug you, but . . . would it be okay if you drove me home for a change of clothes? I can't keep wearing your sweats, and I don't think Casey wants me raiding her closet. Not that I could fit in her Gymboree pixie clothes anyway."

"Mal."

"Oh, come on, I'm kidding."

I would like to have Casey drive her, or even Angel, with her learner's permit, could technically do it. But the roads are terrible.

"C'mon, Mike. I just want to grab some clothes and a tooth-brush. Is that so unreasonable?"

"Fine. Let me at least clear a path, here."

I put the shovel back on the porch, and Mallory comes out the door with her purse.

"I've gotta tell Casey . . ."

"I told her," Mallory says, brushing past me on the way to the car. "She's fine." Mallory plops herself in the passenger seat. "Didn't this used to be your dad's?"

"My mom's, actually."

"Oh, that's right. I remember."

My mom's old Honda. She never wanted anything flashy, de-spite my dad's love for his SUV, so she tended to drive a Honda until my father would deem it too old and buy her a new one.

Then he'd give it to me, so I've been driving my mother's hand-me-down Hondas for years.

I hate this goddamn car and everything it means. But I don't want to have to choose between paying for band camp or making a car payment.

"You'll have your own car one day," Mallory says, patting my knee as I crank up the cold engine.

★ ★ ★

This is a rare peek for me inside Mallory's apartment. Usually I'm in the car, and the kids go in or out the front door guided by Mallory, when she's home, when she's not "ill." No reason I don't go up to the door, I just don't, and everyone seems to like it that way. Never the twain shall meet.

The inside of Mallory's apartment looks like Mallory's dorm room circa 1993.

Cast-off clothing covers every surface. She's peppered the walls with cheap posters depicting landscapes and sunsets. The ceiling of the living room is covered with greenish plastic stars, the kind that glow in the dark when you shut the lights off. There's a bead curtain between her living room and hallway. It rattles as she pushes through it toward the back.

Strewn on the floor are some toys I've never seen, which must be Jewel's. This rankles, to know that she has a life I'm not part of, even if it's only some of the weekends.

"Sit down!" Mallory calls from within the apartment, presumably her bedroom, where she's packing a bag. "Make yourself comfortable!"

I wander into the dining area, just a nook off the living room, really.

She's got framed photos of the kids on the wall, their eight-by-ten school photos, and I notice that these are the photos from the year she moved out. I know she has the new ones, I always make sure she gets some at my own expense. Is it laziness that prevents her from putting the fresh pictures in the frame? Or is it nostalgia for a time when we were all together?

There are snapshots half spilling out of a photo-place envelope among the detritus on her kitchen table. I tilt my head to look at the top one. It's Mallory wearing a bikini on a fishing boat, a burly guy's arm possessively around her shoulders. They're both pink with sunburn.

"Jealous?" she says, coming from the back and noticing me looking at the pictures.

"Ha," I say. "Good luck to him."

She comes over to stand next to me. She's squirted on some perfume. I don't remember what it's called, but she did used to wear it when we were married. She looks down to see which photo I've seen.

"Oh, him. He's over, anyway."

"Did the kids ever meet him?"

"No. Not that it's any of your business."

"Like hell it isn't."

"Like I have any say in who you date, or get engaged to, or bring into the house to live."

"You knew all about her."

"Not at first."

"It was just a few dates, then."

"You were kissing her. And I had to hear it from Angel."

"I didn't know she'd seen us. And . . . God, just stop."

My voice rings overly loud in the small space. In the silence that follows we glare at each other, and the tinny sounds of the neighbor's television float through the wall.

My cell phone rings. "Hi, Case. I'm on my way back."

Her voice echoes weirdly on my phone, but I can make out "police" and "Cleveland."

"Oh, God, is he okay?" I walk closer to the doorway, trying to get a better signal. Mallory follows like a shadow.

"Yes, he's fine. They picked him and the girl up for shoplifting. He's at the police station, and I've got the address . . ."

With Casey still talking in my ear, Mallory flings herself at me and wraps her arms around my waist, her face on my chest. I put one arm around her, reflexively.

"I'll be right back. Map it for me, will you?"

"Where are you, anyway?" She sounds baffled, unhappy.

"I ran Mallory home to get a change of clothes. I'll be right there."

I hang up and Mallory holds tighter, murmuring, *Thank God, thank God, thank God,* into my chest, and I steal a moment to sink into relief with her, the other parent, who regardless of her faults is the only other person who can really understand how this feels.

Chapter 23

Dylan

W hen the cop hangs up the phone and tells me my dad
will be coming, I'm mostly relieved. So relieved I want
to cry, but I'm embarrassed enough by my stammer
and actually doing this stupid-ass thing that I don't want to add
to it, so I look at the cop again, the one who's pissed at us.

And Tiffany is pissed at me.

"Come on," barks the cop who called the house. "You can
come sit in here." We follow him to a beige room with a table and
a few chairs. He tosses some magazines down, crusty, wrinkled
ones probably borrowed from the waiting area in the lobby or
maybe the break room. I see a *Glamour*, *Sports Illustrated*, and
Newsweek.

He gives us a hard look before he leaves. "You two try to go anywhere, you can wait in a jail cell. Don't think I won't do it. I've got better things to do than babysit a couple kids who run away because Mommy and Daddy are meanies."

He slams the door, and Tiffany jumps in her seat. Then she starts to cry. Again.

"Why did you have to do that!" she yells at me through her tears. "You dumbass."

"That" is get busted shoplifting.

Tiffany had dragged me back to the mall. After risking our lives to dash across the street and risking our lives further by eating these horrible wet hot dogs rolling in this machine for who knows how long . . . she talked me back into the mall.

We couldn't think of anywhere to go after our brief failed attempt at hitching a ride. I was trying to talk myself into it, thinking we'd be in a warm car, there are two of us, so that was safer. But it's so snowy I don't think anyone could see us, or they didn't want to stop for a couple of school skippers. Plus it was a really busy road—even if someone had decided they wanted to stop, someone who didn't look like an ax murderer, someone willing to take us south, the roads were so bad they would have caused a pileup.

When Tiffany said she wanted to go into the mall again for a while, I was so relieved I almost fell down, and I gave up on the hitching idea for good.

I've done a lot of stupid-ass things the last few days, but getting murdered by a psycho was one stupid-ass thing too far. Plus I feel responsible for Tiffany, who, as Mom would put it, is "not the sharpest knife in the drawer."

So we were back in a different part of the mall, and I said we should look like we're shopping so it doesn't look so weird that we're just walking endless loops. So we went into JCPenney, and Tiffany looked at earrings.

I saw someone watching us and got worried about getting caught, until I decided that getting caught might not be the worst thing ever.

I took a pair of earrings and slid them up my sleeve. And when Tiffany was ready to go, we walked out into the mall to the sound of blaring alarms, and that same someone—plainclothes security, it turned out—came to say, "Come with me, please."

"No!" Tiffany wailed, and tried to run away.

I was so embarrassed.

Tiffany is calling me a dumbass again.

"I mean, why did you even take the earrings? I didn't even want some, I was just killing time. I didn't know I was running away with a thief."

This is so ridiculous on so many levels, I don't bother to answer.

She tries a new tactic.

"I thought you loved me."

"I thought I did, too."

It came out too fast, and too late I realize I should have softened that. She's wailing again on the table. I come around to her side and put my hand on her arm, but she shakes me off.

"I'm s-s-sorry. Didn't mean it."

"Yes, you did. And you don't love me because I'm fat."

"No!"

I look up at the ceiling, trying to organize my thoughts. I don't like a lot of talking. It's hard when I'm nervous because I stammer, and I get embarrassed, and it gets worse. That's why

I'm better at writing, and why I like Facebook so much, or really anything on the computer. I'm really fast at typing.

In my backpack I have a notebook. I always have a notebook because I like to draw, and sometimes I write little poems when I'm bored. So I take out my notebook and start writing.

> *I don't know you very well, is all. I thought we could get to know each other in messages and we'd be close that way. But real life is different. I still care about you lots, but that's not exactly the same. Please don't be mad. I just didn't want you to get hurt trying to hitchhike.*

I shove this across the table to her, nudging her elbow with it. She sniffs and wipes her face, and reads. At first she scowls, but then her face relaxes. She slumps back in her chair, but the waterworks have stopped.

I pull the notebook back and add this:

> *You know we weren't going to get very far. We had no money, no car. If we hitched, we'd either get a creepy freak, or a good citizen who'd know we were running away and probably turn us in. It was never going to work.*

I underline *never* for effect.

> *And I'm cold. Aren't you cold?*

I add a little cartoon of our shivering selves.
She reads this and smiles a little.

Then her smile fades. "My dad's gonna kill me."

"R-really?"

She sighs hard now, and suddenly looks older than she's seemed this whole time. "Not *literally*. Guess I might as well tell you I don't really have bars on my window."

Yeah. No shit.

We fall into silence. She flips through *Glamour*. I try to work up enthusiasm for *Newsweek*, but I can't focus. My mother's hysteria on the phone keeps playing in my head, like a mosquito buzz that won't go away. What's waiting for me back home. But why did I expect anything different?

The fact is, I didn't think very far ahead. My future after the bus ride was a big blank, but that blank seemed refreshing and clean. An inviting sheet of paper ready for sketching, without all the messy scribbles of my stupid school I hate and home with its tension so bad I'm surprised we're not all twitching. When that big bus rumbled out of Grand Rapids, I felt dizzy with freedom and pushed all thoughts of home out of my head. Even my sisters. Probably because I knew if I pictured Jewel's face, I'd never be able to leave.

The door swings open, and we both jump. A uniformed lady cop comes in carrying sandwiches and drinks. "Well, if it isn't Romeo and Juliet. Well, star-crossed kids, you're probably hungry."

She plunks the sandwiches down with a couple of Cokes.

"Thank you," I mutter, glad to get that out without stammering.

She regards us with one hand on her hip. "You know, I've got kids. Littler than you, but I've got kids. Most of us do," she says, gesturing out the door to the rest of the police station. "What you two did to your parents, you don't have the faintest idea what that's like, the hell they were going through. You took years off their lives with this stunt."

I can feel a blush creep up the back of my neck. I'm sure thinking of my sisters, now. And my dad, and Mom, because I gave her a reason to freak out, this time. I wonder if Casey was worried. Probably.

"Well, eat already. I don't want your folks thinking we starved you. I'll check on you later. Juliet, your dad should be here soon."

Tiffany isn't eating. She's just picking at the bread.

I know the feeling. But I eat it anyway, because the officer was nice enough to bring it to us. I don't want to seem ungrateful.

Chapter 24

Michael

When my dad pulls into the driveway, Casey's in the shower. I go upstairs to knock on the bathroom door. "Yeah?" she says.

"Hey, babe," I say loudly over the sound of the water. "My dad's here, we're heading out."

She pokes her wet head around the curtain. Tendrils of hair are stuck to her forehead. Makes me want to grab her face and kiss her.

"I'll see if Mallory will go home. Give you some space."

"See if she will? How about *sending* her. Dylan's fine, and this isn't her house anymore."

My head starts to throb, and I pinch the bridge of my nose.

When I look at Casey again, her face has sagged with resignation. "Sorry. It's fine." She pulls the shower curtain back in place with less force than before. "I'll be fine," she says over the spray.

I have more to say, but it's hard to talk over the water.

We'll talk when I get back, about many things that we've put off for too long.

I bribe Jewel with a trip to get doughnuts Sunday morning if she does her homework like a good girl, and make the same offer to Angel, only with lattes.

Angel nods, and then announces she's going to take a nap. I can see that she's caked makeup over the bluish hollows under her eyes. I give her a tight hug before she goes.

Mallory is making fresh coffee in the kitchen.

"So," I say, pulling on my coat and peering toward the front of the house to see if Dad has pulled up. "Everything's going to be okay."

Mallory is radiant. I haven't seen her like this since she was pregnant with each kid. "I know! Thank God."

"So, listen, I can drop you off at your apartment on our way."

She stops in mid-pour of the coffee. She tries to shove it back in the coffeemaker and misses, sloshing hot coffee all over the counter.

She puts her hand on her hip, eyes squeezed to slits. "Are you throwing me out?"

"The crisis is over."

"So? I want to be here when he gets home. I don't want to miss a minute. In fact, I'd insist on going with you if your father didn't hate me worse than Hitler."

"I'll pick you up then, on the way back. You'll see him even quicker, in the car."

She looks up at the ceiling, blinking rapidly. "You are throwing me out. I cannot believe after what we've been through the last forty-eight hours—"

"This isn't your house!" As always with Mallory, my voice is louder than I mean it to be.

"So Casey wants me out, is that it? Can't handle the ex hanging around? Please. As if I'd want *you* back."

"You don't need to be here."

"I want to be here, isn't that enough? What were you saying yesterday, about how of course you want me to spend more time with the kids? If this has taught me anything, it's that I've been too cavalier. Yes, fine, I admit it. I've been inconsistent about parenting time. I get migraines, and you know when I don't *feel well* what it's like for me. And for them." She pauses to stare at me, hard, making sure I understand her code. "But I've been through hell, these last two days. That's my boy, my baby, I carried him in my womb and I thought we'd lost him. Let me unwind with my girls, Mike."

"So you're *feeling well* now? For how long?"

"Fuck off. I'm asking you a favor, and don't think this isn't humiliating for me, to have to beg to stay in the house that used to be mine to spend time with my own daughters, just so your new little girlfriend doesn't feel any discomfort." She makes a mock-sweet face and adds, "I promise not to cause any trouble."

"Mal . . ."

"You want me to beg? Does that make you feel like a big man? Okay, fine."

She gets down on her knees in front of me, hands balled up together as in prayer.

"Jesus, Mal. Get up. Fine. But, listen—"

"Daylight's burning, Mike!" shouts my dad from the living room, and I have to leave it there.

My dad is ruffling Jewel's hair as she hangs off his leg.

"Hey, Dad. Thanks."

"All gassed up, warmed up, Cleveland programmed into the GPS. Your mother whipped up some sandwiches for the road."

I check my watch. Four o'clock. It'll be the dead of night before we get there, the wee hours before we get back, assuming we turn right around and don't stay the night somewhere.

Casey has appeared now, hair slightly damp, smelling like something sweet and floral. I check back over my shoulder. Mallory has remained behind me in the kitchen, sopping up the spilled coffee.

"Hi, Dr. Turner," Casey says.

"Hello, dear," he replies politely. Courtly, almost, with that little nod of his head.

I wish he'd tell her not to call him by his title.

"Angel's napping," I explain to my dad.

I give Jewel another enormous hug, telling her to stay warm and do her homework and that she should go to sleep like a good girl tonight. "Listen to your mom. And Casey."

I pull Casey in for a hug, but she's stiff in my arms. She returns the hug, but it's with formality. For show.

"Sorry," I whisper in her ear. "Just one more day."

Her smile is thin as she waves at me.

I walk out of my childhood home into my dad's huge car and into the passenger seat, with snacks packed by my mother, and wonder if I'll ever shake off this déjà vu.

Chapter 25

Casey

I need a cigarette.

This will cause Mallory to roll her eyes or worse. I will stink. It will blacken my lungs and yellow my teeth and give me throat cancer.

But I may tear out my throat otherwise. So.

I dread the cold, though the wind appears to have subsided, as the snow is falling still heavy but now more or less straight down instead of sideways.

So I leave Angel to her nap and Jewel and Mallory to their channel flipping on the couch and step out to the front porch, which is more sheltered than the back patio.

I test the cut on my lip with my tongue. It seems to have scabbed over, so that it must look like hell but will probably not split open, if I'm careful.

After several tries to light up, my cig finally catches and I suck in, both loving and hating that pinch in my lungs that comes before the light-headed relief.

I'd promised myself I wouldn't contact Tony again this weekend, not until I'd had a chance to decide what to do. How much to tell Michael and when. Ideally before Angel decides to let fly with my secrets.

But it's too much to hold this all in. There aren't enough cigarettes in the world to make this feel better. I'm a boiling pot with the lid bolted.

So I text him, as it's safer than calling.

Dylan found. He's fine. Thx.

Moments later, a return text: *PTL*—which I recognize as Tony's texting shorthand for Praise the Lord—*what happened?*

Ran away. Long story.

Glad he's OK. U?

SHE is still here. Makes me crazy.

Hang in.

I pause in the texting, finishing the last few drags of the cigarette, deciding what else to say, what I can reasonably type with my thumbs that will sum up everything.

Don't know if M. still wants me. Want to stay. Hope I can.

Minutes go by with no response. He's a volunteer firefighter, so he probably got called to a wreck.

I feel better having said it to someone, even though Tony may not have gotten the message yet, even though Tony is a relic from my past, a secret.

We were neighbors during my JinxCorp days. We'd get home at about the same time many nights. He was bartending and operating sound for local bands, so I not only saw him in the hallway in front of my apartment but some nights going out I'd go to his bar. Sometimes I'd see him with a band, fiddling with those knobs and sliding buttons for the budding rock stars who called him Gramps. He called them "Assholes" and smiled, so they assumed he meant it affectionately. For some of them, that was true.

He would later tell me that my rock-bottom moment was also his.

"You're young, Edna Leigh," he told me, when my stitches were itching under the bandage and he'd brought me some stuffed grape leaves and baba ghanoush from Olive Express. "If I did that, I bet I'd be dead, or paralyzed or something. I'm sixty-some, and I'm not made of rubber like you."

"Ha, I only wish I'd bounced," I said back, sounding cockier than I really felt.

He quit his bartending gig and gave up working sound. He went to work for his brother, though there'd been bad blood there for the longest time.

The cold finally gets to me. I should also check in with my mom. She never used to be the "checking up" type, but after Billy, everything changed.

In the house, Jewel has fallen asleep in her mother's lap. Mallory's asleep, too, her head tipped back on the couch. Not sure why she should be so tired, since she seems to be the only one who slept last night. Rather soundly, in fact. So soundly she couldn't hear me knocking on the door just a few feet away, when I was locked out.

I prefer privacy for talking to my mother, anyway.

These two halves of my life will have to mesh if we get married, but I find it hard to imagine this.

The phone rings a few times before she picks up.

"Hi, baby," she says.

"Hi, Mom."

"How was your day?"

"Ummm . . ."

There are tears, now.

"Honey? What's wrong?" I hear her clunk a glass down on the table. I imagine her sitting forward in her chair, concern written in the lines on her face, lines put there by me, Dad, Billy.

"It's okay, now," I tell her, wiping my face hard, shaking my head. "It's just been a hard day."

"Oh, sweetie."

Her concern does me in.

I do tell her, some of it, anyway, an edited version of events, leaving out most of the stuff about Mallory. She interrupts my story with lots of "Oh, honey" and "Oh, baby," and commiserating gasps.

Finally she says, "Thank God he's all right. What happens now?"

I shrug, then remember she can't see me. "I don't know. I'll have to let Michael deal with it, I suppose."

"You can't sit on the sidelines forever, if you really are going to marry him. Are you sure you still want to do that?"

"Yes," I croak out. My throat feels raw.

"Why do you want to put yourself through all this? Edna, honey, you're so young yet, you can have any kind of boyfriend you want, someone who can afford to pay attention to you, who doesn't have to spend all his energy on other people, someone without an ex-wife. And don't you want babies of your own?"

"Of course. And I'm going to, with him."

"Don't be so sure."

"Mom—"

"He's got teenagers, and he's what, thirty-five?"

"Thirty-six."

"I guarantee you he's reaching the end of his rope with kids, especially after this. Would you be willing to give up ever having a baby of your own, to stay with him? Is he worth that?"

"I can't talk about this right now."

"I just don't want to see you throw away your youth by making your life harder than it has to be. Don't do it just to win him. This is not some TV show with the guy as the prize."

"So we're watching *The Bachelor* again, are we? Will you give me a break, please? We've been through hell, here."

"I'm so sorry my TV watching isn't up to your lofty standards."

"I didn't say that."

"I thought that's why you bolted town, to go off and live your dreams. This is what you dreamed of? Teenage stepkids who run away and sneer at you?"

"You make it sound so awful."

"I'm only repeating what you tell me. Why don't you call Pete? He misses you. We all do."

"That's what this is really about. You don't like that I left."

"Of course I don't. I miss my children."

I suck in a breath at her phrasing, comparing my absence and Billy's. "I'm right here, on the phone."

"And never here where I can see you. Are you eating? You sound thin."

Despite it all, I have to laugh. "I *sound* thin?"

My mom laughs, too, and the tension falls away like leaves from an autumn tree.

"I hate to see it so hard for you," she says, her voice softer, still warm with laughter.

"Life isn't supposed to be easy. If it were easy, everyone would do it."

"Smartass."

"My ass has never been smarter."

We banter like this for a few more minutes and talk about my cousin's baby's party and how it's been rescheduled because of the storm, and while I keep up the prattle I'm entertaining my mother's question to me: Would I choose Michael if it meant giving up having babies?

Shortly after Michael proposed, we were up late flipping channels while the kids slept. The fire was lit and the room was dark and the ruddy light danced across his face. I kept turning the ring around and around on my finger.

Steel Magnolias was on. Julia Roberts and Sally Field were fighting over Julia wanting to have a baby, despite her character's delicate medical condition. Michael was about to flip past, but I took the remote out of his hand.

"I understand that," I told him. "Wanting to have a baby of her own."

"Real subtle, Casey," he said, smirking at me and taking the remote back.

"I was just talking about the movie." Such a reporter. Always suspecting ulterior motives.

"But you do want to have a baby." He said this matter-of-factly, flipping to a poker tournament on one of the ESPNs.

I shrugged, trying to act like I could take it or leave it, like he'd asked if I wanted some popcorn. It had taken a lot for Michael to risk getting married again. I feared if I pressured him, he would bolt like a skittish horse.

He playfully nudged me. "C'mon, you have baby radar. If there's a baby within a mile of you, you'll find it and start playing peekaboo."

"I'm practicing for the peekaboo championship."

"So you *don't* want a baby with a broken-down old man like me?"

I was almost afraid to look at him, but I dared it. He was smiling at me softly.

"Well, I guess if you can manage it," I said.

He kissed my forehead. "I think I'd manage just fine." He moved on to my neck. "I'll have a baby with you."

I shivered with delight as he continued kissing my neck.

Then he said, "It would make a nice change to make a baby with someone not crazy."

The delicious shivers evaporated, and I moved away from the reach of his lips. He looked at me with a wrinkled brow.

"I think I hear a kid on the steps," I lied.

I know it was a favorable comparison. I know I should have ignored it and kissed him back. But his ex-wife, his old life, seeped always into our most intimate moments.

And now she's here. In our house.

I hang up from my mother and return to the fridge to rummage for some dinner. The children will be hungry soon, and life must go on.

Chapter 26

Michael

T he leather interior of my dad's Navigator makes me feel like a dwarf. I'm not short, but compared to how cramped I feel in the hand-me-down Honda, there could be a conga line in here.

"Go on, lean the seat back," my dad tells me. "Get some rest."

At the push of a button the seat glides down soundlessly.

I jerk back to consciousness with my mouth feeling pasty and my stomach roiling with the confusing motion of rolling along while everything in my sight is stationary. For a few seconds I don't understand any of it.

Then my nap amnesia wears off. Dylan. Casey and Mallory at home with the girls.

"Where are we?" I ask Dad.

Now I understand what woke me up. We've slowed dramatically, and can see little through the windshield but taillights and snow so thick it's like a wall.

My father is tense on the wheel, his mustache twitching, eyes narrow as he searches for passage.

The appeal of a big vehicle has never been clearer.

"We're only to Ann Arbor," he says.

He was right to drive me. I never could have been alert enough to manage this alone. I'd have caused a hundred-car pileup by now.

I consider telling him this, but he knows he's right. It must be nice to have such confidence.

My cell phone rings, and I snatch it up, visions of disaster at home flicking to life.

It's Evelyn. My boss.

"Hello, Evelyn. Sorry I didn't come in today."

"That's fine, Michael, we understand. Any news?"

"Yes, he's in Cleveland and we're going to get him now. He's fine."

"Thank God," she says, but she says it without emotion. I know her mind is already on the very next thing she has to say. "Look, I hate to talk to you about this over the phone, but rumors are swirling, and as we always tell our readers, it's best to get the truth at times like this."

"Yes" is all I can manage.

"We will be offering you a severance package, Michael. Please know it is not in any way personal or a reflection on the work you've done for us. There were any number of factors involved, and the decision making was an arduous, complicated process."

"I'm sure it was. So who else got the ax?"

"Michael—"

"Evelyn. Just tell me."

She rattles off the list. I notice Kate's not on it. I would like to be glad for her, but she has no children to support, she's beautiful and charismatic. She'd bounce back, probably higher than she is now.

"When's my last day?" I ask.

"We're keeping everyone on through the end of the year."

"December 31?"

She pauses. "Yes."

Happy goddamn New Year.

I become aware of my father sneaking looks at me.

Evelyn and I exchange businesslike pleasantries, and she thanks me for my years of service, but I'm not really listening as the conversation winds down and I hang up, still wondering why I didn't make the cut.

Kate must be the rising star of the *Herald*, what there is left of it, anyway. She's been using Twitter and has gathered quite a following of loyal readers who hang on her every post.

I never could figure out that damn Twitter, and it made me want to gnaw off my own hand every day when I read the comments posted beneath each of my stories on the newspaper's Web site, from such insightful pundits as "Tigerrrfan32" and "Gdawg." They picked apart the content of my stories, the syntax, even what I did at council meetings, reading hidden agendas into my every action: when I looked bored, when I was taking notes, whom I interviewed first after a meeting.

My dad begins to pull off the road.

"What are you doing?"

He nods toward the signs advertising places to eat. "Can't see anything anyway. We might as well stop to eat and hope the snow lets up. Anyway, I want to talk to you, and I can't do that very well while I'm driving."

"We need to get to Dylan, and we've got sandwiches in the car."

"I can't see anything, Mike. We've got to stop. So we'll eat."

Minutes later we're at a Wendy's. My dad orders a baked potato and a salad and a glass of water.

I order the biggest, most cheese-drenched sandwich I see and a large fries. Plus a Diet Coke.

My dad raises his eyebrows at me, and I ignore him.

Dad leads the way and chooses a seat in the far reaches of the restaurant away from the counter, where the employees are joking around now that we've walked away. Except for a couple other storm refugees, we're the only ones in here.

I drench my salty fries with more salt.

I have to acknowledge I might be doing this just to bug him.

Dad spreads his napkin carefully over his lap and picks at his plain potato. Not even butter.

"I've been meaning to talk to you anyway," he says, squeezing his packet of fat-free Italian dressing.

"What about?" I ask, as if I don't know, and take a giant bite of burger.

"So you'll go to grad school."

I chew the burger carefully, and decide not to reply. I'm just too tired.

"I'm not supporting you forever."

I swallow hard. "You're not supporting me now."

"I could get much more in rent for that house than I do from you, and you haven't purchased your own car in years. And I know you need the help, but the time has come to face facts, Mike."

"Do tell." I gaze out the window, but there's nothing to see. Just bright dots piercing the white: headlights, taillights, gas station signs.

"Your career is a dead end. Journalism is dying, especially print journalism. You can't make a living as a blogger; that's a joke. What are you going to do, teach? I'm sure all the local colleges will be buried in ex-journalist résumés first thing Monday. It's time you got a serious education."

I swipe fries through a pool of salt on my paper placemat and dunk them in ketchup.

He goes on. "I will loan you the money for grad school provided you choose a field with some promise, something that can support three children and however many more you'll have with your new girlfriend, in the proper fashion."

"Ha. Proper fashion?"

"So you don't have to ask me for money so that you can pay for the fancy jeans Angel wants to wear so she can fit in, for Dylan's band trips. So you can save for their college educations and your own retirement. So you can own a real house." Dad points at me with his plastic fork. "The way I raised you. The way your kids deserve to be raised."

"I work hard."

"Of course you do. But you also married an unstable woman who couldn't hold down a job and kept having kids with her while she ran up debt."

"Nice way to talk about your grandchildren."

"I love my grandchildren. That's why I'm doing this."

"Threatening me?"

"Telling you that I'm charging you the market rate for rent in that house, and letting you buy your own car, and letting you figure out yourself how to pay for your own life. Unless you go to grad school for a decent job. In which case you'll have all the help in the world."

"Blackmail, now. With my children in the middle."

"It's your children I'm thinking of. I'm not going to subsidize your fantasy world any longer. I always said reporters don't make enough money, and if you ever could, you certainly can't now."

"Unbelievable."

"I'd think you'd jump at the chance."

"So I just found out I got fired, and we're going to fetch my runaway son, and this is when you decide to dump this on me?"

"Giving you time to think about it. You know, you could be an engineer. Your math grades were always excellent."

"Fuck you."

His mustache twitches. I think he might actually be smiling.

I throw down the burger. It slides apart, spilling condiments all over the tray. "Fine. Raise my rent. I'll drop off the Honda this weekend. We'll figure it out ourselves. I am done."

If only I could storm off and slam a door.

Instead I reassemble my sandwich, and then discover I have no appetite for it anymore. In fact, I feel ill.

Dad is still eating his salad, so I'm forced to sit there, listening to the tinny speakers in Wendy's play "White Christmas."

A young couple comes in then, hanging on each other and laughing. The boy is thin and tall, with piercings. The girl's cheeks are pink with cold, and her dark blond hair trails out from under a funny-looking knit hat. She's got her arms wrapped around the boy underneath his unzipped jacket. They're both white on one side of them with wind-whipped snow.

They gaze at each other as their giggles subside, then their faces meet and they plunge into a romantic kiss, the kind that happens in movies over a violin crescendo.

The fast food workers hoot their approval.

My dad snorts his disgust.

I stare down at my half-eaten meal and think about how much that girl looks like Casey, and wonder what she's doing right this minute.

Chapter 27

Casey
_____

I t's like we're sister-wives!" giggles Mallory, as she chops up
some vegetables.

I'm dropping spaghetti into a pot while the girls set the
table, and try to laugh gamely because the girls are here.

I imagine having Michael to myself. The freedom and money
to dash out for dinner just because we feel like it, having sex
whenever we want, loudly if we want. Sleeping in until noon on
Saturday, eating bagels in bed. Choosing a home together that
would be ours, and always just ours. Starting fresh with our
baby. Growing into a family gradually, and with care.

It's impossible; Michael and his kids are a package deal. It's
like my daydreams as a kid where I could fly. My mom tells me
I once thought I could grow into flying, like it was something
grown-ups got like breasts or a beard. I was just little, but I do
remember the crushing sensation of a collapsing dream when
my mom told me, having to stifle her laughter when she realized
I was in earnest, that I would never fly.

I steal a glance at Mallory and allow myself to savor the resentment I usually choke down and ignore. If she were a normal, stable person, she could have the kids, which is the natural order of things, and we'd get them every other weekend and the rest of the time be a normal couple.

But it's not her fault, Michael says. With her history. She's *unwell*.

At the table, Jewel giggles over a joke Angel has just told, and I remember my journal and then I'm swimming in shame. How could I wish them away, even part of the time?

My mother could be right. Maybe I'm not up to the challenge.

We manage to cook spaghetti together without incident, and as we go to sit down at the kitchen table, I notice that Mallory has chosen my usual seat. I move to Michael's chair without comment.

I look at the clock and imagine Michael and his father might be as far as the Ohio border. Well, in good weather, they would be. I'm grateful for his dad's four-wheel-drive monstrosity, today.

"Casey keeps a journal, don't you, Casey?"

It takes me a moment to realize it is Angel speaking. She sounds like her mother, too.

"I'm sorry, what? I was distracted." I heard her; I'm stalling. My heart throbs in my ears.

Jewel pipes up. "We were talking about journals in school. We write in them every day. I was writing about alligators yesterday. Did you know they're as old as dinosaurs? But not extinct." She says it "ess-tink."

Angel twirls her spaghetti around her fork. She's only playing at eating, making stage business out of it. She turns to me, her face placid. "Yes, and I was saying that I just learned you write in a journal, too."

I reach out for my glass of water, my hand just on the edge of shaking, and take a sip. "Yes, I do."

"Really?" Mallory says, leaning forward over her plate. "I had this shrink once who told me to do that, but I could never find the time, what with Mike always working at the paper, and I had three little kids to deal with at home."

"It can be therapeutic," I say, settling my glass down with extra care. I turn to Angel and add, "You can vent things you don't really mean. You know, get things out when you're frustrated."

Angel shifts in her chair to face me. "But you must mean it, at least partly, or you wouldn't feel it. It's not like you write lies in your own journal."

"But sometimes you're overreacting to a situation, and then you settle down and realize what you were feeling wasn't real."

Angel shrugs. "That doesn't feel like a very honest way to live, if you ask me. I'm up-front about my feelings."

"You could say that."

Angel's eyes narrow at me, and I gulp. She goes on, a little smirk playing at her lips. "Anyway, I'd be afraid a journal would be discovered, and read. Then what?"

It's drafty in here, but the air feels jungle-hot to me right now.

"Well, you hope people will have enough respect to leave your things alone."

Mallory breaks in. "One thing you'll realize, my dear young Casey, is that mothers don't get any privacy. You give that up along with sleeping through the night. You can't hide anything from them."

Angel has not looked away from me yet. "And why would you want to?"

Jewel says, "Does your diary have a lock, Casey? I've seen them with locks on them."

"No, it doesn't," I say, standing and taking my plate to the sink. "I'm going to eat later. I'm not feeling very well."

I walk to the stairs, willing myself not to turn around. I can feel Angel's eyes on my back the whole way.

I crawl under the covers of the unmade bed. The sheets are cold. I huddle into them, cocoonlike, trying to warm them with my body heat.

Angel says she's up-front with her feelings, and she's not kidding. But I can't believe she doesn't have secrets, thoughts so deep and scary she can't post them to the Internet.

Maybe she senses what I know for sure, that exposure makes you weak. Maybe that's why she won't admit to having any at all.

I can see the allure in that.

When I was in middle school, I was dumb enough to take my diary to school. It was a real diary back then, with a purple cover that said "My Diary" in silver letters, and a little lock. Those little lockable diaries were the "in" thing at my school back then. Ashley, the popular girl on the student council, had one, so I heard. It had been a Christmas gift, and I remember excitedly waiting until January 1, so I could start writing on the first dated page.

I'd wanted to show my friend Tina. We were all showing off our Christmas gifts, after all. Backstreet Boys CDs and stuff like that.

I took it to fourth hour because lunch happened in the middle of fourth-hour class. I'd stuck it in my binder, and then because I got to class really early, I ran to the bathroom to check the cover-up on a super-ugly nose pimple.

As I walked back to the doorway I heard a bunch of laughing, and I still remember feeling excited, quickening my step so I could see what was so funny.

When I turned the corner, I saw Big Mike standing on a chair. We all called him that because he was big like a high schooler already. He had my diary open, and was holding it up and gesturing as he read out loud. The class stood around him, faces up like little birds waiting for food, laughing and laughing.

" 'I think I'm growing breasts!' " he read in a falsetto, over-emoted voice. " 'There definitely seemed to be more roundness than before when I checked this morning, turning sideways in the mirror so I could get a good look. I can't wait until I have a true woman's body, then maybe I can get Tyler to look at me! Tyler is so handsome, I just want to melt every time he says hello to me . . .' "

At this point no one had yet seen me. I felt sick like on a ride at the fair, nauseous and out of control. In the time he was reading that paragraph I saw Tina, my friend, hopping pathetically up toward his thick arm as he leaned out of her grasp. I saw Tyler pull his shirt up and bury his head inside, turtle fashion. From inside his shirt he made retching noises.

Then someone saw me, and one by one they stifled their laughter, but their faces were still flushed and pink from the glee of my exposed secrets.

Big Mike looked not at all ashamed. He hopped down from the chair, my own chair I could see now, and tossed my diary carelessly down on my desk, making kissy noises. Kids started shoving Tyler toward me, and he was backpedaling with his feet. Big Mike grabbed me, and he smushed me into Tyler, shouting, "Does she have a real woman's body? Does she?"

"Enough," shouted Mrs. Thomas from the doorway, walking in as the bell rang. "Everyone to your seats."

Her stern demeanor was for everyone at once. She always regarded her class as one organism, behaving or misbehaving as a unit. It never occurred to me to tell her what had happened.

I slunk into my chair and glanced at the lock before I buried my diary back in my binder. The flimsy thing had simply been busted open.

I later heard from Tina that she'd mentioned my diary to Jenny, something about how she heard I had a cool purple one and I'd brought it to show her, and Big Mike had overheard and run right to my desk.

For weeks afterward it was the cool thing to do, to grab Tyler and shove him at me. Once Nick Allen smashed me up against a locker, feeling my chest for a woman's body, declaring it not there yet.

If Tyler happened to glance my way, he always looked like he might vomit and he'd scurry away as fast as possible. All things considered, I couldn't blame him.

I threw away the purple diary in a Dumpster at the grocery store. I eventually bought a plain notebook and hid it between the mattress and box spring in my room, publicly declaring that diaries were lame anyway.

Because if I learned nothing else in seventh grade, I learned that one flimsy lock is hardly enough to protect your secrets.

Chapter 28

Angel

It's kind of nice doing dishes with my mom. It's so . . . normal. When my phone bleeps in my pocket, I dry my hands and reach for it. I have to hold the phone out of my mom's view because she's stretching her neck to see.

It's Scott. I've been trying to get his attention for weeks now.

Ru OK? Found him?

I hadn't told him about Dylan, but word gets around. And he's concerned! It's sweet. I feel a little guilty being happy about his concern, considering the reason.

Yeah. He ran away, he's fine.

Cool. Coming 2 the party?

I hadn't even had a chance to ask my dad about Hannah's party. It's not the kind of thing he normally lets me go to. It's not chaperoned, and there will be booze there. Not that I'd be up-front about that, but he's not an idiot and he'd figure it out on his own. I pause, my thumbs over the buttons, not wanting to say "My dad won't let me go" because that makes me sound like a baby.

Sure, I type in. I'll figure out a way to make it work. Later.

The floor creaks behind me and it's my mom, trying to peer over my shoulder. She rubs her hands together, like something really exciting is coming. "A boy, huh?"

I roll my eyes and walk past her, accidentally bumping her arm.

"Hey! You're just going to shove me out of the way, now? Since I don't live here, you think you can treat me like crap?"

I turn slowly on my heel, my heart starting to beat hard, like it always used to when she shouted.

Then she shakes her head a little. "No, I'm sorry. It's been a long day, hon. I just love a budding romance. What's his name?"

"Scott."

"Ooh, how old is he?"

"He's in my grade."

"How do you know him?"

"I said, he's in my grade."

"Do you have classes with him?"

"Yeah, some."

"Which ones?"

"Algebra Two and drama."

"Is he cute?"

"Mom, please."

"What? I just like knowing what's going on with you. In case you haven't noticed, we lost a kid recently because no one knew what was in his head."

"What does that mean?"

"I mean, someone thought I was such a horrible mother, but then look what my stand-in does?"

I'm no big fan of Casey, but this is *so* not fair.

"This is no one's fault but Dylan's. He's the one who ran away. Be mad at him if you're going to be mad at somebody."

My mom puts one hand on her hip, looking at me with her mouth hanging open. "You sound just like your father. When did you get so judgmental?"

"So running away was not his fault? He just *accidentally* got on a bus?"

"I mean, there's got to be more to the story. There always is."

Oh, I get it. We're talking about her, now.

"Well, fine, okay, something must be upsetting him. But seriously, he's the one who did it. It's not Casey's fault."

"Why are you defending her?"

"Why are you attacking her? Why not Dad? He's the parent."

"He works all day."

"So? Dylan's in school all day."

"So you like her better than me, is that it?"

Her hands are shaking. I can see it from here. She's also twisting her rings around, and working her hands like she's ripping up pieces of paper.

"Hardly. In fact, given what she thinks of me, I'm surprised she can stand to be in the same house."

This seems to snag my mom out of whatever she was fretting about.

"What do you mean?"

I glance around me quickly, not seeing Casey nearby, but I whisper, just in case. "I mean, I found her journal."

My mother takes my hand and pulls me to the couch, patting the cushion next to her. "Talk to me," she says.

★ ★ ★

Jewel comes up to sit next to me on the couch, after the dishes are all done. Casey hasn't come down yet, so it's weirdly like it was before the divorce, and Dad was working late, and it was just us kids and Mom. Dylan's not here, but he could be practicing up in his room, or doing his homework. He likes to do his homework alone, upstairs. I like to be at the dining room table, so I don't feel alone. I like to be part of things, and he doesn't. Maybe that's why he never talked to us about anything. I should be a better big sister.

I look down and see Jewel's got her blanket. I haven't seen that in a while.

"You okay, J.?"

She just nods, and snuggles up more. I take an afghan off the back of the couch, which Grandma Turner crocheted for us, and toss it over the both of us. I grab the clicker and change the channel. It was a cop show, and lots of people were getting shot and stuff.

"Hey," Mom says from the armchair. "I was watching that."

I nod my head toward Jewel.

Mom rolls her eyes. "Oh, she doesn't even pay attention."

I raise an eyebrow at my mom, surprised she doesn't realize that Jewel hears everything. Just like I do.

I put it on *Hannah Montana*, and Mom raises her hands, making a little annoyed snort, and then wanders off to the computer.

Jewel shifts under my arm, and I remember holding her when she was a baby, and I felt so grown up. Eventually I realized that I did more for my baby sister than most kids, how I fed her a lot when Mom would get distracted, or Mom would be taking her extra-long naps, or be really upset or something and not notice the time, and how I'd change Jewel's diaper when it started to hang down.

But she was such a funny little baby, and I liked how she pulled my hair and tried to stuff it in her mouth. I didn't mind so much, except for when I had a lot of homework it was hard to remember to check on her all the time.

It's a relief now that she's bigger, and can remember these things by herself.

Of course, if Casey and my dad get married, they'll have another baby and maybe it'll start all over again. I'll probably have to babysit so they can go out on dates. And they'll probably get all kissy-face and stuff.

Awkward.

"Angel?" Jewel says, her voice extra young sounding because she's so tired.

"Yeah, J?"

"Why did Dylan leave?"

"I dunno. I guess you can ask him."

"Doesn't he love us?"

" 'Course he does. Boys are dumb, though. They don't think."

"Dylan's not dumb."

I sigh. "Everyone's dumb sometimes."

I actually hate *Hannah Montana*. So I pick up my phone with my free hand and send a one-handed text about the big party.

Mom suddenly stands up from the computer and snatches her coat off the couch. "I'm walking to the store," she says.

She asks me if I need anything, and I wave her away with my phone.

"Keep an eye on Jewel," she says.

Duh. What else is new?

Chapter 29

Michael

My father and I have not spoken in miles and hours, except to remark that the snow is letting up.

The roads are still tricky, I can tell from the way other cars fishtail in front of us, and the way my dad's jaw clenches. I wonder if he used to do that in surgery, tighten his face in concentration. No wonder he was always so tired. He would be standing up for hours, awake for hours. I suppose he's conditioned himself to this kind of thing.

He thinks I don't appreciate his hard work because of his financially cushy life, relative to mine at least. I just don't need to give him more credit because he gives himself plenty already.

The sameness of the Ohio turnpike is hypnotizing and, given my exhaustion, makes me feel a bit delirious.

I try sending Casey a text, but she doesn't reply. Maybe she's sleeping; it's late. I hope everyone is asleep by now. I imagine my house dark and calm and peaceful, as a home should be.

My dad clears his throat and I look over. I've been stroking my jawline scar.

"What's on your mind?" he asks.

"Nothing."

I fold my arms and lean back against the seat, watching the highway lights blur past me out the window.

It was one of the worst fights. I'd gotten an overdraft notice from the bank, in fact, several of them. We should have had plenty of money. Enough, anyway.

I was tired from work, and I should have broached the topic carefully, because there were ways I could handle Mallory to minimize the theatrics. But there were always days when I wasn't up to it, my resolve to be the stoic weakened by late hours at the office.

This was one of those days.

Dylan and Angel were in bed. This was before Jewel, and when the other kids were young enough that we could tuck them in at a reasonable hour. I'd finally opened the mail.

Mallory was at the table with a travel coffee mug full of beer. She had mints in her pocket she would chew between mugs, as if that fooled anyone.

"Dammit. Mallory!"

"What?"

"What have you been spending money on now?" I threw the papers down in front of her.

"The kids needed clothes."

"What clothes? I haven't seen any new clothes."

She rolled her eyes. "Like you do the laundry."

"I see them every day, I—" I flinched. I'd been sucked into her trap. Arguing the minutiae, missing the point. "We'll never get ahead if you keep taking money out of the ATM."

"I need money sometimes."

"For what?"

I knew damn well for what. I wanted to hear her say it. In fact, a desperate irrational urge seized me, a need to hear her just once come clean about something.

"Stuff." She took another sip, leaned back in the kitchen chair. She couldn't look more bored.

"Give me your ATM card."

She snorted. Didn't move.

I walked around her to the dining room table, where she always put her purse. It was a rule my mother had pounded into me: never, ever go into a woman's purse or a man's wallet. I was past rules, past reason.

When Mallory saw me grab her purse, she jolted to life. She raced to me and got her hands on it. We tugged back and forth, and the sacklike purse exploded onto the floor in the struggle.

In the middle of the wreckage—tampons, loose change, makeup—I spied a flask. Had she started drinking on the go? Her face was warped in fury, her eyes huge and wild. I broke away from her stare and saw her wallet, which I snatched up.

She leaped on me like a feral cat. I turned my back to her, hunching over her wallet, tearing through its contents to repossess the ATM card.

Part of me knew I'd gone too far. Maybe I was right to repossess that card, I was always goddamn right, in fact, but my error was in tactics. I'd sunk to her level, as I later would analyze, but then, right then, my reason had been burned away.

I seized it and held it up over her head. This was a childish action, but I was elated with accomplishment.

She leaped at it, raking her fingernails down my arm.

She slapped my face, but I barely felt it. I continued to hold the card out of her reach and circled back into the kitchen. Coming down from the high of my victory, I was realizing that I had a bigger, more present problem.

Mallory was drunk and crazy-mad, and the kids were upstairs.

"You controlling fascist Nazi sonofabitch asshole," she spat.

"I only wish I could control you. I wish I didn't have to."

"Oh, no. No, you love it. You love dominating me."

I laughed at this. She controlled everything, in fact, by virtue of her unpredictability setting the tone for my every waking minute.

"Don't you laugh at me."

Her hair had gotten ruffled in the scrum over the wallet, and stiff with hair gel, it was sticking out crazy. Her lipstick was smeared.

Something about this struck me as inappropriately funny.

"Shut up!" she screamed.

I found myself unable to stand it.

My wife, my life, everything was ludicrous.

I was a fool, and I deserved every bit of it. That was funny, too, in the way funerals are funny when they shouldn't be, when you giggle about some little goof and it becomes the funniest thing you've heard in years surrounded by mourning on all sides.

I didn't see her rearing back, I think I was probably looking somewhere else in the kitchen, trying to stop myself from laughing.

But the motion from the corner of my eye caught my attention. I saw something fly at me and flinched and heard something shatter against the cabinet next to my head.

That's when I saw Dylan emerge from the darkness of the stairway like a specter, dragging his stuffed bear by its leg. He never did talk much, especially under stress. He let his face say it, with his huge eyes and hanging open mouth.

Mallory saw me see him, and she whirled around, unsteadily. "Oh, baby, I'm sorry if we woke you, Daddy and I were having a little argument."

Dylan pointed at me, then touched the side of his own face.

I put my hand up, and it came away red. That's when I started to feel dizzy.

I went wordlessly up to the bathroom, concerned—but in an oddly detached way—that if she'd sliced an artery in my neck, I might bleed out right here in front of my son. I figured I should probably go upstairs if that were the case, to spare him the sight.

When I used a wet towel to rinse off the blood, I saw that a shard of whatever she'd thrown had sliced my face. It was a long cut, bloody, but not fatal.

I called Mallory's sister—back then we were still on speaking terms—to come keep an eye on things, telling her I'd had "an accident" and that Mallory "wasn't well," euphemisms with which Nicole was familiar.

And when I got back from the med station with stitches and a bandage, I saw the blood had been cleaned up. I saw, too, that the ATM card, which I'd dropped, was gone.

I'd thought that was my breaking point, that night. I'd thought, as I packed up the kids and we arrived at my father's doorstep, leaving Mallory passed out from spent rage and beer,

It's finally over. I'd failed in my marriage, but I thought staying would be failing worse, recalling Dylan's expression as he saw my cut face, wondering how long before both kids witnessed something worse.

I let my father photograph my injury, prepared for the humiliation of labeling myself a "battered spouse," looked at his handwritten list of expensive lawyers who would help me keep my kids. I slept in the guest bed in my old childhood room, with a child in the crook of each arm.

The next morning I got that call from Mallory, and I knew I'd have to go home.

Chapter 30

Mallory, 2000

I woke with my limbs shaky and my tongue tasting like paste.
My anger spent, the house now rang with emptiness like
a struck gong.

He'd done it. He really had left me.

I'd been expecting it, really, from the first moment we'd met.
At every milestone I found myself more surprised he hadn't
bolted, and more afraid of how much I needed him not to.

Because that meant when he finally did, I'd be destroyed.

I pulled myself upright in the double bed.

I hadn't meant to throw anything, certainly hadn't meant to
hit him with it. He was belittling me, just like they all did, my
whole life, only from him it wasn't supposed to happen. That
wasn't part of the script. He was good, the others were bad.

I couldn't process it, him joining *them*.

But he did. He belittled me, and when I got angry he ran away and took my babies and I was alone once again.

When this happened as a teenager, when they abandoned and shunned me, I had a solution. Temporary it was, and a poor substitute, but it would obliterate everything else for the time being, and that worked well enough.

But I was old now, my body softer, stretched and marked by two pregnancies. Finding a random screw would not be so easy, these days.

Speaking of my body, I needed to pee. And, despite it all, I was hungry. And thirsty.

Rising from the bed was like peeling apart strong magnets, but I did it. I pulled myself along the wall to the bathroom.

I was searching for another roll of toilet paper under the sink when I saw something that reminded me why I might have felt so unstable yesterday. Oh, yes. Over five weeks since I'd last needed a tampon.

I replaced the toilet paper and then dug in the bathroom drawer, where I kept all my "feminine supplies," as Michael called them.

I could hardly keep my hand still, and splashed myself with urine. I set the stick on the sink and did not look at it as I scrubbed my hands clean.

I looked back and saw it clearly: two lines.

I clutched it to my chest, sobbing now with relief.

Even when I'd asked my ob-gyn to take out the IUD, I hadn't really believed I'd conceive again. For one thing, me and Michael barely made love anymore, and I certainly didn't deserve a third baby. But it was an effort worth making, I thought, in case it was meant to be, in case this time I could get it right.

I never got around to having that conversation with Michael. I definitely had never expected such rapid success. I wasn't so young anymore, after all.

I brought the stick in the kitchen with me as I dialed the Turner home, knowing that must be where Michael had gone. I stared at the stick like I was afraid the second line would vanish if I blinked.

Michael's voice was tight and hard when he picked up. He objected when I told him the news, kept saying, "That's impossible!" and "I thought you had an IUD?"

I'll go to the doctor today, I told him, and I'll find out. And I'm sorry, I told him, I'm so sorry you're hurt.

So very, very sorry, and it's so lonely here, I told him. I can't be alone, I said. I just can't be, not now. Please come home to me. I beg you.

I would tell him later that the IUD had gotten dislodged, skewed, and that my obstetrician removed it that very day I first came in, and what a miracle, but the embryo was unharmed.

When Michael came back home with the children, I was brimming over with apologies and joy and new potential baby names.

And I believed, then, it would all be okay.

Chapter 31

Casey

I gasp myself awake, as if an alarm bell is clanging in my chest.

I squint at the clock. Midnight.

I leap out of bed, and tiny dots of light swarm into my vision. I sink slowly back to the edge of the bed. I've been asleep since dinner, leaving the kids and Mallory unattended. Michael didn't say I had to keep watch like a jailer, but I know he expects me to make sure everything is okay, and I can't let him down.

I listen at each child's door, approaching Dylan's door out of habit, even, but it stands open, his room light still on, casting shadows over the emptiness. I flick off the light to save electricity, plunging the upper story into darkness, except where the moon slips in through Dylan's open curtains.

The moon. That means the clouds have parted. The storm has stopped.

I pick my way carefully down the stairs, feeling my nap clinging to me, slowing me down.

I find Mallory downstairs in the living room, watching TV.

"The girls are asleep," she says.

I resist the urge to ask her if she made sure Jewel brushed and flossed. It doesn't matter now, anyway.

I sit on the opposite edge of the couch, wishing I'd stayed asleep. If the kids are asleep, there's no reason for me to be up. The few hours' rest has made me feel off-balance and foggy-headed. Worse than when I'd been awake on the adrenaline of the sleepless.

"I don't bite," Mallory says, smirking at a cop show rerun. Some CSI team is standing around a corpse, frowning at it.

I notice that I'm plastered into the far corner, feet tucked up like I'm afraid of her. I shift a little to the middle.

"You hungry? I made you a plate."

I jerk my head away from the TV in surprise. She walks out to the kitchen, and I hear the microwave beep a few times. In a couple of minutes she emerges with a steaming plate of spaghetti and sets it down on the coffee table in front of me.

"Go for it," she says.

My sleep-deprived brain briefly entertains the notion that she's poisoned me. This makes me chuckle before I dive in. I realize I'm starving.

"What's funny?" she asks.

I shake my head, not daring to tell her.

I polish off the plate of spaghetti, and before I even get up, she takes it from my hand. "Here, I'll put it away."

She's being too nice. Maybe cyanide really is coursing through my veins. Doesn't that smell like almonds? Did I smell almonds?

She flops down on the couch again.

"Don't look at me like that. Seriously, what do you think I'm gonna do?"

I'm glad she can't see me blush at this.

"I'm going to have to tolerate you, I guess," she says with a heavy sigh, stretching her arms over her head.

"What happened to 'You will never raise my children'?"

She waves her hand at me. "I thought Michael would have explained by now not to take anything I say seriously. I get sort of worked up, if you hadn't noticed. I would like to play a more active role. Maybe I can work my way up to shared custody."

I hold my breath, not knowing how Michael would want me to answer.

"Would that be so bad?" she says, turning her smile on me. "More time for just you and Mike? Newlyweds?"

Michael has talked about her smile during one of the conversations we had early on when he was trying to explain her to me, before I told him to stop trying. He said her smile was magnetic and powerful. I thought he was full of it, just trying to rationalize his lust for a foxy coed, but I never said so.

It is a charming smile, but that's all. She doesn't have magic powers.

She has turned back to the TV. "I know. You don't want to say anything. I get it." She seizes the remote and jabs it at the TV. "God, this is boring. I'm bored. Aren't you bored?"

I nod. Seems safe enough to agree.

"I'll make some popcorn and put on some music. If it's quiet, it shouldn't wake the girls. Maybe we can talk, you know?"

I'm wary, but also pleased. I can see Michael now, smiling and relieved that he doesn't have to worry about us in the same room anymore, in awe, in fact, that I made friends with his crazy ex.

He will be so proud of me.

For several minutes we just snack on popcorn, and then I start to feel stupid for thinking I could talk to her.

"So, how did you meet Mike?" she finally says.

"You never heard?"

She snorts. She has turned on her end of the couch to face me, sitting cross-legged. "Yeah, we've never much discussed his current love life."

So I tell her the story about meeting at the med center when Jewel was sick.

She sniffles a little, wipes her eyes. I'm not sure I get it, it's not *that* romantic.

Then she answers my unspoken confusion. "I should have been home to take her to the doctor."

Normally I would snap at this, something to the effect that it's her own damn fault. But this would seem cruel to say now.

She pulls her knees up to her chest and rests her face on her knees, looking out to the middle of the room.

I want to break the mood, so I turn the question around on her. "How did *you* meet Michael?"

She snaps her attention back to me. "Really? You want to know?"

I nod. Frankly, I'm curious to hear her version of the story.

This has livened her up. She goes back to cross-legged sitting and nabs a fistful of popcorn.

"Well. I was at a party at MSU. I was a social work major, he ever tell you that? Ha. I was going to solve all the world's problems. I was going to make sure what happened to me never happened to any other girl." She says this as if mocking herself, with exaggerated earnestness. She laughs, shakes her head, and eats some more before resuming. "Anyway, so my guy of the moment was giving me a hard time. He'd been so hot, all tattooed and sexy, but a mean drunk, so I ditched him. Then I was all bored and wandering by myself when I saw this nerd . . . Remember that show *Murphy Brown*? Remember the boss, what was his name?"

I've seen it on reruns. I try to think . . . "Miles?"

"Yeah! He looked like Miles! Only taller. And not Jewish. But anyhow, he was the polar opposite of Tattoo Guy—you know, I fucked that guy for two weeks and I don't even remember his name?—and I thought maybe I should try something different. He was so cute, and at first he was all standoffish and sad. Some girl had just dumped him for another guy. But his resistance lasted like, what, a minute? I kissed him right behind his earlobe, and just licked a little bit there, he really loves that . . . Wait, you probably know that!"

She carries on some more about the seduction, but all I can think of is how Michael told me not to kiss his neck at all. He said he found it distracting.

I look up in surprise as Mallory continues her story, reaching over and slapping my knee to emphasize something funny. I tune back in to hear her describing their first night of sex in great, gory detail.

Why did I start this conversation?

She sits back, almost glowing like she just really had sex. "Yeah, he was done for. And I thought, hey, who knew that nerds could be so great in bed? And he was so nice. God, so nice. No one had ever been that nice to me. Especially no man. So it started as a lark, but I kept seeing him. I *worshipped* him back then. I think that's why he stuck around so long, I mean, who can resist being worshipped? I was like a starving person who'd been eating gruel finally given a fresh apple. All I ever wanted then was fresh apples, one after another. And then, Angel."

At this I maintain a diplomatic silence.

"Oh, I know. You think I got pregnant on purpose. Everyone on Michael's side thinks that. My own family thought it, too. No one thought I could actually keep a decent man on my own." She begins to pick at her cuticles, crack her knuckles. "Guess they were right, in the end. But I'd like to think he stayed with me for some other reason than the baby. I mean, these days, having a baby out of wedlock is nothing, right? People do it all the time. Who even uses that word, *wedlock*? Lock, yeah, right. It was meant to be, I guess, however awful it was. Because it wasn't always awful. You know that, right, that it wasn't always?"

"Sure," I say, because it must not have been. Not every minute.

"It won't always be perfect, either," she says, pointing to me. "Don't get your hopes up for *that*."

"Oh, I know that. Believe me."

"Oh?" Mallory smirks. "Really."

I shouldn't say anything. But maybe this is just the kind of girlfriend bonding to heal the rift. After all, it's something we have in common. I opt for a small complaint, something most wives have, as I've gathered.

"Well, I sometimes feel like he takes me for granted."

She sits up straight. "Oh, honey. We have a lot to talk about."

Chapter 32

Dylan

H ey, Romeo," says the female cop again, this time coming
in with a bottled water.

I've been dozing on a chair, my feet up on another
chair, leaning on the wall. I sit up and nod, swinging my feet
down to the floor.

"Not much for talking, huh?"

I shrug.

"Alrighty. Well. Your dad just called from the road. The
storm has slowed him up, but he'll be here in a few hours."

Oh, jeez. I'm such a baby. I can feel my eyes getting wet again.
At least it's a lady cop and not that mean detective.

"So, what was so bad you had to run from, huh?"

"N-n-nothing." I wipe my eyes with my sleeve.

She sits in a chair across from me, leaning on the table. "You
don't fool me, kid. It wasn't just your Juliet, not that she isn't
a lovely girl. What's up? You have trouble at home?" Her face
shifts, just a little, from her relaxed, just chatting look. Her eyes
harden a little. "Anyone hurt you at home?"

"NO."

Her eyebrow goes up, and now I think, Shit, she'll think I'm lying, I'm trying to convince her too hard. I don't want to get my dad in trouble, or Casey.

"I hate my school."

She nods, a look of recognition on her face. It's embarrassing to think she's heard it a million times, but also a relief. Maybe I'm not such a freak. She might even understand.

"My grandpa made me go cuz they f-f-f—" I take a deep breath. Slow down, calm. "They found a gun at my old school. Now I'm not even in band. Hate it."

She notices my sax case on the floor next to me. "Why didn't you just talk to them?"

I shrug. Like that would help. My dad is all about doing "what's best," whether the kids want it or not. Nothing ever changes around my house, anyway. Even the divorce didn't change that much. Mom is still nuts half the time, and they still fight. Only now we have to stay in her shitty apartment every other weekend where I can't practice because my sax disturbs the neighbors.

"I made friends with this . . . girl and it sounded like she had a bad . . . time of it." Sometimes I pause instead of stammer, but that's only slightly better. It still sounds weird. Anyway, I could talk for an hour, and it's not like any of it would make sense.

It sounded great just to go away, when Tiffany suggested it, like hitting a big "delete" button on everything bad.

"You know," the lady cop says now, "adults can help you. But you have to say something. There's no reason to suffer alone."

I look at her from under my hair, which I've let fall over my face.

"You know, most adults were once teenagers. The ones that

didn't spring into being from a pod in a lab. Give your folks a chance, will ya? Better than running off."

The cop slaps the table. "Well. Gotta do some paperwork. So much paperwork. If I'd known about all the paperwork I might have been a lumberjack or something. Anyway, I'll let you know when your dad is here."

When she goes, I rest my head on my arms and let my eyes go unfocused. It's like being in a cave.

I really want my dad to hurry up.

Tiffany didn't look at all relieved when her dad showed up. It didn't take too long; he lives right in town, after all.

Tiffany got up to leave with the officer, and looked back at me. I didn't get why she looked so wrecked exactly. I thought she was going to barf.

"He's never going to let me talk to you again," she croaked out.

I stood up and came over to hug her. She hugged back, too hard. "C'mon, it won't be that bad. You'll be grounded, but not forever." I was thinking of her "bars on the window" story and was convinced by then that he was just a normal strict dad.

"No, he's going to take away my phone for good and ban me from the library and everything. He'll find a way."

I didn't know what to say to this. I couldn't tell her she was wrong because I didn't really know. And even though she'd been annoying me pretty much from the moment I saw her in person, my heart dropped when I thought of never chatting online again, or talking on the phone.

She hugged me one more time, and then the cop sort of pried her off me, and she looked back over her shoulder the whole way out, her face soaking wet by then. There was a circle of her tears on my shirt.

They didn't let him in the room with me, but I heard him bellowing outside, probably loud enough for me to hear him on purpose.

"I want that kid charged!" he screamed.

They'd already explained to us that running away was not a crime, after Tiffany had started to panic about going to juvy.

Still. It made me nervous to hear that. I thought of all the e-mails I had that would show she went willingly. Anyway, she met me at the bus station. I didn't drag her out of her house.

The cops' voices were lower, so I didn't hear them. But he screamed again. "I will take out a restraining order against this little pervert! He better not contact my daughter ever again, or I'll make him regret it!"

"Dad!" Tiffany's voice was panicked and squeaky.

"That's enough! I made a mistake trusting you even this far, haven't I? And to think I could have lost you like we did your mother . . ."

At this his voice broke.

All I heard after that was Tiffany sobbing her way down the hall.

And by then I figured she was probably right and I would never hear from her again.

I'd never felt so lonely in my entire life and I decided to sleep. While I was drifting off, I kept thinking about what her dad had said, about "lost you like we did your mother." Tiffany didn't talk much about her mother, but she didn't mention not having one, either.

Geez. With that kind of history, she doesn't stand a chance.

Chapter 33

Michael

I 've been awake so long, it feels like I've got sand in my eyes, but I'm at least some semblance of alert. My dad has refused to relinquish the wheel, so the unspent fury building inside me at being treated like a helpless child has brewed strong enough to jolt me to life.

The rest of the drive has been spent in hours of prickly silence. Eventually Dad switched on the stereo to classical music. I was grateful that it seemed to be all the thundery, angry classical tonight, not the sleepy-weepy stuff. Must be lots of Wagner.

Now my father's GPS interrupts Wagner to tell him to get off the highway, turn left, turn right. My dad has selected a British woman's voice for his GPS. It sounds like Kate Winslet. Maybe it is. Maybe if you can afford a luxury SUV, you get Kate Winslet telling you where to go.

The snow has faded to a few wispy flakes, now, and the plows and salt trucks are carving furrows into the slushy gray of the roads. The only other cars out seem to be police cars, tow trucks, and semi trucks, who don't stop for anything or they don't get paid.

If Dylan had climbed into a trucker's cab, he could have made it to New York by now.

We get out of the SUV and I embrace the cold as opposed to the close, oppressive interior. I'd even started to resent the seat warmer.

The lights inside the police station burn my eyes. It's quiet in the lobby, but the cops behind the counter look busy as ever.

We tell them why we're here, and the officer, placid and calm, picks up a phone to dial somebody.

My throat feels thick with held-back emotion. It's clear why they call it "choked up." Haven't felt like this since Jewel was born.

He comes around the corner led by an officer, his eyes on the floor.

"Dylan!" I run and grab him, and I don't care if he doesn't want me to. For a second I'm surprised how tall he is; with him away from me, I'd regressed him to a smaller, younger child. He has to push back twice before I let go of him.

His skin looks sickly in the hot fluorescent glare. He's got a little peach fuzz sprouting on his lip. His eyes are red, and it might be from crying, but it might be from sleeplessness, too.

My father claps Dylan on his far shoulder, then pulls him in for an awkward, sideways, one-armed hug.

I apologize to the officers for the interruption, and thank them profusely for watching him. When they leave the lobby, giving us relative privacy, I weigh what to say to Dylan. I want to shake him by his shoulders and scream at him what he did to us, and demand to know why he did it. I also want to hold him in my arms like he's a toddler because it was so much easier to protect him back then.

I decide to save the heavy stuff for later, when we've both slept. When I've had time to think. First things first: a logical consequence, and a safety precaution in case he goes temporarily insane and decides to try this shit again.

"I don't want you contacting that girl."

He shrugs. "Sh-sh-she wasn't what I thought, anyway."

I know that feeling.

Dylan falls asleep at once in the backseat. I'm so relieved I'm feeling sleepy again, too, though each time I close my eyes, my stomach roils. Lousy fast food.

I send Kate a text so she can tell everyone at work that I've got Dylan and he's fine.

Then I call the house. Mallory answers.

"Oh, thank God," she gushes. "Can I talk to him?"

"He's sleeping."

"Sure, poor kid."

"Poor kid nothing. He did this himself, don't forget."

"You're such a hard-ass."

"Let me talk to Casey, please."

"Hi," Casey says, and her voice makes me smile in spite of the evening. I tell her we've got Dylan unscathed, the storm has stopped, and we're on our way back.

"Good," she says, and there's something funny about her voice I can't place.

"You okay?"

"Just really, really, really tired."

"Everything okay with Mallory?"

"Sure!" She sounds almost chirpy. "We're getting along famously."

I don't detect any sarcasm, which confuses me so much I wonder if I'm dreaming. "Well, great. Good. Why don't you get some rest, it will be a long time yet before we're home."

"Sure, you bet."

Mallory and Casey getting along?

I try to remember Mallory at her best, and imagine for the thousandth time what it would be like if she could stay that way. She was most calm immediately after delivering a baby, that baby euphoria carrying her like a wave over whatever rocks and cliffs lay under her surface. Most dads I know groused about those months. The grumpy wives, lack of sex, colicky kids keeping them up even if the wives were the ones rocking and feeding.

Not me. Three times, I had hope for a future with my wife.

And it wasn't awful in the early days, either. Not immediately.

In college, during those months we dated, before she got pregnant, she was wild and passionate, but back then it came off as impulsive and freewheeling. If she was quick to anger, she was also quick to forget, like a water droplet on a griddle that would sizzle away: hot for one second, but gone the next.

Her jealousy flattered me. To think that any other girl would look my way. Not after Heather, anyway. Who was supposed to be "the one." My parents loved her. My roommate thought she was awesome. Heather was the perfect easygoing girlfriend, I thought, until she went easy with my roommate.

I still remember Tom going, "Dude, there was a hat on the doorknob," as if the fact that I'd barged in on sex—with my girlfriend!—was the bigger sin.

Then I went to that party, trying to drown my sorrows in beer—I couldn't stand the dorm room, every time I glanced at the other bunk I remembered him screwing Heather—and that's when Mallory swooped in on me.

Her smile was bright, her eyes narrowed like she was sizing me up, which of course she was.

My thought process—such as it was—ran something like, *Take that, Heather.*

And what Mallory and I did had nothing to compare with the boring missionary sex I'd had with Heather. We slammed up against walls, she hung from the towel bar, we got rug burns every which way, not that we noticed until much later, comparing our scars gleefully like prizefighters.

I have to stop thinking about this, or I'm going to get a hardon right here in the SUV.

So instead I think of the day she threw a mug at me and sliced my face open.

My dad thinks I married her to be a rebel. My mother thinks I did it out of love and a sense of old-fashioned responsibility.

They're both wrong.

Actually I did it for Angel, before Angel even had a name, or discernible gender. Because one day I came home to the apartment—we'd moved in together by then, assisted by my dad's bank account—to find her glassy-eyed and giggly, her belly poking up under one of my old shirts, empty food wrappers all around. She'd gotten high.

She can't do this, I thought. She's not ready.

But ready or not, the baby was coming. And that's when I knew I couldn't leave her.

For our whole marriage I insisted to all doubters that I loved my wife, right from the beginning and right up to the end. It's what a good person does, after all.

That's a phrase my mom always used, my whole life, whenever she was giving me a life lesson, either directly or by telling some anecdote for my benefit.

You share your sandwich with your friend, Mikey . . .

Don't honk from the driveway; walk up to the door to pick up a date, Mike . . .

Love your wife, Michael . . .

That's what good people do.

She never told me out loud to love my wife. But I heard it anyway. It wasn't until I met Casey that I started to second-guess all those strident assertions. I began to think I hadn't loved her, genuinely, so much as I'd talked myself into loving her. To be a good person.

My dad startles me so much I almost spill my bottled water all over the heated seats.

"I'm sorry" is what I'd heard.

"For what?" I was so lost in thought, I almost forgot where I was.

"For all this trouble."

Then I realize it's a "sympathy" sorry more than an apology. Still, these are two words I never hear coming from my dad.

"Teenagers," I mutter, not knowing how else to respond.

"He's a good kid," my dad says, peering out over the road. "I don't understand it."

"I don't either."

"Must be his mother."

"Dad."

I look back. Dylan is sound asleep. He always could sleep in the middle of a marching band if he had to, so I relax about him overhearing.

"What else could it be? Maybe you should take him to a psychiatrist. My friend Arnold—"

"We took the kids to a counselor once, remember? It cost a fortune and they faked the proper answers and it kept them from getting their homework done and going to practices and stuff."

"I'm trying to help."

"I thought you weren't going to help me anymore."

He shifts in his seat, and it's childish of me, but I enjoy his discomfort. "I'm worried about him."

"Me, too."

"What if he's . . . got problems."

This is unlike my father, to soft-pedal something. "Obviously he does, Dad. He ran away."

"You know what I mean."

I do know, of course. But I shake my head. "It's not like that. He's too calm, too steady."

"Still waters run deep."

Now this is familiar territory for Dr. Turner. The platitudes and proverbs.

"You remember my brother," my dad continues.

"Yeah?" I ask quizzically. Uncle Joe was a factory worker last I knew, out in Oregon. We don't see him; there was some kind of rift years ago, and Dr. Turner doesn't discuss it much

"Our parents believed in letting us sink or swim. They figured we'd rise to our potential, or we would not, but that would be up to us. So they didn't supervise our studies, or do more than grunt at our grades. If I hadn't had Mrs. Ellis as a teacher, I might have gone half deaf in a factory myself. But she saw that I was goofing off in the back of the class, and she took me aside and she told me I was wasting God's greatest gift. This was back when teachers could still talk about God in schools, you know."

"Don't start." I spit that out automatically, but I sit up straight, intrigued in spite of myself.

"Anyway, she challenged me. She knew I was competitive in sports, so she used that spirit, and challenged me to get an A in all my classes that semester, and if I did, she'd get me a scholarship. Not a huge one, just a few hundred bucks from the Chamber of Commerce, where her husband was president. But a few hundred went a lot further than now. I had a lot of ground to make up, but I did it. Yes, I damn sure did."

He smiles under his mustache.

"Huh," is all I can think of to say. "Well, good for you."

"Didn't get the scholarship, though. She was a little overconfident that she could have a hand in picking the winner. Or maybe she knew she couldn't, and just figured I needed some kind of carrot on the stick. But the thing is, it wasn't that hard once I sat down to do the work. Obviously I was smart, smart enough to do well. I'd just never really tried before. And I thought then—and think often, now—what if Mrs. Ellis had never challenged me?"

"I thought we were talking about your brother."

"Ah yes, my brother. Still waters running deep."

He taps on the steering wheel, some rhythm I don't recognize.

"He died in the factory. Got his hand caught in a machine; bled out before they got him to the hospital."

"What? When?"

"This week."

"What the . . . Why didn't you tell me?"

"I was going to. The funeral is this weekend. But then this with Dylan came up. And Joe and I weren't close. We hadn't talked in years. He thought that I believed myself better than him, and in an argument years ago I told him he was right, that I *was* better. But in the last few days I've been thinking maybe the only difference was that he never had Mrs. Ellis as a teacher. He had Miss Collins, who was very young and always seemed to be on the verge of crying."

He taps some more on the wheel.

"Yes," he says with finality, as if solving a difficult medical mystery. "I do believe if he'd had Mrs. Ellis, he wouldn't have been a factory worker. And he'd be alive right now."

"Dylan's not going to be a factory worker."

"My son the newsman. So literal."

"I'm not taking him for granted, either."

"No? Ah look, we're back in Michigan. Lots of hours left, but that feels like a milestone to me."

My dad turns up the classical music to indicate he's done with the revelatory conversation.

I turn back to look at Dylan, the highway lights flashing on his face, and try to remember the last time I had a serious heart-to-heart chat with him, the quiet one in the family.

Chapter 34

Casey

Yes! Exactly!" Mallory slaps her hand on the kitchen table so hard I jump. "He's so nitpicky. Like it matters how you load a dishwasher, especially when he's not the one unloading it."

Lucinda Williams sings from the CD player, "*It's a real love, a real love . . .*" We have moved on to potato chips and dip in the kitchen, under a circle of yellow light from the hanging fixture.

I should feel bad about this. Unloading to his ex-wife, of all people. But it feels like I've been straining under the pressure of holding stuff in, and now I finally let it go and the relief is so powerful I could weep. I don't have any girlfriends anymore, not since I left JinxCorp. No one I know from school will talk to me since I dumped Pete. I don't even have Billy, who I think would have understood, despite not being a wife.

The dishwasher thing almost made me start throwing plates on the floor. I'd had a horrid day. Jewel was home sick with an earache, and I was trying to program a database for a grouchy, demanding client, and then I had to arrange a new ride home for Angel when her carpool canceled, and Michael was working late and came in just as I was loading the dishwasher.

I didn't get a "Hi honey" or "How was your day?" or anything. He hung up his coat, looked at me, and said, "Those pans will never get clean in there, you have to scrub them in the sink."

I told him I'd use the pots and pans setting.

"It doesn't matter," he said, sighing. "And all the bits of food will get caked on there and it will be twice as hard to scrub, later."

I tell Mallory now, "I used to think I was lucky that he's so domestic, but it's like, everything has to be done exactly his way. He gets after me about the way I fold the socks, too."

"It's like living with your parents, isn't it?"

"I went on strike for a couple days. I figured if he was going to nitpick how I did stuff, he could do it himself. But he was working so hard it just didn't get done, and I felt bad for the kids not having clean laundry. It's not their fault."

"Yeah, kids. They mess up all the best revenge plans." Mallory winks at me.

"The bitch of it is? He was right about the dishwasher. I had to spend twenty minutes scrubbing the stupid pans the next day."

Mallory flops her head down on her arms. "Oh, the rightness!" she says, her voice muffled by the table. Then she pops up again. "My God, he's right all the time. I wish he were a fuck-up, you know? So then I could be relieved at not being awful in comparison."

I nod, knowing what she means. It's hard enough for me, and I'm a pretty stable person. These days, anyway. As far as Michael knows.

She goes on, "I used to try to lighten him up, but whenever he relaxes, he always assumes the world is going to crash down on him. And look what happens? Dylan ran away anyway. You can't control this kind of thing, no matter what kind of grip you have." Mallory shakes her head suddenly. "Enough. Tired of thinking about it now. Want something to drink? I'm thirsty."

"Sure."

She roots around in a paper bag on the counter I hadn't noticed before. She must have ducked out when I was napping.

She smacks a bottle of Jack on the counter. The sound is like a gunshot.

"No thanks." My voice comes out funny. Overly high, fake-casual.

"Aw, what'll it hurt? The girls are asleep, the guys won't be back for hours. Just a nightcap to shake off this day."

"I thought you gave it up?"

"Not entirely, one hundred percent. Just . . . mostly. But today," she says as she twists off the cap, "is an exceptional day."

There's nothing I want more than to call Tony right now. Or to see Michael, to hear him tell me that we're going to get married and pick a date and have a baby.

A baby. I can hold on to that. I close my eyes for a moment and imagine a pink receiving blanket, tiny fists pinwheeling in the air. Toes like little round peas. Can't have that while drunk. I can't.

"You okay?" asks Mallory, and because I can't tell her, I say, "Yep, just really tired."

But I can't go to bed, either. I can imagine crawling into bed, and Mallory going to sleep, and then it's just me and a bottle of Jack in a dark, quiet house.

Mallory pours herself some. "Oh, I'm going to get some Coke." She turns to the fridge.

Despite the agony it will be to watch her drink and not have some, I'm relieved to see things slipping back into their normal pattern. She was acting so normal and regular I was beginning to think I'd gone through the looking glass.

"So, why don't you drink, anyway?"

I shrug. "No reason."

"Yeah, right, come on. There's always a reason. I don't *care*, Casey. I'm just asking."

She's not going to let this go. I have to give her something, something plausible, something that won't indict me.

"Well, my brother. He died, and it involved drinking, so . . . It's just not the same anymore."

This is sort of true.

Mallory's face goes soft. She reaches out and puts her hand on my arm. Her fingernails are all ragged, but her touch is gentle. For a moment I wonder how I will explain to Michael that I acknowledged my brother first to his ex-wife, before ever telling him. For a long time I assumed he'd dump me, and I'd never have to talk about Billy. Then he proposed. After that, I could never find a moment when the words would come. How could I tell him that story without telling him what I really was?

Too late now, anyway. Mallory leans forward on her elbows, staring at me. Waiting.

So I start my story, and in doing so it's like Billy is right there with me in the kitchen, nodding his head along, tipping the chair back on its rear legs, which drove our mom insane. I can even smell that stupid Polo cologne he wore, trying to cover up the cigarette smoke.

It was one of those random, accidental parties, where people just started drifting toward a particular house in town. There was a game on TV. People were playing cards in the kitchen, but mostly everyone was just lying around, draped on each other like housecats.

This was Lisa's place, and we could still smoke there. A haze hung in the room. The doors and windows were open to the summer outside. It was one of those delicious nights when the evening air is a pleasant kind of cool.

Someone started a bonfire outside. I, myself, was at that stage of drunk where I felt so relaxed I was made of liquid, and walked around smiling at everyone. I wandered from the house out to the bonfire and plopped myself in Pete's lap, tipping us both over in the aluminum lawn chair he'd been sitting in. We all found this hysterical. We detangled, and I picked leaves out of my hair. This time I sat down with exaggerated care, which we all found hysterical once more.

I'm telling Mallory about the poker game that started it all, but my memory is working on another level, going over scenes I much prefer to linger on, scenes that are too private to share. Pete's strong arm behind my back as I perched sideways on his lap, curled up. His callused fingers stroking my waist inside my T-shirt. The smell of his cigarettes mixed with aftershave, which was not lovely but comforting.

It was just after my college graduation, and that may have been the last moment I was purely happy.

We all heard a ruckus after that. As the noise from the house increased, our talk around the bonfire died away, and Pete removed me carefully from his lap. He exchanged looks with several other men, and they strode off in a pack. The women followed, also swapping looks.

Inside, my brother was wrestling with someone on the kitchen floor, the rest of the party in a circle around him. It was mostly women in the circle, who were ineffectually yelling at Billy and the other guy, someone I didn't recognize.

Pete and the others strode up and with much tussling and struggle, pulled the two apart. In the melee, someone knocked over the kitchen table. Poker money and cards scattered.

"What the fuck is the problem!" yelled my cousin Rick.

Billy angled forward at his foe. I could see the bulging veins in his arms from all the way across the room. "You take it back," he said to the man.

"You're psycho," the guy replied. "I was just jokin' around."

Billy lunged again, and that's when I recognized him, the other guy. He'd grabbed my ass at the bar the previous week.

"Okay," the guy said. "Fine, fine. I take it back. Sorry. Jesus."

The hands holding Billy back relaxed. There was some dusting off among all the men, Billy and the ass-grabber, and the men who pried them apart. Someone righted the table.

Lisa finally appeared from a back room where she'd been screwing her boyfriend, hollering about her kitchen being a mess and how she didn't want any fighting in her place. "I've got valuable things in here!" she shrieked, and lots of us giggled at that. Yeah, her shot glass collection. So precious.

"No problem, Lisa," said the ass-grabber. "I was just telling Billy what a good fuck his sister is."

Billy was across the room before anyone could blink, and then it was more prying-off and tussling.

Lisa yelled at them to get out, get the hell out.

I scrunch my eyes before I tell this next part to Mallory. She leans forward and squeezes my wrist. I look at her, and she bites her lip a little, shakes her head.

So Billy took off. He didn't have a car, having smashed his up over the winter. He used to get everywhere on his bike, an old racing-style ten-speed you had to ride all bent over, only he'd perfected the art of riding it without holding on.

I assumed he'd just go outside, maybe head a few doors down to his friend Larry's house, cool off.

Pete returned to the bonfire, bringing me along with him, his arm around my waist.

When we heard the sirens a few minutes later, no one even looked up.

Then Larry burst through the door, screaming, "Billy's been hit by a car!"

I was drunker by then, so I tripped three times running down the road.

The cops wouldn't let me near him.

It was dark, the road was narrow. The driver—a second-shifter coming home from work—was sober as a stone and just plain never saw him. The next day's paper said, "Cyclist Killed in Laingsburg," and police said that according to witnesses, he'd decided to go out for a refreshing nighttime ride.

"Refreshing nighttime ride," I say to Mallory. "I laughed at that. Who rides for refreshment that time of night, I ask you?"

I imagine Billy next to me, laughing, too.

Mallory says, "But honey, if the other driver was sober, why does that mean you don't drink?"

"My brother got in a fight because he was drunk, got thrown out because he was drunk, went on a frickin' bike ride at midnight in the dark on a two-lane rural road with a gravel shoulder because he was drunk. He probably swerved in front of the car, too. Alcohol was not a *factor*, it was everything. Alcohol killed him."

In the version of the story I'm telling Mallory, this is when I quit drinking. This is when I realize just how much I've been swilling, not just me but everyone around me, and how normal it all got to seem but how unhealthy it must be. I turn my back on it all and move on.

This is where I would be very brave and smart. If only that were true.

Instead, I drank more, and so did everyone else. We managed to hold off during the church service and the graveside ceremony, but back at the house, aside from the dark suits and dresses, the wake would have been indistinguishable from a Super Bowl party.

Pete had been distant since the accident. Girl crying had always freaked him out, and every sober minute, I was crying and sick with blame. Pete was inadequate to the task of convincing me otherwise.

Billy had gotten in a fight defending my honor, and then thrown out of the house over that fight and died.

Lisa felt no guilt, and for this I hated her.

I sat at the wake, sipping a Miller, watching her talking to her boyfriend and smiling. If she hadn't made him leave, he wouldn't be dead.

It was ill-advised of me to tell her this, I realize now. And "tell" isn't the right word. "Scream semicoherently" is closer to the truth.

But it was not one of Pete's more sensitive moments when he got between us and took Lisa's side, telling me in front of everyone—at my brother's funeral—that I was being a crazy bitch.

Lisa started crying then, clung to Pete's arm, and turned in to his chest. He wrapped his arm around her and left me, his grieving girlfriend, to stand alone in a circle of gaping mourners.

My mother missed all this. She was in the kitchen, having thrown herself into cooking and hostessing. My dad was out back with the older men, talking baseball and trying not to think about why he was wearing a tie.

On Monday I took a bus to Grand Rapids, renting the first apartment I could manage with my savings, temping as an office worker until I found my job at JinxCorp.

Pete and I reconciled more or less, supposedly. He sent a dozen roses with an apology note, which I assume his sister scripted for him. To say it was out of character doesn't even come close.

I broke up with him by e-mail a few months later, already screwing other people on my own nights out. He took up with Lisa eventually, after loudly complaining to anyone who would listen how "cold" I'd been.

In the story of our couplehood back home, I became the villain, the one who took off for the big city and cruelly disposed of my hick boyfriend, the one that I was expected to marry. Not to mention I abandoned my grieving parents.

My mother reminds me occasionally that Pete is single again, and asks about me all the time. Pete has no children, she likes to say. Pete is your own age. Pete has a good job working on campus at Michigan State. Being a custodian is honorable work, she tells me, as if I'd ever said otherwise.

In the version I'm telling Mallory, I just say we had a fight at the funeral and broke up.

Mallory stands up and gestures for me to do the same. I stand as well, and she wraps her arms around me.

This is surreal.

But it's kind of sweet, too, and maybe it's the exhaustion, or the aftershock from spilling this story, but a few tears spill out before I can stop them.

She sets me back and makes as if to wipe off my face, but I flinch away and do it myself.

She turns from me to refill her glass at the counter. "You know, hon," she says, getting another glass down from the cupboard, "you don't have to punish yourself. You were both young, just kids, really, you and Billy. You didn't do anything wrong. Billy didn't either, did he? You are way too hard on yourself, and I don't know if that's your personality, or if Michael did that to you with his expectations, which believe me, I know are impossible. But we've been through hell today. The girls are fine. It's late. Have a drink to unwind so you can sleep." She turns to face me, one hand on her hip, head tipped at a sympathetic angle. "Because, sweetie, you look awful."

I laugh, feeling a little dizzy. I settle back into my chair. The lack of sleep crashes on me then, like the ceiling falling in. But mentally I'm sharply alert, my mind skipping from one thing to another: Billy, Michael, Pete, Dylan, all the men who have complicated my life.

Mallory pushes a glass of Jack and Coke across the table. "Go on. After what you've been through? You deserve it."

I reach out my hand and stroke the cool side of the glass. The sharp tang of the smell takes me right back to that velvety, unwound feeling after a drink or two. I feel Billy next to me, raising his own drink as always, nodding his encouragement. *Live a little, Sprite.*

Chapter 35

Mallory

She's staring at that drink like she's going to fuck it.

If she weren't trying to replace me, I'd feel sorry for her. She's not such a bad girl, but she doesn't belong with Michael and she's not going to mother my kids. She should go back to her hick Pete and go have ten fat hick babies. Everyone would be happy.

I go to the counter and refill my glass with Coke, pantomiming adding some Jack Daniel's. My back is to her, and she's not looking, anyway. She's still staring at her own glass.

I'll get her talking some more about Pete, anything to keep her going so she doesn't stop to think. So I ask her how she met him, her hick Pete. So she blabs and I put on my "listening" face.

It all came into focus when Angel came to talk to me about that diary, and the awful things she wrote about my girl. I pressed Angel for more detail, and that's when she told me about the drinking this Casey girl used to do, and how she *loved* Jack Daniel's, and must have some boyfriend named Tony on the side, and how Angel was pretty sure her dad didn't know any of it.

But he will. And I won't have to be the bad guy, for once.

Then I can put the rest of my plan in motion.

It seemed like a good idea at the time, letting Michael have the kids. Angel was making me crazy. We'd have epic screaming fights, and Dylan would hardly talk to me, and Jewel was all over me every minute. I couldn't breathe. And worse, I couldn't keep track of all the stuff. Girl Scouts and school reports and she needed money for this or that and Dylan needed reeds for his sax and every time something got missed I could just feel them all hating me, the bad mother.

Only, Michael never helped, did he? Oh no, he flounced off to work every day, leaving me to deal with it, and in all his criticism over the forgotten permission slip and my napping and how *tired* I was, which he always said with a sneer, did he ever offer to help me? Did he inquire as to *why* I needed to have a glass of wine or five just to get through the day without jumping out of the second-story window?

No, the smug righteous bastard would come home and just be full of complaints.

So one day I was having a really bad brain day. It was like my mind was full of static turned up loud and I wanted to scream and run through the neighborhood tearing my clothes off, so instead I poured a drink, just to settle me. No one was supposed to be home for *hours*. I was going to calm myself down, sleep for a while, and then wake up feeling better so I could be Mom for them.

It wasn't my fault Jewel got sick. Probably his fault that she has stomachaches all the time, as much as he demands from those kids, always frowning when they get anything less than a B. And I *felt* fine. To this day I think the cop fudged the paperwork on my breath test out of revenge, because I yelled at him. But then, my little girl had just been in an accident and they were trying to haul me off to jail right in front of her. I was supposed to be a good little obedient girl and go quietly?

That will be the fucking day.

Then Michael kicked me when I was down by presenting me with papers. He should have stood by me and sued the police department for false arrest, he should have had his dad hire a hotshot lawyer to get the breath test results thrown out, but *no*. He divorces me and takes my kids.

And this was the guy who once was so chivalrous and kind that he carried me up my apartment stairs when I felt dizzy during my first trimester with Angel.

My first instinct when he told me about the divorce was to break a wine bottle and slash his face. So I'm actually proud that all I did was cuss him. I went all mother-bear and psycho and screamed that he couldn't take my kids away.

Then, after I wound down, I gave it some thought.

I imagined Dr. Turner hiring the best lawyer in town, and hauling out every bad thing I'd ever done. I imagined them going through the wine bottles in the recycle bin, visiting the liquor store to see how often I went. Michael would be testifying about how much I drank in a week, how I'd slur my words when he came home.

I could sit there all day protesting that I waited until the kids were in school, and anyway, if they thought I was bad with some drinks in my system, they should see me without any, that I'd probably climb a clock tower and take out half the neighbor-hood.

All they'd see is a substance abuser with big tits and a spotty record of attending parent-teacher nights, versus the esteemed Dr. Henry Turner's son, Clark-fucking-Kent who never takes a wrong step.

I'd still probably win if it stopped there, because mothers don't lose their kids much, but then there would be the day of the accident. Driving under the influence with my daughter in the car. Unseatbelted, though Jewel was old enough to do it her-self and should have remembered.

Hell, if I heard that story on the news I'd hate that awful woman, too.

So I started to think again.

I started to think of my lost twenties, spent raising babies and cleaning house, my carefree days over and done.

I could have my freedom back. I could see my kids, and we'd spend our time together doing fun stuff, like going to the zoo and getting ice cream. Let Clark-fucking-Kent manage the homework and buy new shoes and see if he can get all the per-mission slips straight all the time. He can get up with Jewel when she has midnight tummyaches. Let him deal with Angel's sassy mouth.

Meanwhile, I'd get my own place, decorate it any way I want. I could date again, guys who didn't make me feel like I was the worst vermin to crawl the planet because I'm not perfect. I could go out at night and not get grilled the next morning about where I was and what time I came home and how many I'd had before I got in the car.

And so I caved, though when the day came to actually move

out I cried so hard I threw up in the bushes by the front porch. Like most things, it was better in theory than real life.

Turned out that making a living was pretty hard. I'd lost my license after the accident. And since I didn't have custody, I didn't get child support. The alimony check Michael sends me is a joke, really, included in the settlement, I suspect, to soothe his guilty conscience.

And then the bosses and coworkers every place I *did* work harassed me constantly, or screwed with my hours, or promoted other people ahead of me. I'm not going to stand for being treated like that, not for some T. J. Maxx fitting room gig. Hell to the *no*.

So I found some boyfriends, and usually they help me make rent, or I borrow from my sister if I'm desperate, but she's such a snoot about it, nose so high she can't smell her own farts.

And the visitations don't exactly go like I'd hoped. The kids complain about sleeping all in the same room, or in my room, but I've only got two bedrooms in my place. Dylan always wants to practice his sax, but that's not allowed in an apartment. They argue about what kind of ice cream on our "happy" excursions, then sass me back as if I'm not their mother anymore. Angel even said that to me once, "You don't even live with us; you can't tell me what to do," and I slapped her so hard she staggered back three steps.

I had to beg her not to tell her father. I thought that time I'd lose the kids totally.

And sometimes I'd have bad weekends I wouldn't be up to taking them, bad brain days, filled with those climb-on-the-clocktower feelings. I can't take them like that, not with no help and backup like I would have had when we were all together and

I could go in my room and let Michael deal. And I can't very well pour a drink first because Michael watches me like the fucking CIA and he'd run to Friend of the Court saying I was parenting under the influence. It's not cocaine or something, but it's not like he cares.

So now I'm also the evil mother who doesn't want her children to visit.

Still, I thought it would work out in the end, that Michael would eventually get tired of the saintly single-dad gig, and my kids would come to live with me. Only now he's gonna get married, and Miss Girl Scout will slide right into my place, and from the looks of it, she'll do all the dirty work and never complain. And probably never throw a glass at him, either.

She needs to go. Obviously.

My new boyfriend, Dean, has a big house in Forest Hills, and he keeps hinting that it's time I move in and he's got *lots* of bedrooms and I bet Dylan could play his sax all he wanted there.

Plus I can show the Friend of the Court all this great stuff I've been working on—I haven't had a drop to drink in weeks—and I bet they would *love* to reunite a mother with her children.

Casey's babble is trailing off now, she's looking away from the glass. She looks tired. Maybe ready for bed.

"So, Casey," I say. "You guys gonna have some kids, soon?"

Her eyes dart down, and I detect a tiny flinch.

She shrugs. "We'll see. After we're married."

"Right. Do things in the *proper* order."

"What's wrong with that?" she says, eyes narrowed at me.

"Nothing. Don't be so defensive." I stretch, swill my fake drink, and get up to make myself another fake drink. This time I pour some Jack into the sink, so it looks like I'm making a dent.

"I'm surprised he wants another go-round. He always told me two was his limit, and we had three."

Her hands are trembling. She thinks I can't tell. I know it by the way she's got this supercasual posture all of a sudden, leaning way back in her chair, fooling with a fingernail.

"We'll work it out."

"Or maybe you won't have any. Man, pregnancy is hard. Stretches you all out in every which way. You think PMS hormones are bad, whew. Pregnancy. Makes the men run for the hills."

Her pretend-casual has crumbled completely. She's leaning on her elbows now, her hands deep in her hair like she's going to rip it out.

"Oh, sweetie. I can see how bad you want a baby. Sure you do, you're so young." I pat her arm. "Wow, a fourth baby for Michael. That'll be a tough sell."

"I know," she says, almost whispering.

"He's not into it, huh?"

"He used to be. He said he would, but . . . Whenever I try to bring it up, or set a wedding date, he changes the subject. Says we'll talk later."

"Oh, the famous *later*."

"I don't know what I'm doing wrong."

I shake my head. "He's got you feeling like you're the one taking every wrong step. And look, you're not me, okay? You haven't pulled half the shit I did. In fact, it looks to me like you're a goddamn Girl Scout. So what's this 'what I'm doing wrong' bullshit? Doesn't he have a part in this? Don't let him saddle you with the whole thing. He does this all the time, he expects perfection out of everyone. It's his dad who fucked him up like that. And he's barely even aware of it, is the funny thing. Sad thing. Whatever."

I lean in close. "You gotta ask yourself. If he doesn't want to have a baby, or set a date, what's *his* problem? Because from where I sit? You're doing your damn best, and he doesn't give you any credit at all."

She picks up the glass without even appearing to notice she's done it, and pours half of it down her throat.

I take a drink, too, to hide my smile.

That's it, sweetie. Drink up.

Chapter 36

Michael

I jerk awake to discover we're pulling off the highway. I look back to Dylan in the seat, and he's awake, too.

I stare at him until he flinches away from me, relishing the fact that I know exactly where he is.

"Almost back," says my dad. In the weak yellow glow from the streetlights he looks older than he should, far older than he did just two days ago when I was so irritated with him at lunch.

"Thanks, Dad," I say, because I have to. He drove all that way without complaint. I never would have made it, tired as I was, in a blizzard.

He nods in response, then checks for traffic and changes lanes.

It's the blackest part of night. No one seems to be around at all except for salt trucks and plows. A taxicab passes. My dad's driving is more relaxed and assured. The roads must be better by now.

Just a few turns to the house.

I turn back to Dylan. "Everyone's probably asleep. But there's a chance your mother waited up, and you know how she can get."

Dylan cringes. Looks out the window.

"I'm just saying. Brace yourself. We'll talk tomorrow. Right now we all need sleep."

I can see through the front window that the kitchen light is on at the back of the house. Someone may have just left it on. I'm hoping no one is awake. I'm in no mood for an encounter of any kind.

My dad says, "I'll idle here until I see that you're in, then I'm going home myself. Call me if you need anything," he says, and I remember again that he is going to cut off support unless I do his bidding. I can't come up with a retort; far too tired.

Tomorrow. I'll deal with it all tomorrow.

I have my hand hovering behind Dylan's back. The walk is slick, he might fall. I also have this vague sense that he might bolt again. Illogical, but the feeling is there. Will I ever be able to send him in to school with blithe confidence again?

I shove the door open hard with my hip. Voices in the kitchen stop at our arrival, and I hit the living room light switch as Mallory and Casey come scurrying in.

Mallory flings herself at Dylan, wrapping her around him and stroking his hair. He shifts uncomfortably but allows it, maybe sensing he owes her this much.

Casey walks over to me and leans heavily into my embrace. I feel like I'm holding her up. She must really be exhausted. I bend down for a kiss, and smell the alcohol. I set her back to look at her. "Casey?"

"I had a drink. I've been very stressed."

The very comes out "vurry."

I glare over at Mallory. She releases Dylan slightly—leaving one arm around his shoulders—and rolls her eyes in Casey's direction, adding a light shrug. Like she's saying, *What are we going to do with her?*

Casey looks at Dylan. "Oh, kid. I'm so glad you're back." She releases me, and in walking to Dylan her step is visibly unsteady. She makes to hug him, but he flinches away, shrugging out of his mom's arm, too.

"I'm—" He pauses here, his face working to prevent the stammer. "Going to bed."

He walks away to the stairs, but turns just before going up. "S-s-sorry."

Casey leans against me again for support. It's all I can do not to shove her off me.

"So, how was *your* night?" I ask them, unable to keep the edge out of my voice. I can't believe she got drunk. And I can't believe that Mallory is not. She seems to be perfectly functional.

"Oh, fine," Mallory answers. "The girls were up a bit late, but they are both sound asleep. I thought maybe we'd have a drink, just one, you know. But Casey here got a little carried away."

"I did not. I'm just tired." At this she tumbles unconvincingly down to the couch, where she stretches out. "Just really, really tired."

I walk away from her to the kitchen to get myself some water. On the table stands a fifth of Jack Daniel's, half empty.

"I was going to have a drink myself," Mallory tells me, sighing. "But when I saw her plowing through it I figured there ought to be one sober adult in the house. I guess the kid cracked under pressure."

"Where did she even get that?"

"Well, that's on me, I guess. I bought it. I was going to have a drink, like I said."

"You bought a whole fifth for one drink?"

"Well . . . I don't know. Wasn't really thinking, I guess. I'm sorry. If I'd known, I wouldn't have even brought it in the house. I thought she didn't drink."

"Yeah, so did I."

Now Mallory leans into my chest. I'm forced to either hug her or stand there like a pole. I hug her back briefly. "Thank God he's okay," she murmurs into my neck.

I let go, and she lets me go, and I finally get that glass of water. My brain has gone numb, and there's a buzzing in my ears.

"Well, let's find you some pillows," I say to Mallory, having thrown last night's couch bedding down into the laundry pile already, not expecting she'd be here another night.

As I pass the living room on the way to the linens, I see Casey is snoring, taking up the whole couch.

I nudge her with my finger. She doesn't move.

I suppose I could scoop her up and carry her to bed, like I might Jewel if she fell asleep on the couch.

Or she could stay there in her drunken sleep and throw up in her hair.

"Mal, you can take the bed. I'll sleep on the floor."

"Oh come on, just sleep in the bed. I won't touch you, promise. I'll stay way over on the other side."

I hesitate, imagining what Casey would think if she saw us.

Mallory laughs bitterly at my hesitation. "I think I can resist your incredible allure."

"Don't bust my balls now, okay?"

Casey snores. Given her drunkenness, she'll probably sleep until noon. I don't relish the thought myself of sleeping on the wood floor, or trying to find a sleeping bag right now. Nor do I feel like making my children's mother sleep on the floor, especially considering—miracle of miracles—she's the sober one.

"Fine. I'm too tired to care."

I drag myself upstairs, brush my teeth, and fall into bed, welcoming the sleep that overtakes me like a Mack truck.

"Daddy!"

Jewel is jumping on my chest.

I squint at her with eyes unfamiliar with bright daylight in my bedroom; I am typically up before the sun.

"Dylan's home! He's home!" She jumps a couple more times and I cough with her weight, but smile at her glee. I straighten her glasses and then pull her down for a kiss on the nose. "Yes, he is."

"Hi, honey!"

"Mommy? You're in Daddy's bed again?"

I'd forgotten. Casey passed out on the couch.

Mallory stretches out her hand and ruffles Jewel's hair, then pulls her in for a hug. Jewel burrows into the covers between us, and slips one slender arm around each of our necks. "Yay! Just like it used to be!"

I prop up on my elbow and put my serious Dad face on. "Hon, it's just because Casey fell asleep on the couch and we didn't want to move her."

Mallory catches my eye over Jewel's head.

"So Dylan's awake?" I ask Jewel, craning my neck to see my alarm clock. Ten in the morning. This is late for me.

"Yeah, he made us pancakes."

"He did?"

Mallory says, "Aw, what a great kid."

I want to ask Jewel if he's talked about last night, but she's just a child. I don't want her in the middle of this any more than she already is.

Knowing Dylan, he's not saying anything, anyway.

I sit up and pull on a pair of jeans and a T-shirt from the basket of unfolded laundry. Casey normally folds the laundry right away. But normal is out the window.

Downstairs, I go first to the kitchen. Dylan is turning a pancake over onto a plate next to the stove. The stack is already about six pancakes high. Angel is at the table, texting. She's already showered and dressed.

"Planning to feed an army?" I ask Dylan. I grab him in a sideways hug around the shoulders.

He blushes a little, and doesn't answer.

"Thanks, pal," I say.

He points with the spatula to the coffeemaker. He made some coffee, too. Would that I could forget all that happened, just ignore it all and go back to the way it was, and enjoy the fact that my son made us breakfast.

I pour some coffee, and Angel says, "Dad, can I go to a party tonight?"

"Geez, Angel, let me get my eyes open here, first. And good morning to you, too."

She rolls her eyes at me.

The coffee's too bitter, so I splash in some milk and with a sigh of resignation go to check on Casey.

I hear the shower turn on upstairs. Must be Mallory, freshening up. Good. I don't need her hovering over my shoulder.

The bright sun reflecting off the snow outside bounces into the room and puts Casey in a spotlight. She's got dried spittle in her hair, and she's sprawled in much the same position as we left her last night.

She hardly looks like the girl I proposed to.

I crouch down next to her face and shake her elbow. I have to do this twice.

She groans to life and immediately throws her arm over her eyes.

"Oh, God," she says.

"Well, good morning, Sleeping Beauty." I wish that had come out playful, instead of hard.

Casey cringes under her arm. "I'm sorry," she squeaks out. "I didn't mean to get . . . I didn't . . . Mallory convinced me."

"So the devil made you do it?"

"I said I was sorry."

She turns away from me, facing the back of the couch. She curls up, holding her midsection.

I lean over, whispering, so the kids won't hear, "I left you in charge, and you got hammered. At a time like this." I'm trying not to sound so hard, like Mallory thinks of me, the mean drill sergeant. I'm failing, my disappointment running away with me. I trusted her.

She curls up more, saying nothing.

"I need to be able to count on you. For better or worse."

"The kids were fine," she whispers back.

"But what if they'd come down with a fever in the night?

What if Jewel had started throwing up? What good would you have been?"

"No good at all."

She covers her eyes with her hands.

I want to feel sorry for her. But I'm tired of coddling. I did it too much with Mallory, for too many years.

I can't think of anything nice to say, so I follow my mother's advice and say nothing at all, instead standing up to go check on my kids.

Chapter 37

Casey

The sun is like knives in my eyes, and my gut feels like a wave pool.

I deserve every bit of it.

Hangovers are just as bad as I remember, but now, new and improved! With extra shame!

Since Michael walked off and left me here, in the few minutes that have passed, I analyze last night. It seems clear that Mallory tricked me. Like the biblical serpent. Of course that sounds hollow to Michael. I'm supposed to be the not-Mallory. The anti-Mallory.

Maybe all is not lost. I can rally. Buck up. Show Michael how sorry I am by being the best stepmom ever, his ally in this time of crisis.

First. Need water. And a smoke.

I stand up too quickly and crumple to my knees on the wood floor.

Jewel is walking past. "Casey? Are you okay?"

"I'm feeling a little sick, honey. I'm okay."

"Do you need some medicine?"

"Thanks, honey. No, I'll be all right in a while."

"Oh. I'm going to get my checkers set. Dylan said he'd play me!"

I'm not the only one trying for redemption. Dylan can't stand checkers.

My phone is still in my pocket. It beeps softly. Must have missed a call.

First, I drag myself to the kitchen for water. Dylan is putting a pan in the sink. I stand in the entry for a moment, watching him, savoring the relief of his presence. He notices me at last. "Hi," he says, points at the pancakes. "Want some?"

I shake my head, my stomach curdling at the very idea of solid food.

Dylan looks me in the eye, and I recognize that look because I just saw it in Michael's eyes.

Disappointment. In me.

I take the water and my parka out to the back patio.

It's shady back here, and the snow comes up over the tops of my unlaced boots. The cold feels like a tonic. Cleansing. I dab some snow on my face, in fact, to perk myself up.

I sit in a patio chair and check my messages while I light my cigarette.

Five texts and three calls, all from Tony, with increasing worry. We missed our early-morning call.

I text back: *Dylan's fine. I'm in trouble, though. I messed up.*

A few puffs later, my phone chimes again.

Uh-oh. What?

Fell off the wagon. Hard.

Can I call?

Better not.

Want to meet?

Not now. Wish I could. GTG.

I let tears run down my face as I ponder how much I need to be around someone who would understand.

Upstairs, changing my clothes, I note that my side of the bed is rumpled. My side, the side I didn't sleep in last night. Of course. Where else would she sleep? The wood floor?

I have to tell Michael the truth, I can see now. All the truth. Starting with my brother, and the drinking. He might not hate me if he knows why, not that grief is an excuse, I'll make sure to say that. He's had enough excuses, I know.

Trouble is, he's got so much happening now with Dylan, and Mallory making herself at home.

If I can get just a minute alone with him, I can start to explain. I can fully apologize, tell him I have a lot to say, which will help explain it, and we'll talk as soon as we can but I'm here for him, for Dylan, for all of them.

My hands shake as I button my shirt. I'm so dizzy I can barely stand. But no. A hangover now is not allowed. He needs me.

As I leave the room, though, I hear his low voice in Dylan's room. They're talking, no doubt, about last night and what else is going on that caused Dylan to do this crazy thing. Such a good kid, too, so we all assumed. Never gave us any trouble. Between Angel's anger and dieting and Jewel's stomachaches and the visitation drama we were so relieved that he was on cruise control.

Michael will handle it, because he's a terrific dad.

As I descend the stairs, a memory worms its way out of my hangover fog. Mallory telling me that Michael won't have another baby with me. This was probably part of her gambit, along with the booze and the fake girly friendliness.

But it is true he won't talk about setting a date. And now I've fallen down on the one important job he gave me.

Angel is playing checkers with Jewel now that Dylan is having his talk with his father. But she's texting in between moves. Jewel is chattering, waving at Angel, practically doing cartwheels.

"Your sister wants your attention," I say to Angel. "Can't you give the phone a rest?"

She sneers at me. "Whatever, drunk."

Jewel's hand halts in the air, hovering over a piece. She's got an exciting double-jump all lined up, I can see. She gapes at me, her eyes wide with shock.

She shouldn't need to know what drunk is, but she does, and she knows it's something her mother did that got her in trouble. She knows it's the reason her mother doesn't live here anymore, much as Michael tries to convince himself that his explanations about how "people can't stay living together happily" covered that part over.

Angel is smiling now. She puts her phone down. "Go ahead, J. Your move."

Jewel looks down at the board, her face serious beyond her years, and barely picks up her checker as she jumps twice and takes Angel's pieces.

I don't see Mallory downstairs. I realize she's probably in with

Michael and Dylan. Of course, she's the mother, and naturally she'd be involved in a serious conversation like this.

Jewel stands up, then. "I don't feel like playing. I'm going to go read."

Without glancing at me, she bounds up the stairs.

Leaving Angel and me alone.

I sit down in Jewel's vacated chair and look Angel in the eye, doing my best to keep my face neutral and stay upright, though my head is hammering and I'm still hangover-dizzy.

"So, you think you know a lot about me, I guess."

"I know enough. I know you're a liar."

"Not telling is not the same. And I'm going to tell your father. As soon as I get the chance, when things settle down."

She slouches. "Yeah, that'll go over well. You're only 'fessing up now because I found your diary and you got drunk. That's, like, a deathbed religious conversion. My dad's a *reporter*."

"That will be up to him, how he feels afterward. There's context here you don't know anything about."

"Ha. *Context* makes it okay to call me a bitch."

"I was *venting*. Getting out my frustration."

"Whatever. You believe it, or you wouldn't say it."

I look up at the ceiling, as if begging God to help me. "You are awful to me sometimes. You treat me like a lackey. You roll your eyes so much I'm surprised you haven't sprained them. You snort in disgust when I walk by wearing something you don't like, and yet I'm expected to do everything you ask. I do it all, without complaint, and still you act like I'm some disgusting leper in your house. And that was before you ever saw a diary, so yes, I vented my frustration, in fact, my *hurt*, that you seem to hate me."

"Oh, like you care how I feel about you."

"Of course I do."

"Because you *have* to, to marry my dad you have to win me over. You think I couldn't see that, after you moved in, how you wanted to do my hair and take me for coffee, and act all buddy-buddy with my friends? It's so fake."

"It wasn't fake," I protest, but she is partly right. I stepped up my attention to her after I moved in. I wanted to make it better because I sensed a shift in her demeanor that day. I sensed her growing suspicion.

"And you're so young you want to have another baby, and there I'll be, a babysitter. Again. Like I practically raised Jewel."

"I'm not like your mother."

"No, you're not. Because she loves me."

"You just said yourself that you practically had to raise Jewel, and I'm telling you, I'm different, isn't that a good thing?"

"Right, you're so much better than my mother, tell me that again how she sucks. Please, I love hearing that."

This conversation is speeding out from under me.

"Angel. I'm really sorry about what I wrote. I'm really sorry I got carried away last night. I'm sorry that I tried too hard and I'm sorry that I have hid things about my past I'm not proud of. I'm asking you a favor."

"What." Her arms are crossed, her ankles crossed. She couldn't be more closed if she were behind a steel door.

"Just let me be the one to tell him."

"Fine." She stands up roughly, so that the chair clatters to the floor. "It won't matter. It'll all work out the same in the end."

Footsteps on the stairs. Her parents coming down. Angel announces, 'I'm going to study my lines," and sweeps past us all grandly, taking the stairs two at a time.

I look at Michael. "What did he say?"

He shakes his head. "I don't feel like repeating it all now. You better go upstairs and rest."

Thus dismissed, I drag myself back up the stairs.

Dylan's door is open. I can see him stretched out on his bed, staring at the ceiling.

I haven't properly greeted him. Whatever else happens, I want him to know I'm happy he's okay.

I knock softly, though the door is open.

He shrugs, so I take this as assent and come in. There's nowhere to sit really. He shifts his legs on the bed, making room for me at the edge.

"I'm really glad you're okay."

He stares up at the ceiling. "Y-y-you read my e-mail."

"Sorry. But we had to." I try for some lightheartedness, but I'm also curious. "You made it pretty tough to track you down. We never did find your laptop. Are you in training for the CIA?"

He shakes his head. "Embarrassed."

"Don't be. Nothing to be embarrassed about."

He sits up on his elbows and looks at me, his face saying, *You've got to be kidding me.*

I can't help but smile sadly. "You're fourteen. You're allowed some embarrassing stuff."

I put my hand on his ankle. Awkward gesture, but it's a part of him I can reach without being invasive, intruding. "I wish you'd talked to me. About whatever it was."

He shakes his head.

"You know I love you kids, right?"

He squints at me.

"Really. I do. If you hadn't come home . . . It's not just be-cause I love your father. I want you to know that."

"Okay," he says. "I know."

I take my hand off his ankle, the moment gone. I should have told Angel I loved her, but it would have been harder to say. She would have noticed, and it would have made everything worse, though that hardly seems possible.

"You gonna practice at all today?"

He smiles now, a real one. Nods. "Got time?"

"You bet."

He hops off his bed and gets his saxophone case from the corner of the room. I scoot back on his bed so I'm propped against the wall as he tunes up.

The sax is going to destroy my throbbing head. But I'll take it. For this kind of moment, it's worth it.

Chapter 38

Dylan

I totally should have talked to Casey.

She's sitting against the wall in my room, obviously hung-over, but volunteering for me to play my sax in here.

I'm all tuned up, and then, from memory, I start playing the solo for last year's band concert, when I was in the school I liked.

All my muscles start uncurling. Over the top of my sax I can see she's got her eyes closed, and she's holding her temples, but she's also smiling.

It never occurred to me to talk to her about stuff. I thought about my mom, and realized she'd flip out, and my dad wouldn't listen, he'd just say, "Excalibur Academy is a wonderful program," repeating exactly what Grandpa Turner said. Like test scores and college placement rates are the only things that matter in a school.

I don't care if there was a gun at my old school. It's not like anyone was gonna shoot me at lunch. That's a whole other crowd I have nothing to do with, but I loved the band, and I had friends there.

At this new school they all make these, like, wide circles around me like I'm invisible. Not to be mean, really, but they were all friends before I got there. And then my best friend from my old school quit talking to me and told me, "Dude, you're trying too hard," when I sent him some messages. I still don't know what that was about.

I could have handled all of it if there had been a real band, instead of this musty old music teacher who plays cello and doesn't even know where the reed goes in a sax. And there are only, like, two other kids who play brass in the whole school. Both of them trumpets.

Whenever I thought of years left in that school, years left in my house with Angel and Casey fighting all the time, and Dad all worn out, and Jewel and stomachaches, I sometimes felt like my heart would explode out of my chest and I wanted to scream. Or other days it would just feel totally black, and endless.

I should have given Casey a chance, though. She might have helped.

Because now my parents are reacting exactly as I'd expected. Except my dad is keeping my mom calmer than I would have thought.

They were in here, and Dad was all, "Son, this is very serious, I wish you'd come to me."

And Mom started crying and cussing.

So I'm grounded until they decide I'm not, which is no big deal because I have no life to be grounded from. And my dad is going to monitor everything I do online, which is no big deal because without Tiffany—and she's got it worse than me, she'll probably never be allowed to touch a computer again—I don't care about that, either.

The worst part is, my dad wants to drag me to a shrink again. They got in a fight about that, right here in my room, my mom saying that's an awful idea and my dad hinting that maybe I'm screwed up in the same way she is.

"Dad!" I shouted.

"I'm just concerned about you," he said with his serious reporter-face.

Too many words to get out what I wanted to say then. Maybe later I'll write him a note.

I close my eyes for the tricky part of my solo. It tumbles out like it was just waiting there for me to turn it loose. And I was thinking I wouldn't remember it right.

I hear something over the sax, and pause, the last notes vibrating in the air.

It's my dad, hollering for Casey.

She looks at me and sighs. She looks like she knows something coming. Something bad, but can't be helped. She heads out the door like she's walking the plank.

Chapter 39

Michael

Sometimes, the only order in my house comes from laundry. It's not exactly a manly thing to enjoy, folded laundry. Not something I discuss over beers at happy hour, not that I ever get to do that, anyway. When Mallory was in charge of laundry, we were forever having to tiptoe among hillocks of clothing, giving socks the sniff test to decide if they were wearable. I tried to keep up on it myself, but I was so tired after work, and when I did run it through the machines, it never did get folded but remained in a heap next to the machine, rendering our dressers and closets pointless.

Then Mallory moved out, and I realized, tired or not, it was my job to do. And I found time to do it, and I insisted Angel and Dylan help me, and we made it work.

Now, laundry heaped in baskets or scattered around makes me jumpy.

So I fold.

And as I fold, I suffer a pang of guilt in realizing that if I have time to do laundry now, I also had time to do it when Mallory lived here. I could have helped, at least.

I snap out a pair of my work pants and match the seams, as if to snap myself back to reality. It wouldn't have helped. Whatever was wrong—is wrong—was far too complicated to be solved with a little laundry help.

Casey normally does this job, these days. She says it's no trouble, she can do it while waiting for her program to compile, or whatever, or while talking to a client on the phone.

If I marry her, will she slide down the same rabbit hole Mallory did? Will I be tiptoeing through laundry piles because Casey is too "tired" to do it?

I ball up some socks and ponder the facts as I know them. She got drunk one time since I've known her. Once.

But it was at the worst time. And that bottle was half empty. That's a helluva lot of booze for someone who doesn't drink. Normally I'd blame that on Mallory, but she seemed so solid last night. Impossible if she'd been dipping into the whiskey with any seriousness.

I ponder what Angel told me about wondering what's "up" with Casey. The fact that she's home alone for hours all day, takes walks every morning, slips outside often to smoke. What if the smoking is just an excuse to nip from a flask?

I cringe to realize I rarely get close enough to her anymore during the day to tell if her breath smells like booze.

I knew Casey was weird about her first name, and private about her past. I could live with that, but now that she's done something that seems so out of character, I wonder if I've been naive.

There's a saying in the news business, that you ruin a good story by checking it out too much. Despite what the movies show, nine times out of ten when a local crank calls with some tale of scandal and vice, once you dig in and find all the perspective and context and actual facts, it turns out to be small potatoes indeed.

Maybe I was afraid to dig too far into Casey's past because she'd turn out not to be what she seemed, either.

I did run her name through the court system, though. I can't be foolish about who spends time around my kids. To do so I had to sneak a peek at her driver's license so I also know her full, real name: Edna Leigh Casey. Edna on a twenty-six-year-old sits weird these days, so I don't blame her for not using it.

I searched her name online, and found her among survivors of a crash victim. So I know about her brother, too. I assumed she'd tell me fairly soon after we got engaged, but as the months have gone by, she's never revealed the presence of a sibling, much less a dead one.

She doesn't trust me. Obviously.

And have I ever given her reason not to?

I start hanging shirts up in my closet and remember one of the good days with Casey, out at the park. The kids had eaten ice cream, Jewel was swinging from the monkey bars. I'd let Angel bring a boyfriend along, so even she was gracing us with her smile. Dylan was quiet as ever, but contentedly pushed Jewel on the swings.

We'd brought a softball and a bat, thinking it might be fun to improvise a game. The kids couldn't be roused to the challenge in the end, preferring boyfriend and playground to playing with me and Casey.

But we played anyway. Playing! Imagine that. I hadn't played since maybe grade school, always so damn serious, and even my fun times with Mallory were serious in the sense of passionate and dangerous, so I always had to keep one eye on her.

I felt ten years younger, ten pounds lighter, as I pitched over and over again to Casey, who laughed harder every time she missed, especially when she would swing so hard she'd swing herself in a complete circle.

Then she said, "Okay, I'm serious now. Just watch me. I'm gonna get this one." Then she imitated Babe Ruth, and pointed toward a water tower, and got herself in a parody of a batting stance, making a face something between a scowl and constipation.

I had a camera in my back pocket, and before I pitched, I snapped a shot.

I bring the socks over to my dresser and lay them inside my top drawer. There's the picture, in fact. She's trying hard to hold on to the serious face, but it isn't working, I can see the laughter in her eyes. I never even managed to pitch the ball. I ran over and kissed her, and for those brief moments we were just kids and we loved each other and it was all so clean and simple. Like a freshly washed shirt.

Something white on the top of the dresser draws my eye. It's an envelope, with my name written on the front, in Casey's hand.

Chapter 40

Casey

I walk into our room, and Michael's holding a letter.

Oh, God. The letter.

"Mike . . . ," I begin.

"You were going to walk out on me in the middle of this?"

"No, I wasn't. I—"

"Then what the hell is this?"

"Let me . . ." I put my hand to my still throbbing head. I sink down to the edge of the bed. "Let me explain."

"Try me."

I can't see him from here, but I bet he's folding his arms. He always does that when he's mad. He looks like an angry school principal in that stance.

"I wrote that Thursday morning. Before we got the call that Dylan didn't go to school."

"So why are you still here?"

"Because I was worried."

I dare to face him. His beard stubble makes his face look dirty. He's frowning deeply, but there's something in the softness of his eyes that tells me he's more hurt than angry, and that does me in worse than any insults he could hurl.

"But I changed my mind. I don't want to go."

"You sound pretty convinced, here." He shakes the paper, then begins to read aloud. "Don't," I say, but he raises his voice to speak over mine. My own words boomerang back at me, overly loud and deep, Michael's voice projecting like he's onstage.

"'Dear Michael, I know I'm a coward for doing this in writing. Something's been wrong for a long time now. I don't feel like you really see me anymore, except when I screw something up.'"

Michael emphasizes the "see" and carries on, oblivious to the fact that I'm curling up on the bed, trying to shrink down and vanish.

"'And instead of getting closer to the kids, my moving in has only driven them further away. Even Jewel treats me like a funny aunt, but still wants her mom home. This kills me to leave. I wanted a life with you, with them. But this is not my house, my bed, my family. I'm in someone else's space and I don't fit right. This is probably because you don't know everything about me, and for that I'm sorry. I thought not saying certain things out loud would make my past extinct, but it doesn't work that way. It's all still there, and I'm still me, no matter how much I try otherwise. Tell the kids I'm sorry and I love them, whether they believe it or not. I wish I could have been the girl you thought I was. I'm sorry. A thousand times.'"

At this he lets the letter flutter down to the bed.

What am I supposed to say now? I've said it all.

"But you've changed your mind," Michael says, sounding like a reporter now. "What exactly has changed in forty-eight hours? Did I suddenly start *seeing* you enough? Did you suddenly become the girl I thought you could be?"

"I was having a weak moment."

"No. A weak moment is feeling bad for fifteen minutes. Walking out the door without a word is . . ." He drops his arms from their locked and folded position, drooping at the shoulders. "I can't afford weak moments that result in you taking off. Did you know I lost my job yesterday?"

"What?"

"You know it's bad when losing your job isn't the headline of the day."

I start to stand up and go to him, but he stiffens at my approach. He holds up a hand.

"I can't do it. Not knowing if one day you'll get fed up and leave. Or get drunk. Or reveal some dire secret."

"That was—"

"Just once. You were stressed. Guess what? Parenting is stressful *every single goddamn day.*"

"So what, then?"

"Can I count on you?"

"Of course."

"No. Not 'of course' without thinking. Not the answer you are supposed to give. The truth."

His cold logic freezes me. How do I know I won't want to leave tomorrow? How do I know I can stay off the booze? He still doesn't know all there is to know about me.

And then there's this: the shouting, and the lecturing, and his rigid unforgiving face. Where is the kind, tender father who stroked his daughter's back that day we met at the clinic? He used to share some of that tenderness with me.

I wish he would again, but that seems past hope, now.

Michael shakes his head. He walks around the bed, back to the bedroom door. I lunge across the bed and reach for his hand, but only manage to brush his limp fingers before he disappears from my view.

Chapter 41

Jewel

I'm so happy I'm jumping on my bed! Just for fun! I'm going to see how close to the ceiling I can get. Oooh! That was close!

My mom was back in my dad's bed, her bed, right where she belongs. And it's all because Dylan left, so she came home because of the problem, so it worked out okay. Maybe Dylan knew that would happen, and that's why he took off. Ooh, he's smart.

Casey probably knows it, too, that's why she has a hangover. Maybe my mom told her she was moving back for good and it made her sad.

I stop jumping while I think about this. I'm sad Casey is sad. I like her. Maybe she can be dad's friend, like before, and we can see her sometimes.

I'm so happy I jump into Dylan's room.

He's putting his sax back in the case, and he looks soooo sad. I run over and jump on him.

"Hey, take it easy, sis," he says.

I'm so proud he hardly ever stutters when he talks to me. He says it's because I'm a magic Jewel.

I know I'm not really. But I like for him to say it.

I lie on my back on his bed and kick the wall with my feet a little.

"That was really smart of you to run away," I tell him.

"What?" he asks me, his face all wrinkled up like he thinks I'm nuts.

"Cuz Mom is back now. Good work," I say in my teacherish voice.

He sits down next to me and puts his hand on my belly. "J., I didn't do this on purpose. Not to make Mom come home. And I—"

He bites his lip, and I stop kicking the wall. That's his "I don't want to tell you something bad" face. I saw it when my hamster died.

He goes, "I don't think she's here to stay. She and Dad fight all the time, remember? That didn't change."

I sit up now to face him, sitting "crisscross applesauce" like in school. "No, it's different, can't you tell? Mom's being calm."

He shakes his head. "I don't want you to get your hopes up. Anyway, J. It wasn't always very good when she was home. Remember?"

I cross my arms. "You're harshing my buzz."

He cracks up. I wasn't trying to be funny. "What?"

"Where did you hear that?"

"Some movie I was watching the last time we were at Mom's place. It means you're ruining it, right? Did I say it wrong?"

Dylan tries hard to stop laughing. I like seeing him smile,

even if it's because I did something dumb. "No, it's not wrong, just . . . weird coming from a kid. You probably shouldn't say that."

"Oh, it's a swear?"

"No, not a swear, just . . . Don't say it, okay? It's not nice talk for a little kid."

"Bees buzz."

"Yeah. They do." He shakes his head, smiling again. There's a joke I don't get. I can't wait until I'm grown up and I'm in on all the jokes.

I stand up and start bouncing again. "Take me downstairs, Dylan! Horsey ride, like when I was little." I jump on his back, and he goes *ooof*! But I know he's just kidding. He's way bigger than me.

So we gallop down the stairs.

The sun is out, and everyone's home. I can't help myself but leap around the room some more. I'm a frog, and the furniture is lily pads.

Dad's putting on his coat.

"Where are you going, Daddy?" I ask him, and leap up into his arms. He swings me around in a hug, but it's a small swoop. He must be really tired.

"Just for a walk. I need some fresh air."

"It's cold!"

"I'll bundle up, kid." He plants a smack on the top of my head.

He stops when he hears the creaky steps. Casey comes down to the bottom of the stairs, and they trade a really long, serious look before Dad goes outside.

"Mom!" I shout. "Can I have some Halloween candy? Pretty please?"

"Sure, honey! Go right ahead."

I bounce on into the kitchen and get my bag of candy out of the pantry. Oh, there's a red jawbreaker. I like the sound they make when they rattle on my teeth.

When I bounce back in—it's a sour one, it makes me pucker— this time I'm a kangaroo.

Dylan's already back upstairs, and my mom and Casey are having a secret adult conversation over by the computer. Casey still looks really sad. Maybe my mom is telling her that she's moving back in for good.

Casey glances up at me and at first it's like she doesn't notice I'm there, then she says, "Hey, J. Don't bounce on the couch with candy in your mouth."

"Oh, leave her alone," Mom says.

Yay! I can keep hopping! Everything feels so good this morning, it's like I could touch the ceiling if I jump high enough. So I try, leaning my head way, way back and reaching my fingers up, up, up . . .

Chapter 42

Casey

She glares at me, all trace of girlfriend kindness from last night gone like frost in the sun.

"Are you going to tell him, or should I?"

"Tell him what?"

"About your secret past. About your boyfriend, Tony."

At this she produces my phone. I make to snatch it out of her hand, but she thrusts it into her back pocket. I can't tackle her for it now, not with Jewel bouncing on the couch next to us.

"Hey, J. Don't bounce on the couch with candy in your mouth."

"Oh, leave her alone," Mallory says, waving at Jewel.

"Where did you get that?"

"It rang in the pocket of your coat when you got back from your smoke break."

"You have no right."

She smirks at me. "I don't care if I do or not."

"He's not my boyfriend."

"Does Mike know about him?"

I don't answer, which is answer enough for her.

She folds her arms and smiles at me like a predator, all teeth. "It won't matter then, who he is. Michael, if you haven't noticed, is a bit of a prude about things. I tried to remove the stick from his ass for seventeen years and couldn't do it. So, good luck with explaining to him why you kept this *innocent* friendship a secret."

And I'm back to Thursday morning again, the hope of a life with Michael and his kids whirling down the drain. I look down at my ring. It catches the bright light bouncing off the snow outside the window.

She's right. Michael grants no mercy. There is right and wrong and lying is wrong and hiding the truth is just as bad.

My heart swells up, and my eyes dart around the room of this house, which now that I'm about to lose it again is not so much drafty and old but inviting and homey, with its archways and moldings, and the kids' things scattered around like leaves on an autumn lawn.

A hard thud in the living room draws my attention, and I see Jewel on the floor.

She's flopping like a fish, eyes bulging and mouth in a large O, but she makes not a sound.

I grab Jewel from behind around her waist, hold my fist at the base of her rib cage, and start thrusting. I'm dimly aware of feet pounding down the steps, frantic shouting.

Jewel is thrashing in my arms, panicky.

"Honey, I've got you," I say. "Hang on."

I thrust again, again.

The candy shoots out, bulletlike, and skitters across the floor. Jewel makes a huge gasp, then coughs, and gasps some more between terrified sobs.

Jewel turns in to me and throws her arms around my neck.

I close my eyes and hold her, letting her tears soak my shirt, and I cry on her hair, and we cling together in a wet embrace. The door flings open and there's shouting and hysteria between Mallory and Michael, but I'm not listening. I'm holding Jewel and crying for what was almost lost to everyone, and is still lost to me.

Michael takes her from my arms, and I let him. She belongs to him, after all. Not me. His coat is still cold from his walk outside. He shrugs out of it awkwardly, trying to hold Jewel at the same time, while Mallory frets, uselessly smoothing Jewel's hair, straightening her glasses.

I notice Angel and Dylan standing under the living room archway. Dylan's face is grim and hard, and he's got one arm around Angel's shoulders; they are nearly the same height. They've grown so much in just the two years I've known them. In two more years, when I'm barely a memory, a blip in some snapshots, they'll be practically adults.

Michael has lowered down onto the couch, where Jewel cuddles up on his lap. Mallory kneels at Michael's feet to get a look into her daughter's tear-streaked face. Red sticky goo from the jawbreaker had leaked out of her mouth and caked on her chin. I go into the kitchen to fetch a wet towel.

I start to wipe Jewel's chin, but Mallory snatches the towel from me to do it herself.

"What happened?" Michael finally says.

"She was jumping on the couch with a candy in her mouth," I tell him evenly. "She must have fallen, and it got caught in her throat."

"Why did you let her do that?" he says. He's actually asking me that question. Me. The one who did the Heimlich and saved her life.

"I didn't." I weigh what to say next. I could swallow my words and say nothing. I could stay neutral, I could even tacitly accept responsibility. But no. I've been doing that all along. Much good as that's done me. "Your ex-wife thought it was a great idea, though."

"How dare you!" she shouts, leaping to her feet. "I told her to stop doing it just before she fell."

My first instinct is to look at Jewel for confirmation of my story, but I glance away: she's a child and should not be put on the witness stand.

And it doesn't matter. I can see from Michael's face he's made up his mind about me.

"N-not true."

We all turn in surprise to Dylan.

"I saw it. M-M-Mom told Jewel it didn't matter, she could keep jumping."

Jewel nods her head in the circle of Michael's arms. "I'm sorry, Daddy," she croaks out. "I didn't know it would happen."

Dylan screws up his face, concentrating on his next words. "Casey was awesome. A hero."

"Oh, some hero!" shouts Mallory. "Some hero getting plastered when her stepson is missing, talking to her boyfriend on the phone, too."

I should point out that I was not plastered while Dylan was missing, but late at night, after he was found, when everyone was asleep. I should point out that Tony is not my boyfriend.

I should point out I've just saved his daughter's life, and the man I thought I'd marry has yet to thank me.

"She was awesome," Dylan repeats, and I see his fists tighten. "You just stood there and s-s-stared."

"I was afraid!"

"Y-y-you . . ." He stops, scrunches his eyes, and sucks in a breath. When he opens his eyes, he says with clarity and volume, "You were useless."

"My own son turns on me, now. I get it. What about you, Angel, huh? You think Casey's so much better than me?"

Angel folds her arms and tosses her hair, an echo of her mother. "She *does* have a boyfriend. I read it in her diary."

Michael startles at this, visibly.

"Casey?"

He's wounded again. He strokes Jewel's hair, and in that moment it doesn't look like he's comforting her so much as soothing himself. Jewel looks at me sideways, her glasses crooked again.

They all stare at me, waiting. A fresh wave of nausea rolls through me, reminding me of my bender last night, of my history, of what I used to be that Angel and Mallory have opened up now.

I stare past them all outside, at the people clearing their driveways, tossing aside the snow.

I walk up the stairs slowly, feeling dreamlike and oddly serene. It's an easy thing to retrieve my duffle bag, which was already packed. My computer is already inside, too. I've probably got angry clients trying to e-mail me, so I should go find some free WiFi soon.

My books and things I will let go. My clothes that I didn't put in the bag can be replaced by one trip to Target.

It's noisy downstairs, but I don't really hear it. It sounds like a loud movie, muffled by the floor.

I pick up the picture from the top of the dresser, consider whether to take it. I place it facedown, instead. My ring slips off easily now, and I leave it on top of the overturned frame.

My vision is blurred as if through a scrim. I only recognize Michael by his size and shape as he blocks my path on the landing in the curve of the staircase. I nudge him aside, forcefully, when he won't move at first.

I drift down the steps. The kids in my peripheral vision look like angels to me, out of focus and distant.

I should get my phone back, but I won't. I'll get a new one.

Change my e-mail, change my number, change my address. Maybe I'll be Eddie again. I liked that nickname, better than Edna at least.

I stroke Jewel's hair once before I go, cup her cheek for a moment, which still feels soft like baby skin, but that might be a trick of my senses, still clinging to the hope I'd had for a baby in this house.

There are voices, but they are babble to me.

I close the door and walk down the porch with a heavy step. The whole world seems muffled by the wet snow as I walk away, up the hill, turning east, then north again, then I stop paying attention because what difference does it make?

I'm not wearing my boots, so before long my feet are cold, my toes numb like the rest of me.

I walk, and smoke, past the Wealthy Street Bakery, full of happy weekend couples, past the Literary Life Bookstore, these landmarks I'd started to feel belonged to me, in my new life.

I have no phone, and no one knows where I am. Out of my numb haze comes a blast of giddiness. No one knows where I am!

Minutes, maybe an hour, pass as I coast on my anonymity. Up ahead I see a huge rectangle of glass with a neon Miller sign hanging in the middle, a cavelike interior beyond. Without a thought I swing open the door and step into the comforting dark of a neighborhood dive. Not my neighborhood, and the patrons can tell, but they merely look up, note my presence, and look back to their tables and drinks and video Keno.

I seek out a corner table. The middle-aged waitress recognizes my silence as a fortress. She bothers me as little as possible, no doubt well versed in the body language of those who'd like to get quietly drunk. As it's afternoon, I go with my standard afternoon drink and order a beer on tap. There's a college football game on a small TV in the corner. I don't know who's playing, and I don't care.

The beer glass is cold in my hand. The bubbles pop against my nose. It's more bitter than I remember, and for a moment my stomach heaves, *No, not again*, but soon settles down to the inevitability of it, the familiarity of it. *Wake up, liver. Back to work.*

I lose myself in the football game. I used to watch with Billy all the time, and he'd explain offsides and downs. I pick a team to root for based on the color of uniform, to keep myself interested, so I don't think too much.

But the game ends, and my cash runs out. It's getting dark already.

I should call Tony. I could borrow a phone, and it's a local call. But I feel myself falling away from him, too, because he would be disappointed in me. Drinking twice in two days, and this time I've got no one to blame.

So I walk some more, not knowing how long, struck that it doesn't matter now. Kid bedtimes, homework routines, band practices, all of it has winked out of my life at once. It's only me again, and no one cares when I do anything.

Pondering this, I unfasten my watch and drop it in the snow.

I investigate the details of my surroundings as if I've never seen them before, as if I haven't cycled past these places a hundred times. But everything looks different when you're walking. Closer. Real.

I start to consider where to spend the night. I figure there's room on my credit card for a hotel room, if I don't go anywhere fancy. But that would require talking to people. I don't want people now. I wonder about overpasses and cardboard boxes. I remember learning in Girl Scouts when I was a kid how if caught in the elements you could dig a trench in the snow and be actually quite warm.

The beer has made me sleepy, and the cold has been so constant now I don't feel it anymore.

From the corner of my eye, I notice a car trailing me. I'm down a side street, I realize. I don't know which street. I haven't been paying attention.

The car pulls almost even with me, and my heart seizes up. The rest of me is unplugged, like someone's cut a cord between my animal self, which wants to preserve my safety, and my higher brain, which is only mildly interested.

I hear the crunch of a door swing open and my feet take over, forcing me to a sloppy, numb, tipsy run.

"Casey!"

I turn before I think better of it, and it's Michael. It's his car, with the door open.

He holds out a hand, beseeching. I just stare at him.

"Please, it's at least warm in the car."

I shrug and allow my feet to carry me back to the car, though the rest of my soul feels banished and locked away, somewhere far from here.

Chapter 43

Michael

Casey didn't get the heavy house door closed all the way, and it swings back open, revealing a sliver of white outdoors, letting in tendrils of cold. I shove the door closed, hard, and the sound punctures the quiet in the wake of her departure.

The color has come back to Jewel's face, and I'm sickened with myself, suddenly, that Casey saved her life, actually saved her, and all I did was criticize.

"See what you all did!" shouts Dylan. I startle at this. "You drove her away!"

"And good riddance!" retorts Angel. "You should have seen what she wrote in her diary about me. All the while pretending to like me just because of Dad and secretly hating me. I expect that kind of crap at school, but not from a grown-up in my own house! Some *stepmother*. She called me a bitch!"

"Watch your language!" I shout back. "Jewel is right here."

Mallory scoffs. "Oh, like she hasn't heard worse a hundred times."

I turn to her. "Yes, and that's exactly the problem."

She throws up her hands. "And we're back to Bad Mallory again, how surprising."

"Well, you make it so easy."

"STOP!"

This is Dylan. His face is florid and visibly sweaty. Angel has stepped away from him, looking askance as if he might bite her.

"I can't take it anymore! Dad, you criticize all the time, and Angel's so mean"—Angel tries to protest, but Dylan steams ahead past her, not appearing to notice—"and Mom is hysterical and no one listens to me and I'm just tired of it! I wish you'd never found me!"

"Well, fine," Mallory spits out. "Maybe I should go, just go forever, you'll never have to deal with my *hysteria* again." She snatches her purse up off the desk at the front of the room, but I recognize the act. She doesn't intend to go, she probably never did.

Dylan puts his hands to the side of his head and utters a low, frustrated growl. "That's not what I meant! I-I—"

Dylan's face is working hard, trying to get words out that stall and sputter on his tongue, and I recognize the anguish in his face over this. Angel has turned pink with fury, and Jewel is sitting cross-legged on the floor; so recently she couldn't breathe, and now she clutches her stomach, rocking slightly in place.

I put my hand on Mallory's elbow, fighting against my animal nature, to bring my voice to a moderate, soothing register. "Come on, Mal, settle down, okay? Let's just catch our breath and talk for a minute—"

"Don't patronize me, you pompous ass!" She swings her arm in an arc to shake me away, and in doing so her purse flies loose from her shoulder, spinning as it does, and spilling its contents across the hardwood living room floor.

I glance down and see prescription bottles. Three or four, and more for Tylenol and aspirin, which I'd bet my useless college degree don't hold anything so innocent.

I make a dive for them, flashing back to the time I fought her for the ATM card. She is on her knees on the floor, too, gathering them up to her bosom. The bottles I get my hands on aren't even in her name.

"Who's 'Patricia Clark'?" I ask, no longer able to screen the contempt from my voice. "And why does *she* need so much Vicodin?"

"They're prescription! And it's none of your business!"

"So this is how you've stopped drinking."

She tosses her head, trying to be confident and failing as she rarely does. "You have to admit I'm much better now, aren't I?"

I suddenly remember a failed visitation from a few weeks ago. Mallory was supposed to be home and wouldn't answer the door, but it swung open with repeated knocking. Angel and the kids came back to the car, said their mom wasn't feeling good and that they had to go home. They'd said she was lying on the couch, seeming too weak to move, or even give them a hug.

At the time, I thought she'd gotten swine flu, or perhaps was sleeping off a hard drunk. I called Nicole and left a message to check on her. Drugs never entered my mind.

How dare I hope she'd changed?

"Get the hell out of here."

She puts her hands on her hips. "I'm visiting my children."

"It's not your weekend."

"I don't care."

"You're not getting any extra time after this little revelation."

She tosses her hair and smiles at Angel. "Well, we'll see. My circumstances are changing, I'll have you know. And so are yours, and not for the better. Did you happen to mention to the children that you lost your job? Or are you saving that pleasant surprise for later? You do need to be able to *feed* your children in order to have custody."

"We'll be fine."

"Oh, that's right, Daddy Turner will save the day. Or maybe he won't, this time. Maybe he's tired of supporting you. And now without darling Casey to pitch in around here—"

I pull my phone out of my pocket. "Dylan and Angel. Please take Jewel upstairs."

"Daddy?" Jewel says, her tiny voice breaking me in pieces with how innocent and scared she sounds.

"Go upstairs with your brother and sister."

The kids scurry away upstairs, whispering.

I hold up the phone. "I'm calling the police unless you're out that door in three seconds."

"I am not leaving until I'm good and ready."

"Can't you see the looks on their faces? You're making them sick. I thought I was doing them such a favor by trying to do everything by the book, everything right, never saying anything bad about you, always trying to keep to the schedule no matter what, and here you are, on drugs now, drugs you've obtained in a fake name, or stolen maybe, who knows, so you're a criminal, too. Are you on them right now? Is that why you let Jewel bounce on the couch with a jawbreaker in her mouth?

What if that had happened at your place, Mal? What if Casey hadn't been here, and Jewel choked to death while you stood there in a daze?"

"That wouldn't happen! I love my daughter!"

"Then why are you doing drugs! Why did you drink and drive with her in the car!"

"It's not that simple."

"Why the fuck shouldn't it be?" I'm roaring now, past trying, past caring. "I'm tired of your excuses, I'm tired of your tragic past, I'm tired of putting my kids in the line of fire every time I drop them off with you. Get out."

"No."

I start to dial one-handed. "Get out now, or I'm calling ʈ police to haul you away, with your illegally obtained drug your purse."

"Maybe I'll tell the police you hit me."

She rears back and whacks herself on the cheek. It leav mark. "How do you like that!" she shrieks, and she slaɼ again.

I recognize this. Mallory is spinning out of contro' dervish. I walk backward up the stairs, slowly. She slap her face, her smile triumphant.

The kids are all gathered in my room, on my b close and lock the door, and call 911.

I hear some breaking of things downsta' Jewel gasp. I pull her into my lap. She pres my chest, and I cover her other ear with the

I hear Mallory scream up the stairs: *"Je*

I press my hand harder over Jewel's ear

"Yes, I'm having a problem with my ex-

After a minute or two, I turn on the radio to drown out the tantrum, which has gone past intelligible speech.

I hear someone shouting on the other side of my front door. I go to my window, and look down to see a patrol car.

I think of Mallory slapping her cheek, and a sick fear spreads in my stomach that if she plays her role to the hilt, I may be the one hauled off in handcuffs.

There's more shouting from downstairs. I look out the window again, and when I hear the bedsprings squeak for the kids getting up I use my best stern-Dad voice. "Stay back."

Jewel does not need to once again witness her mother in police custody. Mallory is in cuffs, being lowered into a police car. This is what needed to happen, I know. But she was once my wife. My children's mother.

A deep voice calls, "Mr. Turner?"

"In here," I answer, forcing myself to be calm.

"Come down the stairs, sir. Make sure I can see your hands."

I tell the children to wait, and descend the stairs, hands palm out, in front of me, and I reach the landing where the stairs curve down into the living room, where I have an aerial view of half the main floor.

The officer's face has a practiced calm. Surrounding him are remnants of my living room. A fireplace poker is in the guts of my TV. Curtains are torn down, the computer is smashed to the floor. DVDs, books, anything she could grasp in the living room, she must have used as ordnance.

This makes the time she threw a mug at me look like an adoring prank.

He asks me who else is in the house and where they are. While I'm on the landing, he ascends the rest of the stairs, peeks into the rooms, always watching me at the same time. When he seems satisfied no one is lurking about, we descend the stairs together.

"We need to speak to you, sir. She says you hit her, and there's a mark on her cheek."

I flinch. "No. This is going to sound crazy, but I swear it's true. She slapped herself, on purpose, trying to get me in trouble. That's when I took the kids upstairs. She's . . . she's not right. Never diagnosed, but—"

"Just tell me what happened."

He writes notes, listening, nodding. He tells me he would like to interview the older kids, separate from me, separate from each other. I'm relieved he doesn't ask to talk to Jewel.

But I'm sick that Angel and Dylan have to go through this, even so. At fourteen and sixteen they can act so adult, but they're not. Not even close.

The officer talks to the kids upstairs while another officer babysits Mallory in the patrol car. I read books to Jewel—she's perfectly capable of reading to herself, but this is comforting, normal, and childlike—and keep her from looking out the window.

He comes down the stairs, asks me to wait, while he goes outside to confer with his partner, a woman I notice now, with red hair pulled into a low ponytail. Dylan and Angel have the wide-eyed look of kids watching a scary movie who are afraid to look but can't tear their eyes away.

"Daddy, are they going to arrest you?" Angel asks me, looking out the front window at the police. "Because I told them it's not your fault."

Dylan nodded soberly. "I snuck partway down the steps while you were fighting. I saw her hit herself."

I relax my shoulders. Wish he hadn't seen that, but it can only help me.

The officer returns.

"I'm not going to arrest anyone today. I'm going to take her out of here, separate you two, basically. We'll write up a report and include your statements and hers. She may pursue charges, though. Just so you know. As it's alleged domestic violence, the report will have to be reviewed as a statutory requirement. Also, if you wish to press charges for malicious destruction of property, you can follow up with a detective on Monday." The officer gives me a card.

I savor the relief that I won't be hauled away from my children, at least not today.

When they leave at last, my joints feel wobbly, and my eyes won't stop watering looking at the wreckage she left, and not just in my living room, but in the white faces of my children.

"Kids. Pack an overnight bag. We're going to stay with Grandma and Grandpa."

Usually this would be greeted with glee by Jewel, a shrug from Dylan, and rolled eyes from Angel, who gets grilled by my dad on her college plans every time he sees her.

Now, they move numbly, quietly.

I call my parents' home. My father answers.

"Dad," I say, my voice breaking like I'm in puberty. "I need to come over."

Chapter 44

Angel

D ylan lines up a ball at the pool table in the downstairs rec room. He says to me, "Do you think that was true? About Jewel?"

I look up the stairway. Jewel is upstairs helping Grandma make cookies still, so it's safe to talk. "I don't know. She says weird stuff when she's like that."

"I'm an idiot," Dylan says, missing the shot. The three-ball bounces out of the corner. He says it without emotion, like he's just reporting the news. I also notice he hasn't stuttered at all since we walked into Grandma and Grandpa's house.

"You're not an idiot," I tell him. "At least, not all the time."

"I should've known better."

I chalk up the pool cue. Dylan rolls his eyes. I always use too much chalk. I don't really like pool, even, but it's something to do. I blow the dust off and try to line up a shot.

I miss the cue ball entirely when Dylan says, "Why did you read her diary?"

I stand the cue on the floor and lean on it. "I didn't know it was a diary at first. It was just some random notebook. But then when she wrote that I was acting like a bitch . . ."

"You probably were."

"Hey!"

"Be real. You're hard to live with."

"Oh, and you're all perfect, running away and starting all this."

He turns away from me, leaning on the pool table with his back to me. In the dim light from the lamp above the table, I can't see his face. "I already said I was an idiot."

"It wasn't just that, anyway. She was writing about this other guy, and how she wanted a drink so bad. Dad didn't know that stuff, and he was supposed to marry her. What was I supposed to do?"

"Not tell *Mom*."

"Shut up."

"Well? Doesn't that seem like a bad idea now?"

"She was seeming okay. And she kept asking me about Casey, and what she was acting like around the house. She seemed concerned for us. And look, Casey *loves* you, always listening to your practices, so of course you'll defend her."

"Mom's not that concerned for us. She just hates Casey."

"Well, whatever, it's all out there now."

Dylan turns around. "It's your shot."

I line up a shot and sink the cue ball. Dylan picks it up and walks around the table, choosing his shot.

"What's going to happen?" I ask.

"I dunno. We might have to go to court if Mom presses charges against Dad for supposedly hitting her."

"Oh, God. He didn't do it, and you saw her do it to herself."

"Totally. But what if she says we made it up to take his side?"

"Shit. You know, I think she got Casey drunk on purpose."

"She's like a puppetmaster or something." Dylan finds his shot, sinks the ball, starts to line up another.

"She was talking about us coming to live with her again."

"In that dinky apartment? Great."

"No, in a big swanky house in Forest Hills."

"And how's she gonna manage that?"

I shrug, not having thought that deeply about it. "I'm sure not sure that's such a good idea, anyway."

"Duh. But you said that's what she wants? She's going to try and get us back?"

"That's what she said."

Dylan looks up from where he's stretched out across the table. "We could run away."

"Ha. Smartass."

Dylan sinks another shot. "It would help if Casey came back."

I cross my arms and glare at him. "How does that help? And, hello? She thinks I'm a bitch?"

"Which you are. Sometimes, anyway. Dad just lost his job, did you hear that? And he's dealing with all this crazy stuff. He'll do better if he's not alone."

"He's got us."

"Not the same."

Dylan's winning anyway, so I go sink into one of the leather chairs at the edge of the room. "She probably hates me forever now, anyway."

He shrugs. "Bet she won't, though."

"How would you know?"

"Because as we found out, she's not exactly perfect herself. Not much room to judge."

I let him go ahead and sink all the rest of the balls and stare off into the dark outside the lamplight. For months I've been annoyed by Casey looking like a kid, butting into my life, sucking away my dad's attention, and then all weekend I've been stinging over that *bitch* thing . . .

I close my eyes and remember Casey, on the floor, saving Jewel from choking while my mom stood there and gaped like, well, like she was stoned. What if I'd managed to run Casey off earlier?

And then I think of my mom trying to get my dad arrested and tearing apart our living room.

"I'm going upstairs," I tell Dylan. "I've gotta talk to Dad."

Chapter 45

Michael

My father, silhouetted in the light from the gas fire in his den, taps the edge of his glass, but is otherwise silent.

After we settled the kids down to various activities resembling normalcy, after my dad checked out Jewel's breathing and peered down her throat to make sure she was fine, after my mom started baking cookies, after I gave him a summary of the brutal events since he dropped us off at the house, my dad and I collapsed into silence near the fire with a drink. Club soda for me.

My earlier bravado in the SUV about not needing his help has evaporated. If I have to be dependent on my father for the rest of my days in order to keep my kids with me, then I'll hand him my balls on a platter.

"I'm sorry," my father says, staring into the fire.

"For what?" I ask, assuming he's going to say something about not having clean sheets on the bed in my old room.

"For trying to run your life. For what I said in the car. Forget it. Take whatever time you need, and I'll help you. And I'll do my best to stop making you feel like shit about it."

I do a double-take, at both the content of his apology and the curse word.

"What brought this on?"

"When you called me, you were on the brink. I could hear it. And then you told me just now what happened, and I saw your kids coming in here looking like shock victims. I've been holding you to an impossible standard. All this time I've been looking at your surroundings, your bank account, the car you drive . . . A proud man, a foolish man—after that big speech in the restaurant about not needing my help—would have done anything at all to keep from coming back here. But." He holds up one finger, like he's giving a lecture. "You knew what was best for your kids was getting them out of that chaos. And you were right. They started relaxing the minute they walked in the door. Dylan stopped stammering. Angel and Jewel smiled. The color came back to their faces." He pauses, staring still into the fire. I dare not speak and break the spell. "It takes a man to put his kids before himself in everything, all the time." He winks at me, but his smile is sad, his voice with no mirth. "Here's to my son, the real man." He leans over and clinks my glass.

My business is words, but words have left me, utterly.

"Dad." It's Angel, looking angelic indeed in the firelight. Her features are soft instead of pulled into a sneer or an eye-roll. "Can I talk to you a minute?"

My father gets up immediately, and gestures to the chair. He bends down and kisses her forehead. Angel looks at me in surprise; physical affection is not generally in his repertoire.

Angel lowers herself into the chair. It engulfs her.

"I'm sorry about reading Casey's diary and talking about it to Mom," she begins, picking at her fingernails. "I didn't mean for any of that to happen."

"I know you didn't. It's not your fault."

"I think you should know that I think Mom tricked Casey."

"Tricked how?"

Angel shifts in her seat. "Well . . . I told her about how Casey always used to drink Jack Daniel's, it was in her diary. And then Mom went out and bought some. She must have, because she went to the store after that. And she brought it out after me and Jewel went to bed. So I think she got Casey drunk."

I put my head in my hand. Of course she did. "But she didn't force it down her throat, Angel. And you can't accidentally drink whiskey and not know it. You and I have talked about peer pressure. It's still your call in the end. She still made the decision."

"I guess."

"Well, didn't she?"

Angel shrugs. "Sure. But I mean, she was up all night with you, wasn't she? And all day? Trapped in the house, in a blizzard, with your ex-wife. She was exhausted. And you know how charming Mom can be when she really turns it on."

"How is it you're Casey's advocate all of a sudden?"

Angel sinks lower in the chair, her head almost disappearing within the deep arms. She stretches out her legs, crossed at the ankles. "I feel a little bad, is all. About the diary. And she did save Jewel's life."

And the first thing I did was accuse her of letting it happen in the first place.

Angel sits up again, leaning forward now, toward the fire. She's threading her fingers together and apart, toying with her rings. "It's just hard. In a year my mom moved out, and she moved in. How could I not feel like she was replacing Mom? And she can't be my mom, she's too young. And then when I read her diary I thought . . . wow, she hates me. Just like the bitchy girls at school."

"She doesn't hate you. And she can't replace your mom. Your mom is one of a kind."

I mean this as a weak joke, but Angel ignores it.

"I'm sorry," I say, meaning for the joke, but also for everything. "I don't think I handled that well, moving her in. I thought you'd welcome her, the normalcy, the help around the house."

"*You* welcomed that."

Her tone is sharp, but she's right. I did. My dad says I always put my kids first, but in this case he was wrong. I just assumed they wanted the same things I did.

Angel softens her voice. "But you like having her around, don't you?"

I smile sadly. "Yeah. I do. I did."

"Did?"

"I don't think she's coming back."

"You sound sad."

"I am."

"You could call her?"

"She doesn't have her phone. The cops found it in your mom's pocket."

"Well, you're a reporter. You can track her down."

"I'm a *former* reporter at the end of the year. Anyway, you're thinking of a bloodhound. My specialty is City Commission meetings. Got an ordinance vote you want covered?"

"You know, Dad? Sometimes when I storm up the stairs to my room and slam the door and I yell to leave me alone? And you charge up there anyway?" She whispers now. "Secretly, I'm kind of glad. I know you'll always be there, even when I sort of don't want you to be."

She gets up and heads toward the kitchen, where I hear my mother singing out that cookies are almost ready.

I'm not hungry, though. Instead I go looking for my coat, pulling my car keys out of my pocket as I head for the car.

Chapter 46

Casey

T he car quickly becomes too warm, so I reach over and flick off the heat. Michael takes the hint and shuts off the engine.

He pulled in at the Sixth Street Park, facing a bright metal modernist sculpture as tall as a house, and beyond it, the Grand River in its smooth shiny blackness.

I tip my head back on the seat, the aftershock of my hangover and the fresh beer making me want to sleep.

Michael told me right away about Mallory's freak-out, and Dylan's defense of me. That bit about Dylan would have made me smile if anything could right now. Michael had been driving, and watching the road, so I guess that's why he wasn't looking at me, but now that we've stopped, he still hasn't.

"You picked me up," I finally say. "So, what?"

"An apology doesn't really cover it."

"Cover what, exactly?" I stare out ahead at the dark so that I almost see shapes and faces. Maybe it's fog, or mist. Maybe my mind is playing tricks. Or I'm going crazy. Is it contagious?

"I didn't thank you for . . . saving Jewel. Not that I ever could, adequately. I mean . . . God." He smacks his steering wheel. "I'm pathetic."

"I know," I tell him, still staring out over the river but not seeing it. I can picture my brother leaning on a couch, the last time I saw him before the big fight to defend my honor.

"You know I'm pathetic? Thanks."

"I know you're grateful, and you have no words. I further know that Mallory did something to you, made you weird and distrustful of everyone. That if you don't supervise every thing every minute, it will all fly apart. And you think you're right, because you walked around the block and look what almost happened."

"But didn't."

"Right. Didn't."

"Why didn't you tell me?"

"Tell you what?" I reply automatically.

"Anything. The drinking. Your real name even."

"I hate my real name."

"Edna's not so bad."

This causes me to jerk around in my seat. "What?"

"I peeked at your driver's license."

I slouch in the seat and cross my arms. "Should have known a reporter couldn't stay out of my wallet."

"Well, you're gonna love the next part then. I ran a background check on you."

"Fuck."

"You were going to move in with me. I couldn't have someone around my kids I didn't know anything about. And you didn't tell me."

"You didn't ask, either."

"Would you have told me, then?"

"Touché."

"Okay. But you still haven't answered me. Why wouldn't you tell me yourself?"

The car still feels too warm, too close. I jump up and shove open the door, slamming it behind me. Michael jumps out of the car, too. Maybe he thinks I'm going to walk away again, maybe he wants to tackle me, and it's true, part of me wants to run run run as fast as I can. Can't catch *me* . . .

But I'm so tired. I trudge only to the metal railing next to the river, brushing off the day's blizzard snow into the dark water, which hasn't had time to freeze. In the reflected city light I can see an oily sheen over the river. He joins me at the railing, hands in his pockets, also looking at the water.

I turn to face him. The tall lampposts in the park behind us give everything a soft glow, like candlelight. Brighter than I would like. "You wouldn't have loved a girl like me."

"You didn't give me a chance."

"Come on! You remember that big speech about how you'll never again date someone who drinks? And you were so relieved I didn't? Every chance you got after that you told me how great it was that I was so unlike your ex, and all the time I wasn't. And the bitch of it is, it didn't work, anyway. You want to know why I left you that letter, why I almost walked out Thursday morning? Because you stopped talking to me about a baby, about a wedding, about anything at all that didn't have to do with field trips and new school shoes and homework. And you let Angel talk to me any way she wanted, and you never stood up for me."

"Angel's been through a lot . . . ," he says, trailing off.

"So have I! I can't absorb every blow like a sandbag and feel nothing. Yet that's what you expect. I get that you're tired of caretaking. And I thought I could handle it, that knowing you loved me would be enough, that I wouldn't *need* you to show it because I'm not needy! I'm anti-Mallory!" I jab my finger in the air, mocking victory. "But I *am* needy. And so I'm saving you the trouble of leaving me. You're welcome."

His voice, when it comes, is gravelly, wet-sounding. "You should have told me. Given me a chance."

"Yeah." My own voice breaks now. "Yeah, probably."

A wind kicks up and blows my hair into my face. I turn away from him, leaning my hip on the railing. I pull out my cigarettes and cup the flame of my lighter as I let the wind blow my hair back. My eyes water from the sting of it.

"Who's Tony?" he asks.

"What difference does it make?" I call over my shoulder, still facing away.

"Is he really a boyfriend?"

"Do you think he is?"

There's a long pause. "No."

"So—" I interrupt myself with a deep drag. "Drop me off at the Holiday Inn, okay?"

He appears in front of me. His face looks wet. "Don't."

"Don't what?"

"Don't go."

I can't think of anything to say.

"I need you, Casey. Edna. Whoever you are, whatever you once did."

"I'm just another problem."

"No, you're a person." He stomps once in the snow, looking down for a moment. His hands had been jammed into his pants pockets. He takes them out, turns them palm up, toward me. His white breath curls around his face, which looks lined and shadowed. "Mallory's gonna try to take the kids. Please, Casey. Don't leave me now."

He looks broken. That's what this look is. I saw it in my dad, after Billy died. That essential part inside a person that keeps him upright and strong against the world, crumbled into dust, and Dad curled up on his recliner chair and that's where he's been all these years, getting heavier, his breathing more labored, his heart straining to keep him going, against his will.

I grind my cigarette on the rail and walk into his arms. I place my head on his chest, where it fits right over his beating heart.

"I can't move back in," I tell him.

"Okay," he whispers. His face is turned sideways, he's resting his cheek on the top of my head. He rocks me a little, back and forth, and I let him.

In a minute I'll ask him again to drop me off at the Holiday Inn, where I'll crawl into scratchy, sterile hotel sheets that belong to no one and decide how much I can stand.

Chapter 47

Michael

I wouldn't have made Dylan come clean up this mess, but he asked to. And as it turns out, I'm grateful for his presence, because it keeps me focused on the task at hand by forcing me to keep up a front.

Alone, it would be hard not to react to the chore of sweeping up broken glass, removing photos from their splintered frames. Picking up the pieces of a ceramic ashtray Jewel made in art class. Her own daughter's lopsided ashtray. She probably didn't even see it.

We did take pictures of this first. My dad's lawyer recommended it.

"Dad? What do we do with the TV?"

I shrug. "Guess we'll haul it to the curb before we go pick up the girls."

Dylan seems to have matured three years in the last three

days. If anything good will come of this, maybe my boy will learn to think things through. To not be so easily led.

Except by me. I'd like it if he still did what I told him to.

After I came back sans Casey last night, they all gave me a wide berth. I ate warmed-up lasagna, and my dad and I zoned out in front of football. Everyone went to bed early. Though I enjoyed the peace and stability, and I sighed with gratitude that all my children were under my roof and my ex-wife was nowhere near us, sleep didn't come.

I lay awake, my mind flipping like a switch between Casey and Mallory.

Casey: Is she thinking about me? Will she come back to me, ever? Is she lying awake, too? Is she drinking right now?

Mallory: Do I have to send the kids to her next week? Will that police report hurt her plans to take the children back, or will it indict me, too? What did she mean about her "situation changing"?

Will I have to hand over my kids to a mentally unstable woman who doesn't have enough sense to stop Jewel from jumping with a jawbreaker in her mouth, who doesn't have the presence of mind to save her own daughter from choking to death? Who could pass out in a daze if she takes too many pills and die right there in front of them?

I bathed in acidic regret for hours, but I kept coming back to my marriage to her and coming out with the same answer: I couldn't have left her to care for Angel by herself, she wasn't up to it.

But then we had Dylan, during a time of relative peace, which now seems like a bad idea, but how can I regret my kids? I could have gotten myself a vasectomy, but I never did. Maybe part of me wanted another shot at fatherhood. With someone normal.

I don't believe Jewel isn't mine. We look too much alike. She looks, in fact, very much like photographs of my mother at this age. This is what I'll keep telling myself.

I look at my son carefully sweeping the hardwood floor, the echo of my sharp chin in his face, and in my mind I hear his sax, soulful and melodic, and of course, I can't regret him.

"Hey, Dylan."

"Yeah?"

He pauses in his sweeping, leaning on the broom.

"Why did you take off?"

He looks at his feet. At the wall, at the broken computer. I continue, "It wasn't just a girl, was it?"

"I hate my school." He tosses his head a little. His bangs are getting long, hanging in his eyes.

His grades at the new school are phenomenal. So I say that.

He scoffs. "That school is ridiculous. Everyone has awesome grades there. I hate that there's no band. It's not enough to play by myself. I want to be part of something."

"But your grades at the old school . . . And that gun."

"I'll study harder. Every night. Get me a tutor. But don't make me go back to that stupid charter school. I don't care if my old school has problems. It's not like I feared for my life. I know how to stay away from trouble. I was happy there, Dad."

I should say no. I should refuse to reward his running away by doing what he wants. Make him tough it out. The new place is supposed to be terrific. Innovative, that's what the experts say.

I start to ask why he didn't just come out and ask me to transfer him, but I've answered my own question before I open my mouth. Same reason Casey didn't tell me who she really was.

"Okay," I say. "First thing Monday I'll call your old school."

Now it's his turn to be startled. "In the middle of the semester?"

"You shouldn't have to wait to be content."

Now he looks younger again, his face glowing with that kind of childish joy little kids have when they go to the park, or, when I last saw it on Dylan's face, when we bought him his first saxophone.

We both turn toward a knocking on the door, and my stomach knots with dread. Knocking, ringing phones, one disaster after another, for days.

I pull open the heavy door, holding my breath.

It's Casey, hands in her pockets, eyes down on the faded welcome mat, inscrutable.

Chapter 48

Edna Leigh Casey

My phone rings as I'm swiping on lip gloss in my bathroom. I'm almost late for work, but I should grab it just in case.

"Hello?"

I'm greeted by an energetic, chirpy rendition of "Happy Birthday."

"Hi, Mom."

"Hi, sweetheart. I know I'll see you this weekend, but I couldn't wait."

"Thanks, Mom."

"Did you like the flowers?"

"Very much. I gotta go, though, okay? Call you later."

"Okay, honey. Love you."

"Love you, too."

I put my phone back in my pocket and smell my flowers on my way to get my purse off the kitchen table. Tulips, perfect for spring. I stroke a silky petal and smile.

I glance around my apartment, which the landlord let me paint a bright salmon pink as long as I promised to return it to beige if I move out. It actually makes my room resemble a child's eraser, but I love even that because it's my own mistake on my own walls.

I still don't have a car, but it's warm enough to bike instead of taking the bus. I snap on my helmet and pedal to my new job doing information tech at the bank. It's not thrilling work, but it's close to home and it's stable, and I felt I needed people again.

Because, as it turned out, isolation wasn't such a great plan.

Forsythia trumpets the arrival of spring, manifesting as flashes of bright yellow in my peripheral vision as I zip down the road.

There's no bike rack at the office, but they let me wheel my bike in and park it in an empty cubicle next to mine, like my very own garage. My boss, Carla, thinks it's precious that I ride a bike and wear a Hello Kitty helmet.

But the helmet was a present from Jewel, so of course I wear it. She's got one, too.

I'm a few minutes early—traffic was so light today—so I call Michael's cell.

"Hi," he answers. "Happy Birthday."

"You ready for today?"

"As I'll ever be."

"You sure I can't come?"

"No, it's fine. I don't want you to have to deal with this any-more."

"You know I don't mind."

"I know. See you tonight?"

"I'll be there with bells on." I pause, waiting for an "I love you" to spring to my lips, but it doesn't. He doesn't say it either. We say our good-byes warmly, and hang up.

We said it too fast last time, both out of relief to have found someone new, someone with whom we could erase history. This time we can wait.

After all, I'm twenty-seven today. I'm not exactly doddering.

I turn on my computer and mentally send Michael good-luck wishes in court.

Mallory took off with some new guy shortly after the disaster weekend, disappearing for three weeks and then calling the house, talking about coming back to town, seeking physical custody again, as soon as she "got things sorted out." She has been absent ever since, except for the occasional rambling e-mail to one of the kids. Today, at Friend of the Court, Michael will petition to have her visitations suspended in light of her vanishing act and erratic behavior. If he prevails, we won't have to worry she'll swoop back to town and pick up the kids like old times, without us knowing anything about her mental state, drug use, or romantic entanglements. It means if she wants time with her kids again, she'll have to petition for it, "as both parties agree."

She could remain with her paramour out of state, or she could turn up today with a powerful lawyer, as she's hinted in the e-mails. We've stopped trying to guess what will happen.

Michael and I, over evenings of Chinese food and bad movies, have dissected her behavior again and again. It might seem unhealthy, but we're both too tired to keep things in anymore, so when the conversation circles back to her, we both give up on clamping down.

Mallory had him in a tight corner after that weekend. His son had run away on his watch, and Mallory pretended that he hit her. She could have blamed the destroyed living room on him, in fact, saying he attacked her. She'd been hinting to Angel that she had a rich new boyfriend who'd pay for a big-time lawyer.

She had Michael in her sights, but didn't pull the trigger. And this was a mystery, and a source of anxiety that she was merely biding her time.

Then Angel showed us an e-mail she'd sent her mother. It was signed by all of the kids.

> *Dear Mom,*
>
> *We will always love you and the good times you gave us. But we want you to know we're happy with Dad. He takes really good care of us, and things are usually pretty calm.*
>
> *We don't want you to feel bad, but we're asking you, pretty please, if you would not try to mess up something that's working. If it makes you feel better, Casey isn't living with us anymore. She and Dad still see each other but they're taking it slow, and it's a lot easier now, on everybody.*
>
> *We still want to see you when you're feeling good.*
>
> *We know you have always done your best, but that it's hard for you. And you're our mom, we won't stop loving you.*
>
> *Your kids,*
> *Angel, Jewel, and Dylan*

Mallory's response was simply: *If that's what you want.*

Angel hadn't showed us the note at first because she thought her dad would be upset with her for meddling in grown-up business. It's taking her some time to adjust to the new Michael, who stops to think before he condemns.

Michael read the note in wonderment, and later, with the kids' permission, shared it with me. Angel assured us the note was a joint project of all the kids, though it sounded very much like Angel when she makes an effort to be her most adult.

It was impossible to tell if that one line—*If that's what you want*—was typed in bitterness or sarcasm or resignation. And some nights Jewel still cries for Mallory, and I don't take it personally because I know she means Mallory at her best. Who wouldn't miss their mother at her best?

But there have been unbroken weeks of peace since then, during which time I've dated Michael like an ordinary girlfriend, returning to my own apartment, taking out my own garbage, and leaving the laundry and homework to him.

My work e-mail is finally up, and I start taking care of business, humming along happily with the rhythm of my new, nicely boring life.

I carry my phone with me all morning, waiting to hear Michael's court news. It buzzes in my pocket when I'm at the coffee machine, and I nearly scald myself slamming the pot down to answer it.

"Well?" I ask without preamble.

"It's done," he answers, sounding weary with seventeen years of dramatic personal history.

"You sound like *The Sopranos*," I say, and he obliges me with a laugh, then says in a cartoon Jersey accent: "You take care of that thing with the guy like I asked you to?"

I respond in kind, "I delivered the package."

Now we laugh together, and say our good-byes once more, because we'll see each other at night.

Angel shows up at my door that night to pick me up, as prearranged, so she can practice driving. I swear she looks taller every time I see her.

"Nice," she says as I lock my door behind me.

I let her take me shopping in the weeks after that one November weekend, allowing myself to be used as a life-size doll to mend some seriously broken fences.

Tonight I'm wearing a dress we picked out together, once the spring clothes hit the stores: it's fluttery, with a subtle yellow-and-green floral pattern. It's got a deep V at the neck, and though I swear it feels too short, Angel insists it's perfect. The green, she tells me, brightens up my dark blond hair. It's what my mom always called "dishwater blond."

Nice, Sprite, my brother says in my memory, on my prom night, when I came down the stairs to Pete.

"Your car, madame," Angel says, smirking at my wobbly navigation down the stairway in these spiky green heels she talked me into.

On the drive we talk about the weather, how it feels to be twenty-seven—old, but not doddering, I report—and the various dramatics at her school, onstage or in the hallways.

I'm not fooled into thinking our connection is magically healed by spiky green shoes. It was always easy to be girlfriends when I was not in charge of her, and that's what we're playing at right now.

It will do. Don't borrow trouble, my mom would say.

We pull up to Michael's dad's East Grand Rapids house, the

edges of the lawn bright with daffodils. I navigate the flagstone path gingerly. The evening chill has already begun to descend, and goose bumps race across my bare legs.

For a flash before we walk in, I want a cigarette, so I rush myself across the threshold, past that thought, and when I hug Michael just inside the door, I know I don't smell like an ashtray. His hand brushes my nicotine patch when he lets go, and he smiles at me, squeezes my hand.

"You look terrific." He looks at Angel. "Good job."

Dylan and I exchange a high five; Jewel hugs my waist, and I ruffle her hair.

Mrs. Turner appears from the kitchen, dusting off her hands. "I made your favorite lasagna. Now go on in and have some punch."

She rushes me toward the dining room, and everyone clatters in behind me. I stop in the doorway to gasp. Jewel crashes into me from behind.

HAPPY BIRTHDAY CASEY reads the banner, decorated with copious amounts of glitter and paint. There are wrapped presents on the sideboard underneath it.

"Did you make that?" I ask Jewel, as if it could be anyone else. She wrinkles her nose under her glasses and beams like a twinkling star.

At dinner, we all try not to watch Angel eat, because from what I hear, nothing sets her off more. There's not much on her plate, but the food actually does seem to be disappearing. Michael told me that after a fraught, high-volume argument Angel agreed to talk to the school counselor, a young woman she's always liked, about why she doesn't want to eat. That, along with her triumphant performance in *The Miracle Worker*, seemed to allow Angel to relax a little. Michael had been quick to add, "Not that I can take my hands off the wheel. Not for a minute."

When Dr. Turner asks Michael how the writing is going, I stop with lasagna melting off my fork to stare between them, to see if Dr. Turner will approve of his son's answer, or judge him lacking in ambition, perhaps.

Michael begins explaining about this online magazine he's started, applying his old-school newsman training, but with stories that are more snarky, more fun. He's getting that off the ground with all of them living here, with his parents, something that would have pained him before, and his dad would have held it over him.

But now Dr. Turner just listens, nodding, twirling cheese around his fork.

I'm sure he's not delighted with the plan, but he's keeping his criticism to himself. That's something.

Michael's also in line for a teaching job at the community college, and substitute teaching at high schools when he can.

"Any offers on the house yet, Dad?" Michael asks, now.

"Nothing realistic."

The Heritage Hill house, which both parents and son decided they should let go, soft housing market be damned.

The phone rings, and Dr. Turner starts to get up, by reflex the doctor on call.

I'm closer, though, so I gesture for him to sit and go answer it myself, clowning for the family with an exaggerated British accent: "Dr. and Mrs. Turner's residence."

"Oh, well, if it isn't the little woman."

I don't answer. The room around me falls silent. Mrs. Turner rises to her feet.

"So. Carrying on with your plan to steal my children? Any more of them run away lately, or haven't you noticed, busy screwing Michael?"

I take a deep breath. I close my eyes and shake my head as if shaking raindrops out of my hair.

She's just a person. As Michael once said, she's not going to eat my spleen.

I hold out the phone and say simply, "It's Mallory."

Michael takes it, listens for a moment, and makes as if to step out of the room to talk. Then he stops, turns back to us, and says quietly into the phone, "Enough." He pushes the button to end the call, and places the phone carefully down. He looks around at the ring of worried frowns around the table.

"Your mom is feeling a little upset right now. I'll talk to her when she's calmer."

We all pause for the phone to ring again, but it doesn't, and Mrs. Turner claps her hands and announces it's time for cake.

When she comes back in, I'm laughing, because there really are twenty-seven candles on a round layer cake.

She says, blinking in the faint smoke, "Quick! Blow them out before the alarm goes off!"

I can barely get in a breath because I'm giggling. Michael reaches out to pull my hair back. "Don't set yourself on fire!" he cries in mock alarm.

I don't get them all blown out at once—my poor ravaged lungs—but it's close enough. I don't wish, either, because I don't believe candles can grant wishes, or that hoping for something will make it come true.

Between bites of chocolate cake I open gifts—a pretty scarf from the Turners, a glittery bookmark from Jewel. Angel bought me a copy of *The Crucible* because I told her that was my favorite play. A homemade CD of Dylan playing his sax nearly has me weeping puddles of mascara down my face.

Michael's box is last.

"I'm sorry to say that it isn't brand-new, but money is tight and all," he says, shrugging, turning pink.

The box is shoebox size, but impossibly light, as if it's empty. Nothing shifts inside, either, when I unwrap it.

Taped to the bottom of the box is my engagement ring, and a note. The note reads, "Dear Edna Leigh Casey, I love you, whoever you are."

My shaking hands can't get the tape loose, and Michael bobbles it, too, so it's Dylan who frees the ring from the box and hands it to his father, who turns to me, holding the ring pinched between finger and thumb.

I take it from him, and for a moment I just hold it, too, and forget his whole family is watching us. The ring blurs in my vision. But this time, no falling-dream dizziness. I feel both bright and weightless. "Wow, I mean . . . how . . . Are we ready?"

"We've got time. No rush."

"Are you sure?"

"Yes." And he smiles, leaning in so close I can spot a piece of basil stuck to a front tooth. He lowers his voice to a near-whisper. "I bet you'll be an amazing mother."

I fumble the ring trying to put it on, and it bounces under the table, and Michael and I crack heads trying to grab for it, and then we sit under the table laughing along with the whole family, all of us ignoring the ringing phone.

A+

AUTHOR
INSIGHTS,
EXTRAS, &
MORE...

FROM

**KRISTINA
RIGGLE**

AND

Wm

WILLIAM MORROW

Discussion Questions

1. Casey seeks to reinvent herself, starting with her name and cutting all ties to her old life. Have you ever wished you could start completely over?

2. What do you think the real motivation is for Casey's attempt to erase her past? Do you think she changed her life for the better?

3. Do you think Michael would have given Casey a chance early in their dating days if she'd been up-front with him about her old habits? Early in a relationship, do you believe it's beneficial for someone to be an "open book," or is it better to hold some things close to the vest?

4. Was Casey prepared to be a stepmother at the time she moved into the Heritage Hill house? Has that changed by the end of the novel? Do you know any stepparents, or are you one yourself? Given the prevalence of blended families, do you think being a stepparent is easier these days than in the past?

5. What do you think lies at the root of Michael's perfectionism? Can you relate to his perfectionism in some way?

6. How does Michael's perfectionism affect him and his family? Does he realize how his actions take a toll on others?

7. Michael and Mallory had sharply different upbringings and seem like a case of opposites attracting. Do you know of couples like this, apparent mismatches who are trying to make it work? Is it ever possible to make it last?

8. Is there a scenario in which Michael and Mallory could have lasted as a couple, or was their relationship doomed from the start?

9. Do you perceive Mallory as villain, victim, innocent, or some combination of these? Does her character elicit compassion or frustration, or both?

10. Do you believe Mallory has undiagnosed mental health problems? How much responsibility does she bear for her own actions?

11. The children each have their own struggles, which they seem reluctant to share with their parents for various reasons. What could Michael have done to get his children to open up? Is it inevitable that children have secrets from their parents?

12. Do you think social class plays a role in the characters' relationships and conflicts? If so, how, and to what end?

13. How does the title relate to each character's story? What are the things they didn't say and what difference would it have made if they'd spoken up?

14. Are there things in your own life you never say out loud? If so, why don't you share what you think? If you speak your mind, do you feel that it always helps the situation, or do you ever regret things you've said?

15. How optimistic (or pessimistic) do you feel for the family at the end of the book? What are some things you imagine happening to the characters after the book's ending?

A Conversation with the Author

What inspired this novel?

I was imagining how an external crisis impacts our internal lives. What if a woman was ready to walk out and leave a situation she could no longer tolerate, but something prevented her from doing so, some kind of immediate and sudden disaster? When the crisis was over, what would she do, then? Would she still go? How would she be able to conduct herself through the crisis knowing what she'd been prepared to do? Oddly enough, this line of thinking came up after watching the movie *Thirteen Days* about the Cuban missile crisis. I'd been imagining someone enduring family strife, and on top of that, this frightening global threat hanging over her head. Casey and Michael's disaster is not of national scope, but it's significant enough to bring everything else in their lives to a halt. I call this book a messy, grown-up love story because real love must be able to endure through the worst, most confusing and difficult times. Sometimes love alone isn't enough to sustain a couple when the storm comes, as it always will.

Why did you choose to write about a blended family?

As I just mentioned, it's a messy, grown-up love story and it's also a contemporary story. Families come in all varieties now, and sometimes that means a young woman falls in love with a man who comes prepackaged with three kids. I'm in awe of the optimism and determination of those who create blended families. By their very nature, these couples walk into a new relationship bearing scars of the past—moreso than those who have never been married before—and I find their willingness to give it another try inspiring. I also wanted to write about a competent single dad who has primary custody of his kids, because it goes against the grain of the pop-culture stereotype of the distant or bumbling divorced dad. These characters come out of my imagination, I should say. I count blended families among my friends, certainly, but I didn't quiz them for this book and in fact spoke very little about it as I was writing. I didn't want to excavate their private lives, or put them on the spot.

You're back to a real setting for this book, as opposed to the fictional town in your previous novel. Why are you back to a real spot on the map?

The Life You've Imagined had a bigger canvas: it took place over the course of a whole summer, and featured many kinds of settings. For that situation I wanted optimum flexibility to make up landscapes as they suited the story. For *Things We Didn't Say*, it's back to a compact time frame, as with my debut novel. Most of the action takes place within forty-eight hours, and most of it within the walls of one house in one neighborhood. I was attracted to the crucible effect this would create, especially with characters who are thrown together unwillingly. I chose the Heritage Hill neighborhood of Grand Rapids, Michigan, for the simple reason that I love it. It's a beautiful, old, and interesting part of town. As with my first novel, this book features a mix of real and fictional landmarks. Heritage Hill is real, the schools mentioned in the book are not. The newspaper where Michael works is not a faithful reproduction of *The Grand Rapids Press,* which is why I called it the *Herald.* But the Meyer May House, the Sixth Street Park, Literary Life Bookstore, the "Castle" building which now holds a dentist's office—all those places are real.

How did the title come about?

Credit goes to my editor, Lucia Macro. This phrase represents so much of what goes wrong for the characters. I think most people in a relationship can relate to this. Think of how many times you want to say something to your loved ones, and circumstances prevent you, or you stop yourself. Why? We fear the results of our words sometimes, but silence does damage, too. It turned out to be so poignant for me, because we happened to settle on this title as my beloved mother-in-law was dying of cancer. It's only natural when we lose someone to think of all we didn't say.

This novel, like your others, has a large cast. Who was the most challenging character to write?

Writing from the perspective of the children was a fun challenge, but by far the trickiest character was the ex-wife, Mallory. She's the first true antagonist I've tackled, but I did my utmost not to turn her into a caricature of pure villainy. She is damaged, but I would not say she's evil. It's an interesting question that Michael wrestles with throughout their marriage, how much control she has over her own actions, and thus how much personal responsibility she bears. I also found the failed marriage between Mallory and Michael to have a life of its own as well, and it was a challenge to portray that relationship in a way that was understandable and relatable. Sometimes the story of a marriage isn't easily understood, especially by those from the outside looking in, and I hoped to give the readers some insight into that story.

John Riggle

KRISTINA RIGGLE lives and writes in Grand Rapids, Michigan, with her husband, two kids, and dog. She's a freelance journalist, published short story writer, and coeditor for fiction at the e-zine *Literary Mama*. Her debut novel, *Real Life & Liars*, was named a Great Lakes, Great Reads selection by the Great Lakes Independent Booksellers Association. *The Life You've Imagined* was honored as an Indie Next Notable Book.

Kristina Riggle

ALSO BY **KRISTINA RIGGLE**

THINGS WE DIDN'T SAY

ISBN 978-0-06-200304-1 (paperback)

"Kristina Riggle writes women's fiction with soul. Her characters are both familiar and quirky, and reading their stories is like spending a weekend catching up with your oldest friends."
—Tiffany Baker, author of
The Little Giant of Aberdeen County

REAL LIFE & LIARS

ISBN 978-0-06-170628-8 (paperback)

"This book has heart. Each of its four stories is compelling and makes you keep turning the page long after you should have turned out the light. . . . Kristina Riggle gets it exactly right."
—Becky Motew, author of *Coupon Girl*

THE LIFE YOU'VE IMAGINED

ISBN 978-0-06-170629-5 (paperback)

"(An) engaging, companionable novel about family, expectations, and adversities overcome. . . . I devoured it and wanted more."
—Therese Fowler, author of *Reunion*